ANNi

THE CRIME AT
TATTENHAM CORNER

Annie Haynes was born in 1865, the daughter of an ironmonger.

By the first decade of the twentieth century she lived in London and moved in literary and early feminist circles. Her first crime novel, *The Bungalow Mystery*, appeared in 1923, and another nine mysteries were published before her untimely death in 1929.

Who Killed Charmian Karslake? appeared posthumously, and a further partially-finished work, *The Crystal Beads Murder*, was completed with the assistance of an unknown fellow writer, and published in 1930.

000003137537

Also by Annie Haynes

The Bungalow Mystery
The Abbey Court Murder
The Secret of Greylands
The Blue Diamond
The Witness on the Roof
The House in Charlton Crescent
The Crow's Inn Tragedy
The Master of the Priory
The Man with the Dark Beard
Who Killed Charmian Karslake?
The Crystal Beads Murder

ANNIE HAYNES

THE CRIME AT TATTENHAM CORNER

With an introduction
by Curtis Evans

DEAN STREET PRESS

Published by Dean Street Press 2015

All Rights Reserved

First published in 1929 by The Bodley Head

Cover by DSP

Introduction © Curtis Evans 2015

ISBN 978 1 910570 76 0

www.deanstreetpress.co.uk

The Mystery of the Missing Author
Annie Haynes and Her Golden Age
Detective Fiction

The psychological enigma of Agatha Christie's notorious 1926 vanishing has continued to intrigue Golden Age mystery fans to the present day. The Queen of Crime's eleven-day disappearing act is nothing, however, compared to the decades-long disappearance, in terms of public awareness, of between-the-wars mystery writer Annie Haynes (1865-1929), author of a series of detective novels published between 1923 and 1930 by Agatha Christie's original English publisher, The Bodley Head. Haynes's books went out of print in the early Thirties, not long after her death in 1929, and her reputation among classic detective fiction readers, high in her lifetime, did not so much decline as dematerialize. When, in 2013, I first wrote a piece about Annie Haynes' work, I knew of only two other living persons besides myself who had read any of her books. Happily, Dean Street Press once again has come to the rescue of classic mystery fans seeking genre gems from the Golden Age, and is republishing all Haynes' mystery novels. Now that her crime fiction is coming back into print, the question naturally arises: Who Was Annie Haynes? Solving the mystery of this forgotten author's lost life has taken leg work by literary sleuths on two continents (my thanks for their assistance to Carl Woodings and Peter Harris).

Until recent research uncovered new information about Annie Haynes, almost nothing about her was publicly known besides the fact of her authorship of twelve mysteries during the Golden Age of detective fiction. Now we know that she led an altogether intriguing life, too soon cut short by disability and death, which took her from the isolation of the rural English Midlands in the nineteenth century to the cultural high life of Edwardian London. Haynes was born in

1865 in the Leicestershire town of Ashby-de-la-Zouch, the first child of ironmonger Edwin Haynes and Jane (Henderson) Haynes, daughter of Montgomery Henderson, longtime superintendent of the gardens at nearby Coleorton Hall, seat of the Beaumont baronets. After her father left his family, young Annie resided with her grandparents at the gardener's cottage at Coleorton Hall, along with her mother and younger brother. Here Annie doubtlessly obtained an acquaintance with the ways of the country gentry that would serve her well in her career as a genre fiction writer.

We currently know nothing else of Annie Haynes' life in Leicestershire, where she still resided (with her mother) in 1901, but by 1908, when Haynes was in her early forties, she was living in London with Ada Heather-Bigg (1855-1944) at the Heather-Bigg family home, located halfway between Paddington Station and Hyde Park at 14 Radnor Place, London. One of three daughters of Henry Heather-Bigg, a noted pioneer in the development of orthopedics and artificial limbs, Ada Heather-Bigg was a prominent Victorian and Edwardian era feminist and social reformer. In the 1911 British census entry for 14 Radnor Place, Heather-Bigg, a "philanthropist and journalist," is listed as the head of the household and Annie Haynes, a "novelist," as a "visitor," but in fact Haynes would remain there with Ada Heather-Bigg until Haynes' death in 1929.

Haynes' relationship with Ada Heather-Bigg introduced the aspiring author to important social sets in England's great metropolis. Though not a novelist herself, Heather-Bigg was an important figure in the city's intellectual milieu, a well-connected feminist activist of great energy and passion who believed strongly in the idea of women attaining economic independence through remunerative employment. With Ada Heather-Bigg behind her, Annie Haynes's writing career had powerful backing indeed. Although in the 1911 census

Heather-Bigg listed Haynes' occupation as "novelist," it appears that Haynes did not publish any novels in book form prior to 1923, the year that saw the appearance of *The Bungalow Mystery*, which Haynes dedicated to Heather-Bigg. However, Haynes was a prolific producer of newspaper serial novels during the second decade of the twentieth century, penning such works as *Lady Carew's Secret*, *Footprints of Fate*, *A Pawn of Chance*, *The Manor Tragedy* and many others.

Haynes' twelve Golden Age mystery novels, which appeared in a tremendous burst of creative endeavor between 1923 and 1930, like the author's serial novels retain, in stripped-down form, the emotionally heady air of the nineteenth-century triple-decker sensation novel, with genteel settings, shocking secrets, stormy passions and eternal love all at the fore, yet they also have the fleetness of Jazz Age detective fiction. Both in their social milieu and narrative pace Annie Haynes' detective novels bear considerable resemblance to contemporary works by Agatha Christie; and it is interesting to note in this regard that Annie Haynes and Agatha Christie were the only female mystery writers published by The Bodley Head, one of the more notable English mystery imprints in the early Golden Age. "A very remarkable feature of recent detective fiction," observed the *Illustrated London News* in 1923, "is the skill displayed by women in this branch of story-telling. Isabel Ostrander, Carolyn Wells, Annie Haynes and last, but very far from least, Agatha Christie, are contesting the laurels of Sherlock Holmes' creator with a great spirit, ingenuity and success." Since Ostrander and Wells were American authors, this left Annie Haynes, in the estimation of the *Illustrated London News*, as the main British female competitor to Agatha Christie. (Dorothy L. Sayers, who, like Haynes, published her debut mystery novel in 1923, goes unmentioned.) Similarly, in 1925 *The Sketch* wryly noted that "[t]ired men, trotting home at the end of an imperfect day, have been known to pop into the library and ask for an Annie Haynes. They have not made a mistake in the street number. It is not a cocktail they are asking for…."

Twenties critical opinion adjudged that Annie Haynes' criminous concoctions held appeal not only for puzzle fiends impressed with the "considerable craftsmanship" of their plots (quoting from the *Sunday Times* review of *The Bungalow Mystery*), but also for more general readers attracted to their purely literary qualities. "Not only a crime story of merit, but also a novel which will interest readers to whom mystery for its own sake has little appeal," avowed *The Nation* of Haynes' *The Secret of Greylands*, while the *New Statesman* declared of *The Witness on the Roof* that "Miss Haynes has a sense of character; her people are vivid and not the usual puppets of detective fiction." Similarly, the *Bookman* deemed the characters in Haynes' *The Abbey Court Murder* "much truer to life than is the case in many sensational stories" and *The Spectator* concluded of *The Crime at Tattenham Corner*, "Excellent as a detective tale, the book also is a charming novel."

Sadly, Haynes' triumph as a detective novelist proved short lived. Around 1914, about the time of the outbreak of the Great War, Haynes had been stricken with debilitating rheumatoid arthritis that left her in constant pain and hastened her death from heart failure in 1929, when she was only 63. Haynes wrote several of her detective novels on fine days in Kensington Gardens, where she was wheeled from 14 Radnor Place in a bath chair, but in her last years she was able only to travel from her bedroom to her study. All of this was an especially hard blow for a woman who had once been intensely energetic and quite physically active.

In a foreword to *The Crystal Beads Murder*, the second of Haynes' two posthumously published mysteries, Ada Heather-Bigg noted that Haynes' difficult daily physical struggle "was materially lightened by the warmth of friendships" with other authors and by the "sympathetic and friendly relations between her and her publishers." In this latter instance Haynes' experience rather differed from that of her sister Bodleian, Agatha Christie, who left The Bodley Head on account of what she deemed an iniquitous contract that took unjust advantage of a naive young author. Christie moved, along with her landmark detective novel *The Murder of Roger Ackroyd* (1926), to Collins and never looked back, enjoying ever greater success with the passing years.

At the time Christie crossed over to Collins, Annie Haynes had only a few years of life left. After she died at 14 Radnor Place on 30 March 1929, it was reported in the press that "many people well-known in the literary world" attended the author's funeral at St. Michaels and All Angels Church, Paddington, where her sermon was delivered by the eloquent vicar, Paul Nichols, brother of the writer Beverley Nichols and dedicatee of Haynes' mystery novel *The Master of the Priory*; yet by the time of her companion Ada Heather-Bigg's death in 1944, Haynes and her once highly-praised mysteries were forgotten. (Contrastingly, Ada Heather-Bigg's name survives today in the University College of London's Ada Heather-Bigg Prize in Economics.) Only three of Haynes' novels were ever published in the United States, and she passed away less than a year before the formation of the Detection Club, missing any chance of being invited to join this august body of distinguished British detective novelists. Fortunately, we have today entered, when it comes to classic mystery, a period of rediscovery and revival, giving a reading audience a chance once again, after over eighty years, to savor the detective fiction fare of Annie Haynes. *Bon appétit!*

Introduction to
The Crime at Tattenham Corner

Adjoining the entrance to England's famed Epsom Downs Racecourse in Surrey is the village of Tattenham Corner. For many decades horseracing enthusiasts have eagerly alighted at Tattenham Corner railway station to attend the Derby Stakes. Just over a century ago, on 4 June 1913, however, appalled Derby spectators witnessed something deeply shocking take place on the track. Suffragette Emily Davison dashed onto the course, directly in the path of Anmer, King George V's colt, colliding with horse and rider. Davison, who suffered a fractured skull and internal injuries, died four days later—a martyr, in the admiring eyes of her co-activists, to the cause of woman suffrage.

Mystery writer Annie Haynes' companion, Ada Heather-Bigg, was, like the martyred Emily Davison, a firm believer in the principle of gender equality, including woman suffrage. Back in 1881 Heather Bigg had made newspaper headlines in the United Kingdom and the United States when she won the University College of London's Joseph Hume Scholarship in Political Economy, defeating all her male opponents for the prestigious award. Two years before the so-called "Suffragette Derby" of 1913, Heather-Bigg, when filling out the "infirmity" category on the British census form, underscored the word dumb, pointedly explaining in the designated spaces for herself and Haynes, as well as those for the three women servants residing in their household, without a vote.

Presumably Haynes shared her companion's views on woman suffrage, but it seems doubtful that the detective novelist would herself have endorsed Emily Davison's particular form of direct action. One of Haynes' great personal interests in life was racing; and she very much enjoyed having a bit of a flutter on the horses. On the occasion of the 1923 Liverpool Cup, Haynes nearly bet on a specific horse due to a recent dream she had had, in which she had opened the Bible to the following passage: *They shall shout out of their lips and their tongues shall be as poisoned arrows.* Upon awakening from her dream she looked at the list of entrants in the Liverpool Cup and found a horse named Poisoned Arrow, running at 12-1. In spite of this striking coincidence, the author shied from betting on a horse at such long odds; yet in the event Poisoned Arrow indeed won the race, just as Haynes' dream had foretold, in a most impressive upset, with the 2-1 favorite, Pharos, coming in third.

Having narrowly missed her chance at winning riches by descrying the mysteries of the racing form, Haynes at least was able to receive income from her popular mystery novels, in two of which--*The Crime at Tattenham Corner* (1929) and *The Crystal Beads Murder* (1930)—she drew on her knowledge of the horseracing milieu. In *The Crime at Tattenham Corner*, Haynes's series sleuth, Detective-Inspector William Stoddart, is tasked, along with his steadfast assistant Alfred Harbord, with investigating the shooting death of Sir John Burslem, financial magnate and owner of the racehorse Peep o' Day. Burslem's body was found in a ditch in Hughlin's Wood, near Tattenham Corner, on the very day of the running of the Epsom Derby, in which Burslem's horse Peep o' Day was, until its owner's sudden death, the favorite (on Burslem's death, Peep o' Day is automatically scratched).

Suspicion focuses on Sir Charles Stanyard, the sporting baronet, whose horse Perlyon was Peep o' Day's main rival at the Derby Stakes. Stanyard also is known to have been jilted by Sophie Carlford (youngest daughter of Viscount Carlford), who then became the second—and much younger—wife of Sir John Burslem. Lady Burslem certainly acts as if she has something to hide, as does Sir John's valet, Ellerby, who vanishes soon after the murder. Pamela Burslem, Sir John's daughter from his first marriage, needs no convincing from anyone on the subject, insinuating to all and sundry that Sir Charles, likely with Lady Burslem's connivance, was responsible for her father's death. But just what does Mrs. James Burslem ("Mrs. Jimmy"), wife of Sir John's absent Tibetan explorer brother, know about the affair, and what precisely can be reliably divined from the *séances* performed by Miss Winifred Margetson, Mrs. Jimmy's American spiritualist friend? (This aspect of the novel may be a nod to the author's' prophetic horseracing dream.) Much investigation must be done by Stoddart and Harbord--not to mention a little romancing, strictly in the line of duty, on the inspector's part-- before an arrest can be made. "As we follow their disentangling of the mystery," noted the *Spectator* in 1929, "we not only encounter thrilling surprises but are introduced to many admirably life-like characters." Can you solve *The Crime at Tattenham Corner* before Annie Haynes' series sleuths? Ladies and gentlemen, place your bets....

Curtis Evans

CHAPTER I

The big clock outside struck 7.30. Early as it was, Inspector Stoddart was already in his room at Scotland Yard.

He looked up impatiently as his most trusted subordinate, Alfred Harbord, entered after a sharp preliminary tap.

"Yes, sir. You sent for me?"

The inspector nodded. "You are detailed for special duty at once. We are starting in the runabout immediately, so if you want to send a message –" He nodded at the telephone.

Harbord grinned. "My people are pretty well used to my irregular habits, thank you, sir."

The inspector rose. "The sooner we are off the better, then." He handed Harbord a typewritten paper. "Wired up," he said laconically, "from the Downs."

> Mysterious death at an early hour this morning. Some platelayers on their way to work in the cutting beyond Hughlin's Wood, not far from Tattenham Corner, found the body of a man of middle age in a ditch. He is evidently of the better class and supposed to be a stranger in the district. The body lay face downwards in a foot of water at the bottom of the ditch or dyke. Up to the present it has not been identified. But a card was found in the pocket with the name of –

The corner of the paper had been torn off, evidently on purpose. Harbord read it over.

"Hughlin's Wood," he repeated. "I seem to know the name. But I can't think where the place is."

"Not a great many miles from Epsom," the inspector said, as he locked his desk and dropped the keys into his pocket. "Centuries ago, Hughlin's Wood used to stretch all round and over that part of the Downs, but it has dwindled to a few trees near Hughlin's village. These trees go by the name of Hughlin's Wood still. I can tell you the rest as we go along."

Harbord followed him in silence to the little two-seater in which the inspector was wont to dash about the country. He was an expert driver, but it needed all his attention to steer his car among the whirl of traffic over Westminster Bridge, passing Waterloo and Lambeth.

The inspector glanced at "The Horns" as they glided by it. "We will lunch there on the way back, Harbord."

He put on speed as they got on the Brixton Road and, passing Kennington Church, tore along through Streatham and Sydenham, and across country until they could feel the fresh air of the Downs in their faces. Then the inspector slackened speed and for the first time looked at his companion.

"What do you make of it?"

"What can I make of it?" Harbord fenced. "Except that you would not be going down unless there was more in the summons than meets the eye."

Stoddart nodded.

"The body was found face downwards in the stagnant water of a ditch, but the cause of death was a bullet wound in the head. The man had been thrown into the ditch almost immediately after death. In the pocket have been found a card and a couple of envelopes bearing the name of a man high in the financial world. The markings on the linen, etc., correspond. I know this man fairly well by sight. Therefore I am going down to see whether I can identify the remains. See those Downs –"

Harbord looked where he pointed at the vast, billowy expanse around them, then he looked back inquiringly.

"Yes, sir."

Stoddart waved his hand to the north side. "Over there lie Matt Harker's stables. He has turned out more winners of the classics than any other trainer. His gees get their morning gallops over the Downs."

Harbord's expression changed. "And you connect this dead man at Hughlin's Wood with Harker's stables?"

Stoddart looked at him. "I will tell you that in an hour or so."

As he spoke he turned the car rapidly to the right, and dashing down the road, which was little more than a track, they found themselves at Hughlin's Wood, with Hughlin's village in the immediate foreground.

Harbord thought he had seldom seen a more desolate looking spot, or a more appropriate setting for the crime they had come to investigate. A few stark, upstanding pines, growing in rough, stubbly grass, were all that was left of the once mighty wood; a long, straggly hedge ran between them and the road that led to Hughlin's village. It stood in a cleft in the hill which ran along to the bottom of the Downs. There was a curious cone-like hill just above the Wood. Harbord learned later that it went by the name of Hughlin's Tomb, and was supposed to contain the remains of a giant named Hughlin, from whom the wood derived its name. On the opposite side of the road was some barren pasture-land, and a little back from the track stood a small hut or barn.

By the Wood apparently the whole of the little population of Hughlin's village was gathered. A policeman was keeping every one back from the ditch.

The crowd scattered as the car came in sight. Stoddart slowed down and he and Harbord sprang out.

Inside the space which was being kept free two men were standing. One was easily recognized by his uniform as a superintendent of police. The other, a tall, clean-shaven man of military appearance, Harbord identified as Major Vincent, the chief constable of the county.

Major Vincent came to meet them. "Glad to see you, Inspector Stoddart. I hardly hoped that you could be here so soon."

Stoddart jerked his head at his run-about. "She is a tidy sort of little bus, sir. This is a terrible job!"

"It is," Major Vincent assented. "This is where the body was found – was flung, I should say – just over here."

The inspector walked forward and glanced down into the rather deep ditch. Long grasses fringed the edges, broken down and trampled upon now; the bottom was full of evil-smelling water.

Stoddart's quick, glancing eyes looked round. "Anything found here?"

The superintendent answered:

"Not so far, but we have made no very vigorous search. We waited till you came."

Stoddart nodded. "Quite right. The body?"

"Over there." The superintendent pointed to the barn in the field opposite. "Temporary mortuary," he explained. "The inquest will be opened tomorrow at the Crown Inn down in the village. In the meantime –"

"The body is here, I understand," the inspector finished. "We will have a look at that first, please, sir."

He made an imperceptible sign to Harbord as he glanced at Major Vincent.

"Any more evidence as to identity?" he questioned, as they walked across the rough grass together.

Major Vincent shook his head. "You will be able to help us about that, I understand, inspector."

"I may be able to. I ought to be if your suspicions are well founded," the inspector answered. "You rang up the house, of course."

"Of course! Answer, 'Not at home.' Said then we were afraid Sir John had met with an accident. His valet is coming down, should be here any minute now."

"Good!" the inspector said approvingly.

The Major opened the door of the barn. "I will stop out here, and have a cigarette, if you don't mind," he said apologetically. "I have been in two or three times already and it has pretty well done for me. It is a ghastly sight."

Stoddart's glance spoke his comprehension as he went inside; the doctor and the superintendent followed with Harbord.

Inside was, as Major Vincent had said, "a ghastly sight." The light was dim, little filtering through, except what came from the open door. The place was evidently used for cattle fodder. The floor was strewn with straw, trodden down and begrimed. The dead man lay on a hastily improvised stretcher of hurdles raised on a couple of others in the middle of the barn.

Stoddart and Harbord instinctively stepped forward softly. The superintendent took off the covering some kindly hand had laid over the distorted face. Then, used though they were to scenes of horror, both Stoddart and Harbord with difficulty repressed an exclamation, so terrible was the sight. A momentary glance was enough to show that the man had been shot through the lower part of the face. The head had lain in the water of the ditch for some time face downwards. It was swollen and livid and grazed, but was not impossible of recognition. Yet, as Stoddart gazed on the figure, still in evening-dress, over the strong-looking hands with their manicured almond nails that had made marks on the palms as they clenched in the death agony, a certain look that Harbord well knew came into the inspector's eyes. He held out his hand. "The card – 'Sir John Burslem,'" he read aloud. He looked at the dead man's wrist-watch, turned it over and looked at the monogram, glanced at a letter that was peeping out of the pocket – "Sir John Burslem, 15 Porthwick Square." The postmark was that of the previous morning.

The superintendent watched him in silence for a few minutes. At last he said:

"Well, inspector, what do you say – is it Sir John Burslem?"

"I believe so," the inspector said without hesitation. "It is Sir John Burslem, I firmly believe. But I only had a casual acquaintance with him."

And, hardened though he was, Stoddart turned aside and blew his nose as his mind glanced from the twisted, broken thing before him to the prosperous financial magnate of whom he retained so vivid a recollection. He replaced the covering over the shattered head and looked at his watch.

"The valet should be here directly. It seems to me we must await more positive identification from him. Until he comes, I should like a few words with you, doctor. How long had death taken place when you first saw the body?"

The doctor coughed. "It is difficult to say with precision. I reached here about half-past seven this morning. I should say the man had been dead at least five hours when I saw him, possibly more, certainly not less."

"The cause of death?"

"Evidently the man had been shot through the lower part of the face. For anything more we must wait for the post-mortem." He added a few technical details.

Harbord waited outside with Major Vincent and the superintendent.

"Sir John Burslem," he repeated thoughtfully. "A financier, you say. I seem to remember this name in some other connection."

"He was a big gun in what is called high finance," Major Vincent told him. "It is said that no international deal, no great scheme of Government stock was launched without his advice. For himself, he was head of the great firm of Burslem & Latimer, the iron and jute merchants, Wellmorton Street, and of Burslem & Co., diamond merchants of South Africa, besides being director of Heaven knows how many companies. Sir John Burslem's name spelt success to any undertaking."

"And will this" – Harbord jerked his head backward – "mean failure?"

The major shrugged his shoulders. "Heaven knows! One's imagination fails to picture the world of speculation without Jack Burslem, as he was generally known. But here's the valet, Ellerby, I expect," as a car stopped.

An elderly man got out and came towards them. He was looking white and shaken.

"Gentlemen," he began in a quaking voice as he got near them, "they say that he – that Sir John has had an accident. He – he can't be – dead!"

"That is what we have brought you here to ascertain, Mr. Ellerby," Major Vincent said, a touch of pity in his tone as he thought of the ordeal that lay before the man. "You will be able to tell us definitely. The clothes at any rate you will be able to recognize. The face has been – in the water for some time and is terribly swollen."

The man looked at him, his mouth twitching. "I should know Sir John anywhere, sir," he said, his manner becoming more composed. "I couldn't be deceived about him. It is an impossibility."

Stoddart went in with him. Harbord stood with the other three at the door. They heard a cry of horror, then a hoarse sob, and Ellerby's voice, broken now:

"Oh, it is Sir John, sure enough! Oh, yes, his poor face is all swollen, but I could swear to him anywhere. There is the dress coat I put on him yesterday evening, and his shoes, and his eyeglass on his cord, and his wrist-watch. Oh, it is Sir John safe enough. And what are we going to do without him? And her poor young ladyship – and Miss Pamela?"

He came out wiping his eyes openly.

"You identify the body positively as that of Sir John Burslem?" Major Vincent questioned authoritatively.

"Oh, yes, sir, there is not no doubt possible." Ellerby's careful, rather precise grammar was forgotten now in his excitement and his own real grief. "I could tell without looking at his face," he went on, "for there's just the things I put out for him last night, little thinking. And her poor ladyship with a big party today going to the races!"

"The races – by Jove!" Stoddart looked at his watch and then at Harbord. "Of course that accounts for all the traffic on the road; it's Derby Day!"

"You are right, sir."

The valet put away his handkerchief and steadied his voice. "It seems but the other day that poor Sir John was telling us to put our shirts on Peep o' Day – 'Best colt Matt Harker ever trained,' he says, 'and a dead cert for the Derby; maybe the last we'll have before the tote comes in,' Sir John said, 'so get the best you can beforehand.' And we did, all of us, at Sir John's own bucket shop."

Stoddart's face altered indefinably. "I hope you didn't build on the colt winning, Mr. Ellerby."

"That I have, sir." The man looked at him half fearfully. "All my own savings and my wife's I have put on, and I borrowed my sister's too. It is a tidy lot I stand to win when Peep o' Day passes the winning-post! Though poor Sir John will never lead her in now."

"Nor anyone else as the winner of the Derby," Stoddart said gravely. Don't you realize what that" – with a nod at the barn – "means to all of you who have put your money on Peep o' Day?"

Ellerby began to tremble. "No, sir, I don't. But we got our money on right enough. Sir John, he said it was as safe as if it was in the bank."

"So he may have thought, though in a gamble there is often a slip betwixt the cup and the lip," Stoddart said dryly. "But don't you know that an owner's death renders void all his horses' nominations and entries. Peep o' Day is automatically scratched. If Sir John Burslem had died one minute before the race was run, and, not knowing, Peep o' Day's number had gone up, he would be disqualified. Today will be a grand day for the bookies. The favourite scratched at the last minute. You get your money back though, but we must wire at once for the sake of the poor devils who are putting on, on the course. Harker's the trainer, you said."

"Yes, sir," Ellerby stammered, his face working painfully. "Matt Harker said that Peep o' Day was the best three-year-old he had ever had in training. He carried all the stable money."

"Well, it is to be hoped Harker hedged a bit," Stoddart said slowly. "For Peep o' Day won't run to-day. And I wonder, I wonder –"

CHAPTER II

Surely, surely, no hour had ever been so long! Sophie Burslem twisted herself round in bed once more. It was morning. Of course it was morning. The sun was streaming through her open window. She could hear the pleasant, familiar sounds of everyday life, but the sound for which she was waiting and watching did not come. At last she caught the echo of voices, distant at first, then nearer. One of the gardeners was talking on the terrace beneath the window.

"Ay! if Peep o' Day brings it off and I ain't no manner of doubt that he will, seeing Sir John himself he said to me, 'You like a bit of a gamble sometimes, I know, Germain. Well, you will have the safest gamble of your life if you put your shirt on Peep o' Day. Best colt I've ever had,' Sir John said. Well, my missus and me we drawed our nest-egg out o' the post office, an' we put it on Peep o' Day, months ago, and we got 100 to 8 then. I reckon we will be made folks tomorrow."

"I am wishing I had done the same," another voice chimed in, "but I thought there's many a slip betwixt the cup and the lip, and so I waited until this morning, and now I'll only get starting price, and they're saying it will be odds on. So 'tain't any good backing Perlyon for a place as I had reckoned on doing. 'Tis sure to be place betting."

"Ay, ay," the first speaker assented. "I had a tip for Perlyon myself, but –"

The voices died away in the distance. As Sophie Burslem lay for a moment perfectly still on her pillow, two tears welled up in her eyes and rolled miserably down her cheeks. Peep o' Day! Peep o' Day! Those poor men had put their savings on Peep o' Day. And now Peep o' Day would never win the Derby!

A minute more and there came the sound for which she had been waiting – a tap at the door. She pulled the lever that raised the latch and her maid came in with her tea. She set it on the table beside the bed.

"It's a lovely morning, my lady. And Sir John was saying yesterday that fine weather was all that Peep o' Day wanted. He likes to hear his hoofs rattle, Sir John said. And if it had been heavy going it would have been all against him."

"Yes," said Sophie Burslem faintly.

She was stretching herself lazily while from beneath her half-closed eyelids her eyes were keenly watching every moment of the maid's. Had she not been called a good amateur actress in the days that were gone? She would have to act today if she had never acted in her life before.

"I have put all my savings on Peep o' Day," the maid went on. "My young man, he has done the same. We shall have something to talk about tonight, I expect, my lady."

Beneath the silken counterpane Sophie Burslem's hands were twisting themselves together in an agony. Then came another of the sounds she was dreading. In the adjoining room some one was moving about opening and shutting drawers; then came silence; then a loud knocking at the door of her room. She made herself speak quietly:

"What is that, Forbes? Just see, will you?" Then she waited again in that blank, awful expectancy. There was a murmured colloquy at the door; strain her ears as she might she could only catch a word or two.

At last Forbes came back. "It is James, my lady; he wants to know if you can tell him where Sir John is?"

"Sir John! I don't know. Has he gone out?"

"I suppose so, my lady. Somebody wants to see him on important business, and he is not in his room. They are saying he has not slept there, my lady."

"What?" Sophie Burslem raised herself on one elbow. Then she laughed. "Nonsense! Really for a moment you quite frightened me, Forbes. I expect Sir John has gone out to put a little more on Peep o' Day. He went over to Oxley last night, you know. Mr. Harker said he had never had a colt he felt so confident about. He is a beauty, Forbes!"

"Yes, my lady."

But the maid still hesitated. Was she really watching her furtively, Sophie wondered, or was it just her own fancy? Was she always going to be fanciful now?

"James says – please what is he to say to the man on the phone, my lady? He has rung up twice before this morning, James says, and it's from Scotland Yard, my lady."

"Scotland Yard!" For one moment Sophie Burslem's heart seemed to stop beating; then went on again with great suffocating throbs. This time she was sure that her laugh did her credit. So had she laughed on the stage in the old days at Elmhurst. "Poor Forbes! You really look quite frightened.

Don't you know that detectives are down at Oxley watching Peep o' Day? It is something to do with that, of course. But why is James up here? Where is Ellerby?"

"I don't know, my lady. He went out ever so early this morning; we are wondering when he will be back, my lady."

"Rather an extraordinary proceeding on Ellerby's part," Sophie commented dryly. "Get my bath ready, please, Forbes, and tell James Sir John will be in directly, I expect."

She slipped on the side of the bed as she spoke and sat there watching Forbes as she went into the bathroom and turned on the tap.

Sophie Burslem looked very young this morning – too young to be Sir John's wife. She was a dainty vision in her soft, silken night-robe, with her pretty rounded neck and arms bare. Her shingled, chestnut hair was ruffled, it needed no permanent waving. The pink and white skin was as clear as ever, only the great, appealing brown eyes had altered indefinably. In the big pier-glass opposite she fancied that others could see the terrible fear that lurked in them, the dark circles round them. Long ago some one used to tell her that she had laughing eyes. Would anybody ever say that again? she asked herself. Just now they seemed to move of their own volition, glancing here and there into every corner fearfully. Suddenly they were caught by a tumbled heap of white by the sofa near the window. It was the frock she had worn last night just as she had thrown it down. She stared at it in a species of fascinated horror. Surely she was not mistaken. Across one fold there was an ugly, dark stain!

She got up and went over to it, her bare feet pattering over the polished boards between.

Forbes came back. "My lady, my lady, your slippers."

Sophie turned round and stood before the heap on the floor, her hands behind her, her breath coming quick and fast.

"Nonsense! I don't want slippers. You can go, Forbes. I will ring when I am ready."

Thus dismissed the maid had no choice but to depart. When the door had closed behind her, Sophie turned, and swiftly, noiselessly, almost threw herself on the tumbled white frock! Yes, she had made no mistake. Right in front, just where the silver girdle was caught up by a buckle of brilliants, a reddish brown stain ran almost down to the hem. She put out one finger and touched it – it was dry, quite dry. But there wasn't one minute to lose. At all hazards that ghastly stain must be done away with. She tore at it with her small, strong hands, but though the silk was soft it was tough, and she could make no impression on it. She caught up a pair of nail-scissors and cut and jagged ruthlessly. Then when she held the long, ragged strip in her hand, she gazed at the remains of what had been one of her prettiest gowns, in despair.

What on earth would Forbes say? But there was no time to think of that now. She caught up the remains of the frock and running into her dressing- room thrust it deep down into the well of the great wardrobe that took up all one side of the room. Then she crammed other things on the top and shut the door firmly. Later on she must think of something to tell Forbes, for now there was nothing to be done but to go on as usual until – She went into her bathroom, crushing up the piece of silk she had torn off in her hand.

She splashed in and out of the warm, scented water, then, when she had rubbed herself down, she lighted a match and tried to set the silk on fire. In vain, it would do nothing but smoulder and make a pungent, acrid smell of burning. What in Heaven's name was she to do? She dashed open the windows as far as they would go; she unstoppered one of the great bottles of scent on the dressing-table and flung the contents about bathroom and bedroom. Then a sudden inspiration came to her.

Inside the dressing-case, with its wonderful gold and jewelled fittings, which had been one of her husband's wedding presents, there was a secret drawer. She ran across, put the silk in the drawer, fastening it with a catch of which she alone knew the secret.

She rang for Forbes. The maid came in, wrinkling up her nose.

"Such a smell of burning, my lady!" Her beadlike, inquisitive eyes glanced round the room.

"I don't notice it," said Sophie. "Perhaps the gardeners are burning weeds outside. Give me my things quickly, Forbes; I must not be late for breakfast. Sir John means to start early."

The maid said nothing, but her sniff became accentuated as she went on with her mistress's toilet, set the soft shingled hair, and finally brought out the gown of grey marocain which Lady Burslem had decided to wear for the races.

Sophie let herself be dressed as if she had been a lay figure. All the while she was listening, listening. At last she was dressed, and her maid clasped a short string of pearls round her neck in place of the long necklace she generally wore.

She glanced at her reflection in the mirror. So she had seen herself look a hundred times – and yet would not the first person she met see the horror shadowing her eyes?

She went down to the breakfast-room. Everything was just as usual. A pile of letters lay beside her plate. Sir John's letters and *The Times*, folded as he liked it, lay by his. She went round the table and sat down. The very orderly, everyday aspect of the room held something sinister, some suggestion of evil to her jaundiced mind.

Though she drank a cup of tea feverishly and played with an omelette, she could not really eat anything. Presently she heard a knock and a ring at the front door.

She caught the echo of a voice in the hall. It sounded like that of her sister Clare – Mrs. Aubrey Dolphin. She was going with them to the races, of course, but She listened again. Another moment Clare came quickly into the room. With a word to the manservant she closed the door behind her. One look at her face told Lady Burslem that the supreme moment for which she had been waiting was here at last.

Clare came swiftly across the room and caught her sister in her arms.

"Sophie, darling, I bring you terrible news. You must be brave, dear, for all our sakes."

Sophie tried to free herself from the encircling arms. "What is it?" she questioned hoarsely. "Not Dad!"

Mrs. Dolphin would not let her go.

"No, no, my darling. It is John –"

"John –"

If there had been one drop of colour left in Sophie's face it was all drained away now.

"Ill," came slowly from between her stiffening lips. "Ill, Clare, not – not –"

"Ah, dearest, he would want you to be brave for his sake. He – he met with a terrible accident last night, Sophie, dear. And, you see, he was not quite a young man, he could not rally –"

"Why did they not send for me?" Sophie gasped.

"Dear, there was not time. He – he died before they could do anything!"

"He died – John died –"

This time all Mrs. Dolphin's strength could not hold her sister up. A dead weight, Lady Burslem sank through her arms and collapsed in a heap on the floor.

• • • • •

Meanwhile from all parts of England a great crowd was making its way to Epsom. It was the people's holiday and the people were bent on making the most of it. All night long, gipsies and parties of nomads had picnicked near the course.

This morning the tipsters were busy. For threepence you could learn the winner of every race. Not of the Derby itself. Nobody wanted a tip for that! It was Peep o' Day's Derby. Had not owner and trainer and jockey all agreed that Peep o' Day could not lose the Derby?

Peep o' Day! Peep o' Day! You heard it on all sides. Peep o' Day, the most popular favourite since the war! Peep o' Day! the crowd exulted.

And over by Peep o' Day's box his trainer, Matt Harker, was standing with bowed shoulders, and Howard Williams leaning up against the door would not have been ashamed to confess that there were tears in his eyes. Champion jockey though he was, he had never yet ridden a Derby winner; Matt Harker, though all the other classics had been taken by his stable, had never yet trained a Derby winner! All of them had been confident that today their ambitions would be realized.

And now Peep o' Day was scratched for the Derby!

CHAPTER III

The inquest on the body of Sir John Burslem had been opened at the Crown Inn at Hughlin's village, but only formal evidence of identity and medical evidence had been taken, and it had been adjourned until the following week, so that the police might have time for further inquiry. Stoddart and Harbord came out last. Stoddart's brows were drawn together in a heavy frown. Looking at him, his assistant felt sure that the case was troubling him more than he would have cared to confess. Somewhat curtly he declined the local superintendent's offer of hospitality, and motioned! Harbord into the run-about.

He did not speak until they had left Hughlin's Wood far behind, and were rapidly nearing London. Then he tossed an envelope over to Harbord.

"Think that can throw any light on the mystery?" Harbord opened the envelope and took out the contents. They consisted of various cuttings from newspapers. He read the first: "Burslem, Sir John, first baronet, born 18 –, eldest son of John Victor Burslem; married first Emma, daughter of Robert Somerville, by whom he had issue one daughter – Pamela Mary; married secondly the Honourable Sophie Charlotte Ann, younger daughter of the fourth Viscount Carlford. Residences: Greystone Hall, Meadshire, and 15 Porthwick Square. Clubs: Carlton Junior; Arts; St. James's.

Harbord put this back in the envelope and took out the smaller one; this was marked "From the Morning Herald": "A marriage has been arranged, and will shortly take place between Captain Charles Stanyard, second son of Sir William Stanyard of Wilton Hall, and Sophie Charlotte Ann, youngest daughter of Viscount Carlford."

Clipped with this was another: "The marriage arranged between Captain Charles Stanyard and Miss Sophie Carlford will not take place."

As Harbord put these back in the envelope he saw that there was yet one more. He picked it out: "A marriage has been arranged between Sir John Burslem, the well-known financier and racehorse owner, and the Honourable Sophie Charlotte Ann Carlford, younger daughter of Viscount Carlford. The marriage will take place early next month at St. Margaret's Westminster."

Harbord put it with the other and gave them to Stoddart.

The inspector looked at him. "You read a story there?"

"Yes and no," Harbord said slowly. "You don't mean –"

"I mean nothing, I think nothing," the inspector interrupted him. "How often am I to tell you that. It is my business to look for facts and to find them. Did you hear what won the Derby yesterday?"

Used as he was to the rapid workings of his superior's mind, Harbord looked his surprise at this change of subject.

"I don't take much interest in racing, sir, except that I have been hearing of nothing but Peep o' Day since we came here yesterday. But I did hear last night – yes, wasn't this Derby won by Perlyon, the second favourite. I thought I heard folks say he would not have stood a chance against Peep o' Day had he run."

"That's as it may be," the inspector observed sententiously. "I have known these hot-pots run nowhere more than once. But do you know who owns Perlyon?"

Harbord shook his head. "Haven't the slightest idea."

The inspector looked at him. "Sir Charles Stanyard, Captain Charles Stanyard – the sporting baronet, they call him. He came into the title on his father's death last year. His elder brother was killed a few months before in the hunting-field."

Neither of the men spoke again for a few minutes; at last Harbord said:

"Peep o' Day's scratching must have meant a good deal to him. But –"

"Thousands," said the inspector laconically. "Heard there was a row between two men at Wilton's the other night?"

"No. I was hard at work at the Barber-Astley case," Harbord answered, his interest growing.

"Well, there was a jolly row," Stoddart informed him. "And the two men who had it were Sir John Burslem and Sir Charles Stanyard, the sporting baronet. Ostensibly the quarrel was over the merits of their respective racehorses – Peep o' Day and Perlyon. In reality, rumour has whispered that the cause was very different. Therefore there are two things we must do to-day. First, we must ascertain, if we can, something of Sir Charles Stanyard's movements on the night of June 2nd and the early morning of June 3rd. Secondly, we must see Lady Burslem and hear what she can tell us of that night's tragedy; or perhaps we had better reverse the proceedings and see the lady first. We will drive straight to Porthwick Square."

He did not speak again as he steered the car carefully through the crowded roads as they entered London and made their way with all speed to Porthwick Square.

Drawn blinds shrouded the inhabitants of No. 15 from the public eye, but the inspector frowned as he saw the crowd outside. That the police were moving people on apparently made no difference. They merely went round and walked back another way.

The butler came forward when the door was open.

"Lady Burslem has promised us an interview this afternoon," Stoddart said, entering and beckoning to Harbord.

"Yes, her ladyship is expecting you, inspector," the butler said at once. "I was to take you to her directly you came. But I heard nothing of this – this –"

He glanced at Harbord as though hesitating as to what description must apply to him.

"That is quite right – I am answerable," the inspector said shortly. "Please to inform Lady Burslem that we are here."

The butler departed, looking as though the foundations of the earth must indeed be shaken when he had to take orders from a mere policeman. He returned immediately.

"Will you come this way, please."

He led them to a small room on the first floor.

Lady Burslem came to them at once. She walked very slowly; her slim shoulders were bent as if under an intolerable burden of grief. There was not one touch of colour in her face – cheeks and lips were alike ashen. There were great blue half-circles beneath her eyes, and her eyes themselves looked only about half their usual size. The eyelids were swollen, and drooped as though the young widow had cried until she did not know how to open them.

There was a great pity in the inspector's eyes as he watched her. He drew forward one of the big easy chairs and she sank into it wearily. Was it force of habit that made him place her so that the light fell on her face, Harbord wondered.

"You – you wanted to see me?" she said, her eyes not looking at him but wandering to the window which looked on to the Square garden and so was without the concealing blind.

"If you please, Lady Burslem."

The inspector went over and stood by the mantel piece, one arm resting on the shelf. Harbord waited; nearer the door.

"You will understand that, while we are anxious to spare you in every possible way, it is absolutely necessary that we should hear all that you can tell us of what took place the night before last."

"Yes, of course?"

Lady Burslem looked at him with wistful, tragic eyes. "Only there is so little I can tell you," she said, feverishly. "I can't understand it, and wonder and wonder until I think my brain will turn and that the mystery of it will drive me mad."

Her words, slow at first, began to come faster, her breathing grew more rapid; she twisted her hands together.

"I understand," the inspector said soothingly. "And that is where we want to help you. Now, if you would just tell us when you saw Sir John last?"

"Why, when we came home," Sophie Burslem said quickly. "We – we had been over to Oxley, you know. It was a lovely night and we had nothing particular on. At least, we had dances and receptions and things, but we made up our minds to go over to Oxley in the two-seater and see how Peep o' Day was getting on. So – so –"

Her voice failed. She fumbled in her bag, bringing out a small handkerchief, and began to dab her eyes.

"Yes?" the inspector prompted, after a pause. "Matt Harker has told us about your Oxley visit. You found Peep o'

Day at the top of his form, I think? 'Fit as a fiddle,' Harker said."

"Yes, he was," Lady Burslem assented, apparently controlling her voice by a supreme effort. "Sir John was so proud of him. He used to say that when Peep o' Day won the Derby his greatest ambition would be realized. Now – now –"

The inspector coughed. "When you left Oxley, where did you go?"

"Why, we came straight home," Sophie said simply. "It was late, of course. We had stayed so long at Oxley, but we had told Ellerby and Forbes, my husband's man and my maid, not to sit up for us. We were never people who wanted a lot of waiting on. We always liked to do things for ourselves."

"What time was it?"

"I do not know – exactly." Sophie hesitated. "I should think it was between one and two. I know Sir John wanted James, the second footman, who sat up for us to sign some paper and he said it must be dated June 3rd."

"To sign a paper?" For once the inspector was betrayed into showing some surprise. "What sort of a paper?"

"Oh, I don't know." Lady Burslem let her hands drop helplessly on her lap. "He signed it too – Sir John. Then he gave it to me and told me to take care of it."

The inspector did not speak for a minute. He took out his notebook and made a hieroglyphic entry.

Lady Burslem leaned back in her chair motionless, her hands lying very still before her. And yet the inspector had an odd fancy that from beneath the heavy, swollen lids the brown eyes were furtively watching him.

At last he spoke:

"Could we see the paper, Lady Burslem? It might help us – might throw some light on the mystery."

"You can't see it just now," Lady Burslem said apathetically, "because I have not got it here. Mr. Weldon, the lawyer, came in this morning and took it away with him. He said it might be important."

The inspector drew his brows together. "I must see Mr. Weldon. In the meantime, when the paper was signed what did Sir John do?"

"As I told you, he gave me the paper," Lady Burslem said tonelessly. "Then we went into the library and we both had some of the things they had put ready for us. Then – then" – the tears sounded vibrant in the sweet voice – "he – Sir John – went out to take the car to the garage. I thought he would be only a few minutes; but now I shall never see him again."

"Why did Sir John take the car to the garage himself, instead of sending one of the men?" the inspector inquired brusquely.

For a moment he fancied that a faint smile glimmered on the pale lips.

"He – he would not have trusted any of them. He was so proud of the two-seater. It had all the latest improvements. He would not let anyone drive it but himself."

The inspector nodded. That there were men and women too who would not let anyone else drive their car, as there were people who would not allow their pet horse, their bicycle to be ridden by anyone else, he knew. But it seemed to him rather a curious fancy on the part of a millionaire, like Sir John Burslem, to insist on taking the car to the garage himself.

"But he did not take it to the garage," he said, rather as if he were answering his own thoughts. "He never went near the garage. The car has been found, you know, Lady Burslem."

"No, I did not," Lady Burslem said, with a momentary accession of interest. "I never heard anything about it. Where was it? Where – where he was?"

"No," the inspector answered bluntly. "It was found on a piece of waste ground on the other side of the river that is used as a parking ground sometimes."

"How did it get there?" Lady Burslem's voice dropped almost to a whisper.

"That," said the inspector grimly, "1 should very much like to find out."

He opened his notebook again. "Has Sir John any enemies?" he asked, fixing a piercing glance on Lady Burslem.

"No, I am sure he had not," she said firmly. "Everybody liked him. He was a general favourite. He was so kind to every one."

"He had had no quarrel with anyone." The inspector's eyes were still watching closely.

"Certainly not!"

"Then," said the inspector very quietly, "you did not hear that a week ago he and Sir Charles Stanyard had a violent quarrel at Wilton's – so violent that the matter was to have been brought before the next Committee?"

The pallid face before him went suddenly scarlet, then rapidly white again.

"Oh, I knew that. Sir John told me there had been some sort of dispute. It was about their horses. I thought nothing of it."

"Naturally you would not," the inspector said in the characterless voice of his which Harbord knew meant that he was getting dangerous.

"But did Sir John tell you that the quarrel was about the racehorses?"

"Yes, yes; he said it was about their horses. Sir Charles owned Perlyon, you know, and he said he would beat Peep o' Day, and Sir John knew – knew he could not."

"And that was all?"

Again there was one of those very long pauses.

"Had Sir John and Sir Charles met since, Lady Burslem?"

"I don't know," Lady Burslem said listlessly. "I don't suppose I should have heard if they had."

"And yet Sir Charles was an old friend of yours – a neighbour of yours in the country," Stoddart suggested.

Again there was that momentary flood of crimson.

"I had not seen Sir Charles Stanyard for ages – until a few weeks ago, when we met accidentally at a dance. I danced with him then. I have not spoken to him since."

"Sir John made no objection to your dancing with him?"

"Certainly not!" There was a touch of hauteur now in the chilly tone. "I am perfectly ready to answer any questions that may help you to find out the cause of Sir John's death, inspector, but really I fail to see –"

"Be assured that I shall ask you no questions that are without some bearing on that subject, Lady Burslem."

The inspector's voice had a new note of sternness in it now.

"Then I am to understand that the last you saw of Sir John was when he left you ostensibly to take the car to the garage?"

"Absolutely the last!" Sophie Burslem assented, her fingers plucking restlessly at the handkerchief she still held, her brown eyes not looking up now, but mechanically following out the pattern of the carpet.

"And he said nothing to you of any intention to return to Oxley or any visit to Hughlin's Wood?"

"On the contrary, he said he should be only a few minutes away; the garage was only down the mews at the back of the house."

The inspector nodded. "And you, what did you do?"

"I went straight to bed." Lady Burslem looked straight at him now. "I was very tired and I wanted to be fresh for the races the next day. I went to sleep at once, and did not wake until my maid brought my tea."

"Quite natural," the inspector said. "Just one more point, and then I will not trouble you any more today. Sir John's relatives – I believe he had a brother and a daughter?"

"Both," Lady Burslem agreed. "The daughter – his, not mine – is abroad travelling in Italy with friends. The brother – you must have heard of him, the explorer – he is hunting about for buried cities or something in Tibet just now. We have cabled to his last known address and wired to Miss Burslem. She is on her way home."

"And the brother?"

"I am sure he will come when he gets the message," Lady Burslem said at once. "He is very charming, I know, though really I have seen very little of him. He was at my wedding. That is the only time I have seen him. The relations were rather strained between the two brothers: James married a variety actress, and although he did not get on very well with her himself he never forgave my husband for objecting to the marriage. So that was why we did not see so much of him as we otherwise should."

"Thank you, Lady Burslem." The inspector took his elbow off the mantelpiece and straightened himself. "Just one thing more – could you give me the name of Sir John's dentist?"

Sophie bit her lip. "No, really I couldn't. I have never had anything to do with dentists, but Ellerby would know." She rang the bell as she spoke and ordered the valet to come to them.

He did not keep them waiting.

"Ellerby –" she began at once.

The inspector stopped her.

"If you please, Lady Burslem."

He put the question to Ellerby.

Ellerby frowned. "I am sure I couldn't; Sir John never went to one here that I heard of. He went to one when he was over in the States, but I don't know where. He told me American dentists could knock spots off the English ones. It is all I know, inspector."

"Thank you. Then that is all this morning and I hope I may not need to trouble you again," turning back to Lady Burslem.

"Thank you, inspector!" Lady Burslem did not raise her eyes. Was it possible that he had not seen the terror in them? she asked herself.

Harbord followed his superior out of the house. Outside the crowd had increased. It needed all the efforts of the police to keep it moving. Stoddart gave a few sharp orders to a man in plain clothes; then he and Harbord got into the run-about in silence. When they were clear of the traffic and had got into a quiet street, Stoddart glanced at Harbord.

"What do you think of her ladyship?"

Harbord fenced. "What do you?"

The inspector did not look at him. "A pretty woman, a very pretty woman. For the rest, I shall be able to tell you more about her when I have seen the paper that Sir John signed that last night, and that Mr. Weldon holds."

CHAPTER IV

"I rang Sir Charles Stanyard up an hour ago, but he is not in town."

Inspector Stoddart was the speaker. He had been out for some time and had just returned. He was sitting before his desk in his room at Scotland Yard, and as he looked up at Harbord his expression was worried, troubled.

Harbord had also been out since early morning, pursuing a different line of investigation. He carried a small brown parcel, which he laid upon the inspector's desk. Stoddart did not take it up. Instead he sat back in his chair and drummed absently on the open flap of his desk as he looked up at Harbord.

"This case does not get any easier, Alfred."

"It does not, sir," his subordinate agreed with emphasis.

"I have just come from the lawyers, Weldon & Furnival of Spencer's Inn," Stoddart went on almost as if he were talking to himself, his eyes not looking at Harbord now, but staring straight in front of him at a map of Old London pasted on the wall opposite.

Harbord waited.

"Weldon & Furnival were Sir John's lawyers," Stoddart continued. "Weldon transacted most of the business. I went to get the paper Lady Burslem said Sir John signed when they came home, which he told her to take care of and which she had given to Mr. Weldon. Well, I had some trouble in persuading Mr. Weldon even to let me see it. He utterly declined to let me bring it away."

"But could he refuse?" Harbord questioned doubtfully.

"Not ultimately, of course. Still, he can put a good many difficulties in our way, as he did. But the point of the whole matter is this" – the inspector paused a moment, and then went on impressively – "that paper was a short will, drawn up apparently in Sir John's own handwriting, leaving everything of which he died possessed to his wife, appointing her sole executor and residuary legatee. His daughter – his only child – is not even mentioned."

"What an extraordinary thing!" Harbord exclaimed. "Why on earth should he make a new will at that time of night? Did he know he was in some danger?"

Stoddart nodded. "Exactly the questions I have been putting to myself, but I can find no answer to them. More especially as he had already made one will since his marriage with Miss Carlford. This former one was drawn up by Mr. Weldon. It left Lady Burslem and his daughter well provided for, but the bulk of his fortune was to be held in trust for any son that might be born to him. Only in the case of his second marriage, like his first, failing to provide him with an heir, was his property to be divided equally between Lady Burslem and his daughter Pamela and any other daughters he might have. It appears to be, on the face of it, a far more satisfactory arrangement, and the questions one cannot help asking oneself are: "Why did he want to make a hurried fresh will in that last moment? And had he any reason to suppose that it was his last moment?"

"Could it have been a duel?" Harbord said in a puzzled tone.

"Hardly!" The inspector laughed satirically. "The duellist does not throw his dead opponent in a ditch and go off with his car. Besides, who would fight a duel in these days?

"I don't know," Harbord said in a befogged tone. Then, brightening up, "I beg your pardon, sir. Of course it was an idiotic suggestion. But this case so bristles with impossibilities that goodness knows what we shall come to before we have finished with it."

"I hope at any rate we shall keep our heads," the inspector said dryly. "This last will is witnessed by James, the second footman, and Ellerby, Sir John's man."

"It is a queer affair altogether," Harbord concluded, "and I'm afraid a little discovery I made down at Hughlin's Wood this morning will not throw any additional light on the matter."

The inspector pricked up his ears. "Discovery! What was it?"

"Well, I proceeded on the lines you suggested," Harbord went on, "and I have found a man who saw two cars, both two-seaters, coming from Oxley at a great pace towards Hughlin's Wood. Each of them had two occupants, a man and a woman. But he did not notice numbers or anything else that would help us to identify either of them. At last I began to think he had taken something that had made him see double. Finding I could make nothing more of him, I thought I would take another look at the ditch and its surroundings. On the other side of the ditch from the road, behind one of those old trees, I found this."

He took up the parcel he had brought in and carefully unwrapping it held up the contents.

The inspector stared. "What's that?"

"One of those wretched little handbags that women carry about and are always leaving behind them," Harbord explained. "And it has just got the usual rubbish they put in them, lip-stick, powder-puff, and what-not. But one thing that most of them haven't got is this." He held out a betting slip – on it was scrawled in pencil, "Put me a fiver on Peep o' Day, fiver each way on Perlyon." "She wouldn't want to make bets after the race was run, would she? Particularly as Peep o' Day was scratched."

The inspector did not look impressed. "No, but that might have been written out beforehand and forgotten."

"Of course it might," Harbord agreed with a crest-fallen air. "But nobody has had the chance to lay the bag where it was found since the murder. And the boys from the Beacon School had been playing rounders among the trees on that very afternoon of June 2nd. A couple of masters were with them, and both masters and boys agreed there was no bag there then. They say they could not have helped seeing it if there had been, as that particular tree was one of their goals."

The inspector shrugged his shoulders. "Umph! Pretty strong evidence that some woman was there on the evening or night of June 2nd. But it does not take us any further."

"No, perhaps not. But what do you make of this?"

Harbord dived into the bag again and brought out another bit of paper.

On it was scrawled in what looked like the same writing as that on the other: "Will probably leave Oxley a little after twelve. Should reach the Wood in ten minutes."

Stoddart knit his brows. "As I said before, it seems strong evidence that some person was lurking there on the night of the tragedy. But I suppose you don't suggest that the owner of this thing" – giving the bag a contemptuous flick – "waited there under the trees and took a pot-shot at Sir John Burslem as he passed in his car, then pulled him out and flung him into a ditch. Besides, you are forgetting when Sir John left Oxley soon after twelve he had his wife with him. He drove her home, drew up and signed his will after that. It was not until he went out again for some inexplicable reason and drove to Hughlin's Wood a second time that he met his death. But the owner of this bag must be traced. It is quite possible that she witnessed the murder, or at any rate knows something of the events that led up to it. The question is, How is this woman to be found? She must have heard of Sir John Burslem's death – the papers are full of nothing else – and she hasn't come forward. The inference is that she has some reason for her silence, and one can scarcely conceive that it is an innocent one."

"Hardly," Harbord assented. He waited silently while Stoddart stood up, took a pipe from the mantelpiece, filled it deliberately and then sat down while he lighted a match.

"There's no doubt a pipe does clear one's brain in a way that this rubbish you younger ones smoke doesn't touch," he said, throwing a cigarette-case over to Harbord. "Help yourself. They are Imperial Regent, quite a new brand, and not bad. So far as I can see, a journey to Oxley is the first thing indicated and a few inquiries as to any strangers who were seen in the neighbourhood that day, or who had made inquiries about Sir John Burslem or his projected visit. Somebody must have given the information away."

"Precisely. But –"

A tap at the door interrupted Harbord before he could finish his sentence. A man in undress uniform opened the door. "A young lady is asking to see the officials in charge of the Burslem case, sir."

"A young lady?" the inspector demanded sharply. "What young lady? What name did she give?"

"I asked her, sir. But she said you did not know her."

"Ask her again."

The man saluted and departed. Stoddart looked across at Harbord.

"Is this your mysterious lady of the Wood and the handbag?"

As he spoke the door opened. "Miss Burslem, sir – Miss Pamela Burslem."

"Sir John's daughter! Show her in at once," the inspector ordered. He drew in his lips as he looked across at Harbord.

Miss Burslem was ushered in in a moment – a tall, slim girl, in a short skirt and with the shingled hair of the period. She looked essentially modern. She glanced at Stoddart, who had risen and put his pipe down, and from him to Harbord.

"Which of you is in charge of the case?" she inquired abruptly. "The case of my father's murder I mean?"

"I am," Stoddart answered. "And Mr. Harbord," with a wave of his hand at the young man, "is my very capable and tried assistant."

"Oh!"

Miss Burslem took the chair nearest her. "Have you found out who is guilty?" she demanded unceremoniously.

"Not yet," the inspector said. "I understood that you were in Italy, otherwise –"

"So I was in Italy," Miss Burslem said abruptly. "You didn't expect me to stay there quietly when my father was murdered, I suppose?"

"No, but I was afraid that you might not have got home in time –"

"We are not living in the days of stage-coaches and sailing boats," the girl said scornfully. "I flew, of course. Reached Croydon this morning and motored straight on."

It was evident to the inspector at a glance that the girl was tired and overwrought. Unlike her stepmother, she did not look as if she had been crying. Instead, her grey eyes were bright, hard and tearless.

"But I will not rest until my father's murderer is punished," she cried impatiently, "and I can tell you who he is – Sir Charles Stanyard, and if my stepmother would speak the truth –"

"Hush! Hush! my dear young lady," the inspector said in real alarm. "Do you know that you might bring grave trouble upon yourself by making such a statement?"

"You mean that Stanyard might bring a libel against me?" Miss Burslem said more quietly. "Now, I am not going to turn hysterical on your hands. Don't be afraid. But" – she pressed her lips together and looked at him squarely in the face before she continued – "I mean my father's murderer to be found and brought to justice if I spend every penny I possess. That is why I came to you at once, as soon as I arrived. Don't think of expense; I am going to offer a reward – oh, a very big reward – the biggest perhaps that has ever been offered, to bring the guilt   home –"

The inspector held up his hand. "Miss Burslem, everything will be done that can be done. As for money" – he shrugged his shoulders – "that will make no difference. Common justice for the rich as well as for the poor demands that Sir John's murderer should be found and punished. With regard to offering a reward, it may be useful. But I must tell you that no member of the police force is allowed to take it."

"Well, if you stand for British justice –" retorted Miss Burslem more equably. "Can't you see the whole thing? Lady Burslem was engaged to Sir Charles Stanyard when they never thought he would come in to the title and the estates. Then she met my father, who fell foolishly, madly in love with her. She threw over Captain Stanyard and married my father. Do you know that she was twenty-one and he was forty-two when she married him? Is it likely that she would care for him?" with the fine scorn of youth for middle age. "And my father's death meant heaps of money for Sir Charles Stanyard. It meant that Perlyon won the Derby instead of Peep o' Day, and they say he was on his colt to any amount. Oh, he knew Peep o' Day wouldn't run!"

"My dear young lady, do you think a man in Sir Charles Stanyard's position would willingly put his neck in a noose for the sake of a few thousand pounds?" Stoddart questioned impressively. "And there is another question: What would your father have said if he heard you bring such a charge?"

"I don't know!"

For one moment Pamela's composure threatened to give way. They could see her throat twitching painfully.

"I haven't seen so much of my father lately," she confessed. "Before his second marriage I was always with him. But since" – forlornly – "I don't think he has wanted me – much." She got up. "Well, that is all. I want to put you on the right track, to tell you to offer the biggest reward that has ever been offered for the discovery of the murderer."

After a moment's hesitation, she held out her hand to the inspector.

He took it in his for a moment.

"We will let you know when it is desirable to offer a reward, Miss Burslem. And in the meantime let me advise you to put all these lamentable ideas out of your head. Believe me, things will not turn out as you expect."

He opened the door and escorted her out of the building.

When he came back he looked at Harbord.

"Nice sort of young person, eh?"

Harbord waited a minute.

"Well, poor girl!" he said at last, "she is evidently overwrought and overstrained, but she has managed to pitch on the obvious clue, hasn't she?"

"She has, but to my mind the obvious clue is generally the wrong one," the inspector observed sententiously.

Meanwhile Pamela had dismissed her car; she felt that she must be alone to think – to try to realize this awful thing that had befallen her. She went to the Embankment and for a while stood watching the sluggish moving waters of the Thames, then almost without knowing what she was doing she turned to the right and in a few minutes found herself in St. James's Park. She was buried deep in thought when, just as she was about to cross one of the bridges, she suddenly collided with a young man coming along quickly from the opposite direction.

He raised his hat with a murmured apology; then stopped short with a sharp exclamation:

"You!"

Pamela stared at him.

"You!" she exclaimed blankly. "What are you doing here?"

The man laughed. He was a tall, fair young man, immaculately garbed and groomed.

"I live near here, don't you know, in Aldwyn Mansions. I am on my way home now. I have just come back from Epsom – looked out for you there, hoped I might see you – and now I meet you on my own doorstep as it were. I should like you to have seen the Derby this year."

"The Derby – don't talk of it!" Pamela's eyes filled with tears. "And Perlyon, I hate Perlyon; I would have done anything – anything to stop him winning."

"You would have liked to have stopped Perlyon winning? Why?"

Pamela did not beat about the bush. "Because Perlyon belongs to the man I dislike most on earth – Charles Stanyard."

The man laughed, his eyes dwelling on the fair, girlish face that had haunted his dreams for the past month.

"Why do you dislike Stanyard, poor beggar?"

"He is not a poor beggar at all," Pamela said decidedly. "He is a terrible man. He has taken care he is not poor. He has destroyed people's lives and happiness to make himself rich –" Her voice broke.

"What?" The man started violently. "Charles Stanyard has – You are getting at me. Do you know him?"

"No, and I don't mean to," Pamela returned uncompromisingly. "Do you?"

"Yes, I know him rather well," the man said after a moment's pause. "He is not up to much, I admit, but I don't see why you should hate him. I should have said he was a harmless sort of chap."

"Perhaps you would not say he was a harmless sort of chap if he had murdered your father!" Pamela retorted.

"Good Lord! murdered your father!" the man ejaculated. "What sort of a story have you got hold of? I know Charles Stanyard pretty well all through, and, whatever his sins may be, I can assure you he is no murderer."

"Well, I think he is, you see," Pamela returned icily. "Perhaps if it were your father he had killed it would make a difference?"

"But why on earth should Charles Stanyard kill your father?"

"Well, some people would tell you because Peep o' Day –"

"What! You don't mean that you are Sir John Burslem's daughter?"

"I am Pamela Burslem," returned the girl with a little air of dignity. "Ah, now you see why I say Sir Charles Stanyard killed my father!"

"On the contrary," the man said with a certain conviction in his tone, "I am quite positive that he did not!"

"Well, you can stick to your opinions and I can stick to mine!" Pamela finished. "Good-bye. I must go home, only" – with a quiver of her lower lip – "it is not home any longer." She turned away for a moment.

In a couple of strides the man had caught her up. "I cannot let you go like this. You don't know how I have thought of you – longed to meet you again ever since that night I danced with you. May I write to you?"

Just the faintest suspicion of one of Pamela's old dimples peeped out. "You forget that I don't know your name. I should not know who the letter came from."

"You don't know my name?" the man repeated in a dazed tone. "No, I was forgetting. My name is Richard Leyton – Dick my friends call me."

CHAPTER V

"It is a wicked will; an infamous will!" Old General Percival was the speaker. "I cannot understand my friend, John Burslem, making such a will."

Sir John Burslem's funeral had taken place that morning. By his own wish he had been buried by the side of his first wife in the great cemetery in North London. Neither his second wife nor his daughter had been present and there had been no flowers, by request.

There had been no communication from his brother, the explorer, and it was doubtful whether the telegram had reached him. Lord Carlford and his son, Alan, had been the chief mourners; there had been a great following of friends and acquaintances, of those who had been connected with the dead man, either in the financial or in the racing world. Crowds, full of morbid curiosity, had lined the roads and had filled the cemetery.

There had been no formal reading of the will, but a few of Sir John's oldest friends had returned with Lord Carlford; and then Mr. Weldon had disclosed the disposal of his property, made by Sir John on the night of his death.

General Percival had been the first to break the silence that followed, and as he finished a low murmur of assent ran round the room.

At the same moment Lady Burslem and her stepdaughter, with Lady Carlford and Mrs. Dolphin, entered the room. They seated themselves at the top of the long library table.

General Percival was not to be daunted. When the little confusion caused by the entrance of the new arrivals had subsided, he began again:

"It is an infamous will! You were good enough to tell me that I was one of the executors, Mr. Weldon – I shall refuse to act! If Miss Burslem takes my advice she will contest the will."

"I beg your pardon, general," Mr. Weldon interrupted; "I said that you were one of the executors of the will made by Sir John Burslem directly after his second marriage. This one, drawn up by Sir John himself on the last day of his life, leaves everything to Lady Burslem, and appoints her sole executrix and residuary legatee."

"Disgraceful!" frowned the general. "I wonder you were not ashamed to make such a will, Mr. Weldon, or to produce it now."

"I had nothing to do with the making of it," Mr. Weldon exclaimed. "I thought I had made it plain, general, that the whole of this will is in Sir John's own writing. Whatever our opinion of it may be, it appears to me there is no possible ground for contesting."

"I do not want to contest it," Pamela said, her cheeks and her eyes flashing. "Daddy was quite right to leave his money as he liked. I do not want it; I have plenty of my own."

There was an uncomfortable silence. Mr. Weldon fidgeted with his papers and coughed.

Pamela glanced at him. "Haven't I?" she questioned.

Mr. Weldon looked unhappy.

"Well, my dear Miss Burslem, under your mother's settlement – you must remember that Sir John was a comparatively poor man in those days – you come into a sum of three thousand pounds when you are twenty-one. Until then you will have an allowance of course, but –"

Pamela turned from white to red, back again to white.

"You do not mean that I have no money of my own that I can use now? But I want a lot at once; I want to engage a smart detective to find out –"

Her voice broke in a strangled sob.

Lady Burslem leaned forward and touched her arm.

"It shall make no difference, Pam, not a bit of difference, dear –"

With a gesture of loathing Pamela shook off the caressing hand and turned away. Then like a small torrent of grief she rushed out of the room.

Lord Carlford, a gentleman of the old school, rose and took his daughter's hand.

"Come, my dear, you have heard all that is necessary," with a glance at his wife and elder daughter.

When they had gone Mr. Weldon looked round. "There is no more to be said, gentlemen; this is a very sad affair. Nothing can be gained by discussing it. I am sure all our sympathy goes out to Lady Burslem and her stepdaughter in their tragic bereavement."

General Percival sniffed audibly. "I am extremely sorry for Miss Burslem," he said pointedly; "this will is a crying scandal.

When this Lady Burslem marries again – as of course she will – Burslem's fortune will be spent on her second husband, and Burslem's girl, who used to be the apple of his eye, will not get a penny."

"It is scarcely decent to talk of Lady Burslem's second husband when her first is only this day buried," Mr. Weldon said expressively.

"Decent! I dare say it is not!" the general growled. "Precious few natural things are! But it is what the widows mostly think of, let me tell you that. Not the one they put underground, but the one they hope to find on top."

Meanwhile the widowed Lady Burslem had walked past the drawing-room, resisting her father's gesture towards them.

"No, you all go in there and have tea and things; I am going back to my room. I must be alone to think."

"Well, I shall see you in, anyhow," Mrs. Dolphin said restlessly, linking her arm in her sister's. "Don't be an ass, Sophie; of course I am coming in to make you comfortable. I'm not too fond of that maid of yours: she seems to me to be always watching you."

"I don't care much about her, either," said Sophie listlessly. "I don't think I shall keep her. I think I shall go abroad in a week or two, and I should prefer some one who speaks Italian."

The door into her room stood open. Forbes was near the window, apparently holding something up to the light. She turned as the sisters entered, and for a moment Sophie fancied she looked discomposed. She recovered herself immediately, however, and came forward.

"You look tired, my lady, quite worn out. A little *sal volatile* and a rest in your favourite chair –"

She drew one up to the open window as she spoke.

Her tone was sympathetic, but Clare Dolphin, watching her, saw a look of triumph gleam for a moment in her eyes.

Sophie lay back in her chair and submitted to her maid's ministrations without the protest her sister had half expected. Presently she looked up.

"I am all right now, Clare. Forbes will look after me. And then I must be alone. It seems to me that I have not had a moment to think since John —"

Mrs. Dolphin did not look quite pleased. "Oh, very well, then, if you don't want me I will go home. Goodness knows, I have plenty to do. But I didn't like the idea of your being alone."

"You are very kind." Sophie received her sister's kisses passively, rather than returned them. "But — but, you see, there is so much that I shall have to do alone now."

"Oh, well, I will come in again some time this evening, just to see how you are."

She shut the door with a decided jerk as she went out.

Sophie sat up. Her languor had momentarily disappeared. "What was that you were looking at when we came in, Forbes?"

Forbes hesitated.

"Well, I had just found your frock, my lady. The one you wore for dinner on June 2nd. I found it all crushed together at the bottom of the wardrobe. It is in a fearful state, my lady. The front breadth is right out."

She shook the dilapidated garment before Sophie's unwilling eyes as she spoke. One glance was enough to show its hopeless condition — dirty, covered with mud-stains. There were still a few ominous dark stains left on the bodice, and the front breadth hung literally in rags.

"What am I to do with it, my lady? I really can hardly touch it."

"It is in a terrible state," Sophie said, staring at it with fascinated eyes. "I knew it was in a mess, but I had no idea that it was as bad as this. Of course I wore it when I went to

Oxley. That, and my purple coat with the beaver collar over it. And of course we did a lot of walking in and out. They – they wanted me to see everything. Earlier in the day it had been raining."

"Yes, of course, my lady." But the maid was not satisfied. "Just look at the front, my lady, all in rags!"

Sophie gazed at it in silence for a minute. "It – there are lots of thorn bushes near the stables, and we left the car a little way away. I suppose I got my frock caught on the bushes going back."

"It looks as if it had been cut, my lady, as if some one had taken a knife and hacked at it," the maid objected, holding out one side.

Lady Burslem sat back and closed her eyes. ' "Well, I am sure I do not know what has happened to it. Put it in the rag-bag, please, Forbes, or wherever you put such things. I don't care what becomes of it. I do not suppose I shall ever wear white again. You can take that white and gilt frock of mine that you f liked so much when it came home last week. It will do for you when you go to a dance with your young man."

"Oh, my lady, and you have never had it on. It does seem a shame. I shall love to have it. Not that I shall be going to any dances now. Tom and me, we lost too much over Peep o' Day."

"Ah! I must have a talk with you about that later on, Forbes." Lady Burslem's accession of energy left her suddenly. "I will have some more *sal volatile*, and – and then I will see you again later."

When at last the maid had retired Sophie sat up and looked round her cautiously. Her cheeks were burning now and her eyes were fever bright. She went across to the door and locked it. Then she came slowly back, her eyes fixed on her dressing-case.

"I must!" she whispered to herself. "I must make sure."

She opened the case. Everything looked just as usual. She felt for the spring that opened the secret drawer. Was it her fancy, or did it work more stiffly than usual? It moved with a sort of creak that she did not seem to have noticed before. And then she uttered an exclamation of horror and dismay. She had put that long strip of satin with its ugly, brown stain in the drawer. Yes, there was – there could be – no mistake about that. And now the drawer was empty!

Frantically she pulled it out. She shook it. She turned it topsy-turvy and felt behind it.

In vain – no silk was there!

CHAPTER VI

"Sir Charles Stanyard?" Inspector Stoddart said inquiringly.

"He is expecting you, sir."

The manservant preceded Stoddart and Harbord along the passage, and opened the door at the end.

They saw a comfortable-looking room, apparently furnished as a study, and a pleasant-looking, fair, young man sitting at the top of the table. He looked up as they entered.

"Good morning, Inspector Stoddart; you wanted to see me?"

"I did, Sir Charles. I am in charge of the Burslem case."

Stanyard raised his eyebrows. "Indeed, I fail to see the connexion. Unless, as somebody said to me plainly the other day, you imagine that I shot Sir John Burslem, so that my horse might win the Derby."

"If I thought that I should hardly be here," Stoddart said gravely. "But because it is my duty to trace every, even the very slenderest, clue that may help to elucidate the mystery of Sir John Burslem's death, I must ask you to give me some account of your movements on the night of June 2nd."

"On June 2nd." Sir Charles Stanyard frowned, as if the effort to remember was too strenuous for him. "Well, I went over to Epsom in the afternoon. I wanted to see how Perlyon was after his journey. Epsom is rather a long way from Maybank, you know, and old Tom Burton, best trainer in the world, brought Perlyon across country in a sort of glorified horse-box, wired to me that the colt was a bit nervous, so I went down to see him. I was detained on the way, so I did not get there till after six. I found Perlyon in first-rate trim, quieted down wonderfully, and as fresh as paint. Naturally I was a bit bucked, and when Tom Burton asked me to have a bit of dinner with him, and then go round and see what news we could pick up about the other gee-gees, particularly Peep o' Day, well, I stopped."

"Ah!" Stoddart looked at him closely. "Did you see Sir John Burslem?"

"No, I did not!" Stanyard said emphatically. "And I may tell you, inspector, that even if I had wanted to win the Derby badly enough to risk my neck for it, there was no need for me to kill Sir John Burslem. Perlyon is a real first-class colt, well bred on both sides by Crown Royal out of Irish Pearl. He could have licked Peep o' Day hollow, given him ten pounds and beaten him. I hope they may meet as four-year-olds next year, and then you will see."

"Well, I was only told that Peep o' Day was the favourite," the inspector returned phlegmatically. "What I know about horseflesh might be written on a threepenny bit. Beyond putting a trifle on the Derby, like everybody else, I never do any betting. May I ask what you did after your walk round with Mr. Burton, Sir Charles?"

"Can't say I did much – there was not much to be done," Stanyard responded. "Stood about, don't you know, talked about Perlyon and Peep o' Day and made up our minds, me and old Tom, to put the shirts off our backs on Perlyon."

"What time did you start back?"

Stanyard got up and, standing before the empty fireplace, leaned against the high wooden shelf.

"Well, really, do you know, I couldn't say positively – about twelve, or a little after, I should think. The beastly old bus broke down a mile or two out, and I had to spend a good half-hour tinkering at it."

"Did Sir John Burslem's car pass you?"

"Shouldn't have been any the wiser if it had," Stanyard retorted. "I shouldn't have recognized Burslem passing quickly in a car. I might have made a shot at him if he had been walking, but just jigging by in a car what chance should I have? Besides, most of the time my old bus was on top of me, and I was poking at her inside; should not have seen Peep o' Day himself, let alone Burslem."

"But Lady Burslem was with Sir John. You would have known her?"

Stanyard turned his head away, and catching up an ivory ornament from the mantelshelf began to turn it about in his fingers.

"Now you are talking! And I know what you are getting at. Because I was a silly ass about Sophie Carlford in my salad days, you think I am keen enough after all this time to do old Burslem in so that I can marry her myself. As if when a chap had been chucked over once he is dotty enough to go on hankering after the girl. If he is – well, his name will not be Charles Stanyard, and that is all there is to that!"

"You were dancing with Lady Burslem at the Ruthwyn Club a week or two ago."

"Now, how did you tumble to that?" Sir Charles inquired, staring at him. "Yes, I just came across her by chance talking to a friend of mine. I had nothing against her. Never do bear malice, you know, so I said, 'Let's have a turn for the sake of old times.' So we did, and that's all there is about that."

"Thank you for being so frank, Sir Charles." Stoddart waited a moment as if considering some point, then said:

"And about the row at the Wilton Club a week before Sir John's death?"

Stanyard opened his eyes wider than ever. "I say, you have been pokin' round, haven't you? Well, it was a bit of a ramp – seemed as if the old chap was trying to get me. It was something I said about Peep o' Day and old Matt Harker, and Burslem overheard and came for me. Bad-tempered sort of chap, I should say. But, bless your life, it meant nothing. Should have got over it and been good friends later on, I dare say."

"Well, you might," Stoddart said doubtfully. "Now, what about this, Sir Charles?"

He drew a little packet carefully wrapped up in tissue paper from his pocket; he threw off the paper and disclosed a silver cigarette-case with a monogram on the side.

"Is this yours?"

"Why, yes it is," Stanyard said, taking it from him. "I was wonderin' this morning what had become of the bloomin' thing. How did you come across it, inspector?"

"It was found in Sir John's run-about the day after his death," the inspector said quietly.

The ivory ornament in Stanyard's hand cracked suddenly. "Oh, I say, that's impossible! How could it have got there?"

"That," said the inspector very softly, "I thought you could explain, Sir Charles."

"Well, then, I can't," said Sir Charles, setting down the broken ornament with a snap and putting the cigarette-case beside it. "I know no more about it than the man in the moon or yourself, inspector; not so much I expect. So that's that! Hadn't you better arrest me and save yourself the trouble of lookin' after me. There's a dirty sort of dodger always at my heels; I guess he's one of your lot."

The inspector made no answer to this sally. "Then there is nothing more to be done now, Sir Charles," he said gravely.

When they had left the Mansions and were walking across the Green Park, Stoddart glanced round at his assistant.

"What do you think of that young man, Harbord?"

"I really don't know." Harbord hesitated. "I thought he was all quite straight and above-board at first; but I didn't quite like his manner over the cigarette-case. He wasn't quite frank about that, I am certain. But he doesn't look like a murderer."

"Murderers never do. If they did they wouldn't get the chance to murder anybody," the inspector observed sententiously.

"When was the cigarette-case discovered?" Harbord inquired.

"The day after the murder, as I said – that is to say, on June 4th. The car was found at the parking place in South London, you remember; at least, the car is said to have been found there. A man who hangs about the parking ground looking for odd jobs said he found it in the car afterwards identified as Sir John Burslem's. His account is that when he saw it he took it out, thinking it would be stolen if left there, and that the owner, when he came back, would reward him. Sir John, of course, did not return, and in the hue and cry about the car, and Sir John's mysterious death, he forgot all about the case, until yesterday morning, when he suddenly remembered it and brought it to the Yard."

"A queer tale, isn't it, sir?" Harbord said doubtfully. "What sort of chap is this man?"

"Oh, William Dawson, his name is – a good character in the neighbourhood, as far as I can make out. Otherwise, of course, he wouldn't be allowed on the parking ground. And I expect his tale is substantially true, but of course it's impossible of verification."

"How in the world did it get there?" cogitated Harbord. "I don't see –"

"Nor I," Stoddart agreed. "Take it all in all, I never met with an affair that bristled with such difficulties as this Burslem case. Granted that Stanyard's case was found in the car, and that, in spite of his denial, Sir Charles Stanyard had been in the Burslem car that night, Sir John himself took the car to the parking ground, so he was alive and well after Stanyard lost the case."

"That seems one point at which our inquiries might begin," Harbord said, wrinkling his brows. "Suppose it was not Sir John himself but his murderer who took the car to the garage, the whole affair becomes more simple."

"Yes. But unfortunately the case does not fall into line with our ideas," the inspector observed sarcastically. "Dawson's description of Sir John is fairly accurate. He picked his photograph out from a dozen others. The only thing that strikes me as odd is that a woman drove on to the ground almost immediately after Sir John and ranged her car beside the other. He did not take particular notice of her, he said, but he saw her stooping over the car. Then she almost ran off the parking ground and hurried away in the same direction as Sir John Burslem, who had turned to the right. But they didn't appear to know one another, Dawson says. They met when Sir John was going out and she was coming in, and they didn't speak. I don't think it helps us much. It is quite likely that the woman has nothing to do with the case."

"On the other hand," Harbord suggested, "suppose this was the woman who watched among the trees at Hughlin's Wood?"

"Was there such a woman?" the inspector questioned. "I must confess I'm rather sceptical."

"The bag seems to me pretty strong evidence," Harbord persisted.

The inspector thought the matter over for a minute or two. At last he said:

"Are you working on the theory that this unknown woman was the murderess? Because against that there is this fact that, whether Burslem was shot in the car or out of it, no woman could have lifted up a man of his bulk and build and pitched him into that ditch."

"No, sir, I am not working on that theory or any other," Harbord answered in an injured tone. "As you have so often impressed upon me, it is fatal to start with a preconceived theory. Besides, so far as I can see, no theory that I can form in any way fits the case. Why should Sir John bring his wife home hurriedly, draw up a will, rush his car to that parking place, and then tear back to Hughlin's Wood and get himself murdered? It sounds quite mad, and yet I suppose it is what really happened."

"Suppose!" the inspector echoed, looking at his young subordinate keenly. "Not much supposition about it. We know it happened. What bee have you got in your bonnet?"

"Well, I expect you will say it is worse than that." Harbord dropped his voice, looking round for possible eavesdroppers. "This case intrigues me more than I can say. I think of it all day and lie awake at night trying to think of some possible solution. Last night, like an inspiration, it flashed across me – impersonation. Has that occurred to you, sir?"

"No, I cannot say that it has," said the inspector in the same low tone. "At least, to be quite candid, I have had such a thought and I have dismissed it as untenable."

"I suppose it is," Harbord said reluctantly. "And yet I cannot help saying to myself" – his voice becoming a mere whisper – "supposing an appointment was made for that night of June 2nd at Hughlin's Wood. And supposing – just supposing for argument's sake – that the murderer assumed his victim's identity, drove the car back to town, forged the new will, and left the car in the parking place. On that theory alone can we explain certain happenings."

"Can we explain them on that theory?" the inspector questioned, his face very grave. "Be careful, Harbord; do you realize what your words imply?"

"I think so," Harbord answered, his face distinctly whiter, but his eyes like steel as he faced his superior squarely.

"A man's nearest and dearest have conspired to get him out of the way before now; also a murderer has passed as his victim. You remember that case a couple of years ago when a lawyer was murdered in the Crow's Inn?"

"Perfectly," the inspector assented. "But the two cases are not on all fours. In the Crow's Inn case no one who knew the victim saw the murderer. In this, if there were any foundation for your theory, there must not only be the complicity of the wife, the drive back to town, but the connivance of the servants who signed the will – which the experts say, though showing signs of being hurriedly written, is undoubtedly in Sir John's writing and on his own notepaper – and the testimony of Dawson, who picked out Sir John's photograph from a quantity of others."

"I am assuming the complicity of the first – I must," Harbord said, his tone troubled. "As for the others – well, people can be made up to look like anybody. Fat people can be made to look thin and thin people fat."

"Possibly," the inspector said doubtfully. "But I must remind you that there were signs of a struggle at Hughlin's Wood and also in the state of Sir John's clothing. No make-up would stand it!"

"Does not the assumed complicity rather settle that?" Harbord questioned.

"How about the servants? The footman who admitted them, and Ellerby, the valet, who witnessed the will?"

"Would it be possible to examine these two with a view to my possible theory?" Harbord asked tentatively. "Their evidence at the inquest was purely formal, and we have had no opportunity."

"Inquest!" the inspector broke out irritably. "The deuce, what's the good of an inquest anyway. Just to allow folks to make a nuisance of themselves, to defeat the ends of justice. Even if you do manage to give the coroner a hint and he takes it some damned juryman is sure to jump up and ask the very question you want to avoid answering, and that gives the whole show away. Tell you what, Harbord, we will just take a taxi to Porthwick Square, interview these two men and see what support we can get for this previous theory of yours."

He put up his hand as he spoke and caught a passing taxi. It was only a few minutes drive to Porthwick Square, and the inspector did not speak. But glancing at his knit brows, Harbord knew that he was revolving some of the knotty problems presented by this new theory.

In Porthwick Square the door was opened by James, the second footman. The butler came forward.

"Mr. Ellerby?" the inspector said inquiringly. "I must see him with as little delay as possible."

The butler opened the library door. "Her ladyship said that this room was to be at your service whenever you wanted it, inspector."

"Very kind of Lady Burslem," Stoddart said as they went in. "Oh, by the way, I should like a word with the young man who admitted us – James, isn't he called? Would you send him in first, please?" The second footman did not, from his appearance, suggest unusual intelligence. As he came into the library he looked thoroughly scared.

The inspector took the chair at the top of the table and motioned James to stand so that the light fell upon his face.

"Just a question or two about the night of June 2nd, or rather the morning of June 3rd. I believe that you opened the door for Sir John and Lady Burslem when they returned?"

"Yes, sir. I did."

"What was Sir John wearing?"

"Just a cap, pulled down pretty well over his ears, a lightish sort of overcoat – it was a warm night, and Mr. Ellerby made the remark that it was too hot for his usual motoring coat. I noticed that he had on a sort of white muffler, though, when he came back."

"Just tell us in your own words what Sir John did after he came in?"

James fidgeted about from one leg to the other. "He didn't do anything, sir, not that I saw. He came into this room, where we are now, and her ladyship with him. She came out again in a minute – her ladyship – and she says, 'James, you must call Ellerby. Sir John told him not to sit up, but finds he must have him now.' So I went and called Mr. Ellerby. Pretty cross he was too, to be roused up at that time of night. But he was not long in coming, and then Sir John called us both into the library and he signed some paper and we both signed after him."

"What did you do next?" Stoddart questioned.

"Well, sir, I came out and waited about, not knowing whether I should be wanted again. But before long Sir John came out and went out to the car that was standing before the door."

"'You can go to bed, James,' he called out. 'I shall not be long and I can let myself in.'"

"Where was Mr. Ellerby?" Stoddart was looking at his notes.

James hesitated. "Well, I don't know, sir. I didn't see him come out of the library again. But then I didn't take much notice, being too sleepy to think of much but going to bed."

The inspector scribbled something in his notebook. "Were you always the one to sit up for Sir John?"

"Oh, no, sir. Henry, the first footman, he generally did the sitting-up. Not that Sir John wanted much, being an independent sort of gentleman."

"How long have you been in the situation?"

"Just over three months, sir."

"Did you see much of Sir John?"

"Oh, yes, sir. Waiting and that, and valeting him sometimes when Mr. Ellerby was out."

"I suppose," the inspector said, keeping his eyes fixed on the young man, "you are quite certain that it was Sir John who came into the house that night – who signed that paper?"

"Certain it was Sir John!" the man echoed. "Why, of course it was Sir John. Who else could it be? Didn't her ladyship and Mr. Ellerby and all see him?"

"We will leave her ladyship and Mr. Ellerby out of it for a moment," the inspector said quietly. "Are you of your own knowledge prepared to swear it was Sir John Burslem you saw the night of his death?"

The man stared at him. "Why, of course I am prepared to swear that it was Sir John."

"You saw his face plainly?"

"Yes, sir! At least" – James hesitated and began to stammer – "not so very plainly perhaps, for he kept his motor cap on all the time, which I thought it was rather queer of him to do. And he wore a white choker thing round his neck, muffled up like, because he was going out again. But of course it was Sir John right enough!"

"Well, I think that is all today, my man," the inspector concluded. "Ask Mr. Ellerby to step this way, please."

James's face had a bewildered expression as he went out.

They had not long to wait for Ellerby, who was evidently expecting the summons. As he entered the inspector was struck by the indefinable change that had come over him. He looked years older than the man who had come down to Hughlin's Wood to identify his dead master.

"Good morning, Mr. Ellerby," the inspector began genially. "I am sorry to trouble you, but there are a few little things that are worrying me, and I thought it might make matters clearer if we had a little talk together – you and I and Mr. Harbord. Shall we sit down to it, Mr. Ellerby?"

He drew a chair into position carefully. It did not escape Harbord's keen eyes that the valet, without moving it, twisted himself round so that he had his back to the light.

"I am sorry to see you are not looking well, Mr. Ellerby," the detective went on sympathetically. "But I am sure you have gone through enough lately to try the strongest man."

"Yes, that I have, sir," the valet agreed. "Nobody knows what the strain of this – this dreadful thing has been but those that have gone through it. Sir John, he was as dear to me as if he had been my own son. And to see him like   that –"

His voice failed. He drew out his handkerchief and blew his nose vigorously.

"It must have been terrible for you." The inspector looked the other way for a minute. "Such a shock too, for you had seen Sir John only a few hours before, hadn't you?"

"Of course I had, Mr. Stoddart, and looking no more like death than you or I do today."

"Yes, that is a true saying – 'In the midst of life we are in death,'" the inspector observed sententiously. "I wish you would tell me the story of that night, or rather the early morning of the third of June. I would not trouble you, Mr. Ellerby, but I know you are as anxious as we are to find out Sir John Burslem's murderer."

"As anxious? My God! I would give my life to have saved him, to avenge him!" Ellerby choked again.

"Take your time, take your time!" the inspector encouraged. "Tell us about that last interview with Sir John and about your signing the paper, in your own words, please."

"Well, it was like this, although I am sure you have heard it again and again," Ellerby began in a shaking voice. "Sir John had told me that he and her ladyship were going to Oxley, and he said I need not wait up for him – he often did. A most considerate master was Sir John; we shall never have another like him. So I was rather surprised when James came to tell me that Sir John wanted me. About one o'clock, I suppose it would be. I dressed as quickly as I could and went to the library. Sir John and her ladyship were both there. Sir John was writing at the table and her ladyship stood at the door. 'Come in, Ellerby,' she says. 'Sir John wants you to witness his signature.' Then she called to James and we went in together. Sir John signed the paper – the will as we know it was now – and I and James signed after him."

"What did you do next?"

Ellerby looked a little surprised at the question. "Nothing, sir, there was nothing to be done. Sir John, he told me to go to bed and he went off to take the car to the garage – he wouldn't let anybody touch her but himself, and me and James went to bed. That is all, inspector."

"Yes." The inspector turned over two or three pages of his notebook rapidly. "There are two questions I must put to you, Mr. Ellerby. The first is – are you certain that it was Sir John Burslem himself who signed the will?"

Ellerby looked thunderstruck. "Am I sure that it was Sir John himself who signed the will? Why, of course I am sure, inspector. I could swear to it in any court of law in the land."

"You don't think you can have been deceived by a clever impersonation – that somebody might have dressed up to look like him?"

Ellerby shook his head; a ghastly smile played momentarily round his thin lips.

"There's nobody on earth could have dressed up to deceive me, inspector. It was Sir John himself that signed that will. There can't be any question of that!"

"Oh, well, thank you, that seems pretty conclusive."

"Now for my second question," the inspector went on. "Did you go straight to bed when you had signed as a witness of the will?"

"Straight to bed?" Ellerby echoed in an amazed tone. "Why, of course I did, when Sir John said he should not want me again. Pretty tired I was and slept like a log until I was awakened by the phone message just before seven o'clock."

"That is all then, thank you, Mr. Ellerby." The inspector closed his notebook and fastened an elastic round it with a snap. "I am much obliged to you." He got up as he spoke.

Ellerby got up too. "I wish I could do something to help you, inspector. Anything to find poor Sir John's –" His voice trailed off to a whisper as he escorted them to the hall.

The two detectives walked to the end of the Square before they managed to pick up a taxi. When they were safely ensconced in it, Stoddart looked at Harbord with a smile.

"Your theory does not seem to hold water, my lad."

"I don't know," Harbord said slowly. "I do not like Ellerby: he is keeping something back."

"I could have told you that on the 3rd of June," the inspector said at once. "The question is: What is it?"

CHAPTER VII

"I thought you said you were going abroad, Sophie."

Mrs. Aubrey Dolphin was the speaker. She looked curiously at her sister. The two were in Lady Burslem's sitting-room, a room that had been specially done up by Sir John in the delicate tints that best suited his young wife's colouring. The walls were grey, and panelled in the very faintest blue. A long strip of wonderful tapestry hung between the windows. Only the old rose in the Aubusson carpet gave a touch of colour. The chairs and sofa were covered in grey silk damask. The cushions matched save that pink and black curves and lines ran riot over them. A couple of Chippendale chairs and a table stood near the window. There were no pictures or photographs or ornaments except an impressionist sketch of Sir John Burslem that hung over the mantelpiece, and a big copper bowl of roses on the writing-table.

"I did think of going abroad," Lady Burslem said wearily. "I thought perhaps when everything was different I might forget. But it seems I can't go until this dreadful inquest is over. They say my testimony may be wanted any time. And – and there is any amount of business that I must do myself. That mine in South Africa – I must see the manager."

"Sophie! What on earth do you know about mines in South Africa or anywhere else?"

"Oh, John has taught me a lot since we were married," Sophie said, her lips trembling. "He – he often told me I was the aptest pupil he ever had."

"I should have said you were one of the most unbusiness-like people in the world," Mrs. Dolphin remarked politely. "However, one never knows. There was a poisonous looking woman asking for you in the hall just now, Sophie. They were trying to get rid of her."

"I am not seeing anyone," Sophie said in an uninterested fashion. "No one but my own people, that is to say. I should be inundated with callers if I allowed myself to be visible."

There was a tap at the door and Forbes appeared. "My lady, there is a person asking for you in the hall. Henry says they can't get rid of her anyhow."

"They must tell her to go," Lady Burslem said impatiently. "Say I am seeing no one."

"Yes, my lady." Forbes hesitated. "Only Henry said, your ladyship said no one but the family, and this lady said – said her name was Burslem – Mrs. James Burslem. And while he was telling her that it was impossible for her to see your ladyship, Miss Burslem came in, and – and the lady introduced herself to her, and Miss Burslem took her into the library."

"Mrs. James Burslem!" Sophie repeated, her white cheeks suddenly flushing crimson. "Oh, I think I must see her. After all, she is my sister-in-law."

"A sister-in-law your husband took care to keep at a distance," Mrs. Dolphin said contemptuously. "Don't be an ass, Sophie. Of course you need not be interviewed by this woman because she married your husband's brother. A nice time he has had with her, I should imagine, from the look of her. But, if you feel she is being badly treated, I will ascertain for you what she wants."

"No," Lady Burslem said firmly, "I must see her myself." She got up as she spoke. "No, Clare, I would rather go alone, really. I don't suppose I shall be very long. You stay here –"

"Certainly not!" said Mrs. Dolphin in a tone as decided as her sister's. "I shall not leave you alone to face the brazen-looking creature I saw downstairs."

Lady Burslem still looked inclined to object, but Clare Dolphin settled the matter by taking her arm and marching her downstairs.

The library door was ajar and they could hear voices inside the room, Pamela's and another's, loud, and with a pronounced cockney twang. As she heard it, Sophie Burslem shivered.

Mrs. James Burslem was standing on the hearthrug with one arm round Pamela, who in her sombre black looked an odd contrast to her stepmother in her loose, white kimono.

Mrs. James Burslem dropped her hold of Pamela and came across the room to greet Sophie. She took Lady Burslem in her arms, the big fur coat she wore, warm though the day was, flopping and seeming to envelop Lady Burslem altogether.

"You poor darling! What you must have gone through! My heart has bled for you!" she said in a loud, raucous tone. "I was just telling Pamela here that I have thought of nothing else since I saw the terrible news in the paper. You had my letter, of course?"

With some difficulty Sophie extricated herself from the voluminous embrace. "Yes, I think so," she said, putting her hand to her head. The flush that had been called up by the news of Mrs. James's arrival had faded now, leaving her by contrast more ghastly looking than ever.

"Just to explain how it was Jimmy couldn't come to the funeral, you know," Mrs. James went on. "Now just you sit down, you poor dear," giving Lady Burslem a push into the nearest chair. "I went to the church, of course, and I thought maybe you would have asked me to come back after; but of course you were not there or anybody that knew me. You expected Jimmy, naturally."

"No, I didn't expect anybody," Sophie returned faintly.

"Then I am sure you would not be disappointed," Mrs. Jimmy returned with a loud laugh that set her sister-in-law's teeth on edge.

"Well, I should have liked to have seen you then, of course. But today I simply had to come. I have a message for you – a special message."

Lady Burslem did not look particularly interested. "I have such heaps of letters and messages every day."

"Ah!" Mrs. Jimmy's raddled face assumed a portentous look. "But not this sort of message. You don't know much about me, Sophie, or you would know that I am possessed of great psychic powers. Now, my friend, Winnie Margetson, is simply the most wonderful medium in the world. We had a séance the other day with the most marvellous results. A message came through to you – I promised to deliver it myself. It is really why I am here today, and I must give it to you alone."

"Why?" Lady Burslem inquired in a lifeless tone. "Was it anything important?"

"Well, it depends on what you call important," Mrs. James said, with a glance at Mrs. Dolphin, which that lady, rightly interpreting as a desire to dismiss her, quietly ignored. It is a message from your husband."

"My husband!" There was no mistaking the effect of the words on Lady Burslem. She sprang up in her chair as if electrified, flushing hotly red. "You couldn't!"

"Now don't get excited," Mrs. Jimmy returned, with the accent on the first syllable. "The message came through right enough and I was to give it to you when you were alone. I have one for you too, Pamela."

"Oh, what is it?' The girl caught her aunt's arm.

That lady quietly removed it.

"Well, first he said that you were not to fret about him. That he was in a beautiful garden and that he was happier than he had ever been on earth."

"Oh, did he say so, really? Do tell me –"

"Don't be so silly, Sophie," Mrs. Dolphin burst out. "I beg your pardon, Mrs. Burslem, but I have not one atom of faith in Spiritualism. As for John Burslem, if he says he is happy in a beautiful garden, his tastes have altered. I can imagine him happy on a racecourse, or reading the Stock Exchange reports, but in a beautiful garden – no."

"Ah, his eyes are open now. Some day yours will be," Mrs. Jimmy retorted.

As she spoke she threw off her coat and stood with her ample proportions revealed in what looked remarkably like a black satin chemise. It was very short and extremely skimpy, and Mrs. James Burslem's figure was not of the kind to look well in short, skimpy garments. Her fleshy arms were bare to the shoulder, her neck betrayed a tendency to lie in rolls of fat. Her hair, obviously owing its colour to peroxide, had been shingled and lay in a fashionable curl on each cheek. Her complexion might almost have been scraped off with a spoon, and the scarlet lips, like those of most of her fellows, owed their colour to the universal lip-stick. Her teeth were her own undoubtedly by right of purchase, and Mrs. Burslem was proud of them and showed them very frequently in an expansive smile. Her eyes were big and prominent and of a very light blue.

Mrs. Dolphin, watching her, observed that, though the full lips smiled, the blue eyes never lost their greedy, rapacious look.

"Everybody seems to have a lot of bother in this world," she went on. "I am sure that while my heart has been bleeding for you, I have been that worried I have scarcely known whether my name was Kitty Burslem or not. Oh, Sophie! – I may call you Sophie, I suppose?"

"Oh, yes, of course," Lady Burslem assented. Her colour had died away now. She was very pale. "I am sorry to hear you have had a lot of worry. I hope it is nothing serious."

"Oh, well, it depends what you call serious," Mrs. Jimmy said with a loud, grating laugh. "You don't ask me to sit down, Sophie. But I suppose I may, even if Pam and this other lady stand."

She dropped into a chair opposite Lady Burslem as she spoke. "It is about Jimmy. You see, I know where he is, but it is jolly difficult to get at him or to get any money out of him. It always is when he is in Tibet or farther away. And I don't know whether he told you, but poor John always made me an allowance. He was good in that way, though I don't say he was as friendly as I should have liked, but if I was in any difficulty, or Jimmy either, he was always ready with his purse."

"Yes, I know," Lady Burslem said with more warmth than she had yet shown. "He – my husband would have wished me to help you, I am sure. He always made you an allowance when you were alone. We will have a talk about it presently."

"You are very good," Mrs. Jimmy said gratefully. "I must say I thought you would be. 'She has just lost her husband,' I said to myself. 'That will open her heart to all widows, grass, or otherwise.' This little talk about – funds now, when can we have it?" Her glance at Mrs. Dolphin and Pamela plainly showed her desire for their absence. But neither of them moved.

"Yes," Sophie said feverishly. "Of course we must have it now. Clare, Pam, do you mind –"

"Certainly not," Mrs. Dolphin said in a huffy tone. "Come, Pamela."

But Pamela looked distinctly unwilling to move.

"I suppose if I go away now I shall see you again, Aunt Kitty?"

"You bet!" Aunt Kitty replied in tones that were an odd contrast to the girl's. "But I don't know about today. I expect I shall have to get on when I have had my little talk with your stepma. So I think I will say good-bye now."

She got up and laying a hand on each of Pamela's shoulders kissed her heartily on both cheeks.

"And, mind, you must come soon to pay me that little visit you spoke of, but I shall be in another day before long and we will fix it up then. I am sure you would be happy in my house, and I should love to have a girl with me. I would take you to a séance." She turned her niece round to the door.

"Now this is nice and real friendly of you, Sophie," they heard Mrs. Jimmy say before they closed the door.

"Well" – Clare Dolphin drew a long breath – "what an appalling woman! I think both you and Sophie must have taken leave of your senses, Pam, to make this fuss of her!"

"I have not," Pam said coldly. "You forget that she is my uncle's wife, and he is my only living relative now that Dad – is dead!" her breath catching in a sob.

"I always understood that James Burslem went exploring to get rid of his wife," Mrs. Dolphin returned. "Now I have seen her I am not surprised. If you want any more relatives like that –"

"I never look down upon people because they have not much money," Pamela said with dignity.

"Neither do I," Mrs. Dolphin returned equably. "I have precious little myself, but I do not fraternize with people of Mrs. James Burslem's stamp. However, every man to his taste. At least I hope that neither you nor Sophie will be silly enough to go to these séances she talks about."

"I want to go to one above all things," Pamela said perversely. "And now that we can get into communication with Daddy –"

"Rubbish! But I have no time to waste talking about Mrs. James Burslem. I just wanted to speak to Ellerby. I suppose we might ask for him."

"Of course." Pamela rang the bell. "Please send Mr. Ellerby here," she said to the man who answered it.

"Yes, miss." The man looked at her rather oddly. "We can't find Mr. Ellerby, miss."

"Can't find Mr. Ellerby?" Pamela echoed. "What do you mean?"

"Well, miss, he isn't anywhere in the house as far as we know. We can't make it out, none of us.

"But of course he must be in the house," Mrs. Dolphin interrupted. "He was here last night, I suppose?"

"Yes, ma'am," James said, turning round to her. "Henry saw him at twelve. But when he did not appear this morning at his usual time, I went to see if he was ill or anything. It looked as if he had just jumped out of bed and gone off!"

"Extraordinary! What on earth should he go out for?" Mrs. Dolphin questioned blankly. Then, after a moment's cogitation, "Stay! did I not hear her ladyship say Ellerby was a married man with a wife living near?"

"Yes, ma'am, married he is, and his wife lives somewhere down Battersea way, and lets rooms to single gentlemen."

"That is where Ellerby is, you may depend upon it," Clare Dolphin said with an air of relief.

"Perhaps he did not feel well after he had gone to his room, and he thought he would go home for his wife to look after him. It is quite natural, but of course he ought to have let some one know. Perhaps he has, or some letter or message has miscarried."

"Beg your pardon, ma'am, but I do not think that is so," James dissented. "Henry rang up Mrs. Ellerby just now, and she said she knew nothing of Ellerby. She hasn't seen him since last Friday ma'am."

"Oh, dear! Is that really so? Where can he be?" Mrs. Dolphin caught Pamela's arm. "Surely no more dreadful mysteries! Misfortune seems to dog this house lately."

CHAPTER VIII

Two policemen were walking backwards and forwards before the place where Sir John Burslem's body was found. A couple of men stood near; one of them held a short scythe, the other had some sort of dredging apparatus beside him. A group of interested spectators stood a little way off. Inspector Stoddart came up from Hughlin village at a sharp pace.

"All right, my men. Now we will set to work at once, and first we will have all this rough growth of grass fringing the ditch mown off, as close to the ground as you can get it, for a couple of hundred yards or so above and below the place where the body was found."

"Ay, sir." The man with the scythe looked round vaguely. "It won't be such an easy job; the grass and the creepers is all grown together and mauled about like."

"You will manage it, I fancy. There is nothing like a scythe for cutting grass. I put it before these new-fashioned cutters any day."

"You are about right, sir." In his obvious pleasure at the compliment the man spat on his hands, grasped his scythe handle and set to work at once.

He with the dredger did not look inclined to follow his fellow's example.

The inspector stood for a minute or two looking up the road and measuring the distance with his eye. Presently he turned back.

"Come, my man, start your dredging and scrape right through the mud at the bottom, mind."

"I ha' bin through this place, mud an' all a dozen times and found nothin'. Don't believe there is anything to find."

"Set to work at once. Clear out all the mud right up to here, and the same distance nearer the village."

The man obeyed sulkily. Stoddart went to meet Harbord, who was coming up from Hughlin village.

"Any success?"

"I can't find any trace of my woman – the one who was behind the tree."

"Your hypothetical woman," Stoddart corrected.

"On the other hand, I met with a man, a sort of hanger-on at the stables at Epsom, who knows Sir Charles Stanyard quite well by sight, and of course had him impressed on his memory as the owner of Perlyon, and this chap had stopped on at the stable doing various little jobs that would crop up on the eve of the Derby. On his way home he came across Stanyard, whose car had apparently broken down, tinkering away at it, and beside him, bending down, apparently giving advice, was a woman."

"What sort of a woman?" Stoddart questioned abruptly.

"Unfortunately, my man does not seem to be able to give any coherent description. According to him she was neither particularly short nor particularly tall; says he didn't see enough of her to know whether she was young or old; but she was plumpish-like, he thinks, and maybe she was wrapped up like for motoring, for the night was not so warm as it might have been."

"H'm! Not very helpful," the inspector commented, "but it is curious that Stanyard should have said he was alone at the time."

"Another curious thing is," Harbord went on as they watched the men casting up the evil-smelling, black mud, "that he did notice that this woman was holding a bag, a bigger one than most folks carry, he said."

"Funny he should notice that, if he did not notice what the woman herself was like," the inspector remarked, turning up the road.

"The yokel mind is strangely constituted – and this man is just a country yokel, taken on at the stable at a busy time, curiously observant and curiously unobservant. Anyway, now we have something definite to connect Stanyard with the woman, or rather a woman."

The inspector nodded. "Can't say any more than that last."

"I say, what is that?" as there came a shout from the man turning up the mud.

He was looking at an oblong, mud-encased object that had been brought up by the dredger.

"'Tis something sure enough," he observed intelligently, stirring his find with his foot.

The inspector looked at it. "A revolver, by Jove!"

Harbord picked it up gingerly, covering his hands with mud. "Looks as if it had lain there some time."

"Wouldn't make much difference after it had lain there a week," said the inspector, taking out a sheet of newspaper to wipe the mud away. "Go on, my man," to the dredger, who appeared to be inclined to rest on his laurels and watch operations.

A minute later the inspector uttered a sharp exclamation: "What's this?"

Harbord looking at the butt end of the revolver, perceived in the middle of the space the inspector had cleaned, the initials intertwined, J.B.

"Sir John's revolver. What on earth was he doing with it? Did he bring it knowing he was going into danger, and did his assassin turn it upon him?"

"If there is anything more unprofitable than another it is asking riddles," said the inspector, scrubbing away at his muddy pistol. "Somebody fired the fatal shot and threw the revolver in here; so much is selfevident. For the rest, the only thing that strikes me is that here we are about fifteen yards from the spot where the body was found. That is just about the limit of a man's throw – outside that of any woman that I know. Besides, a woman never can throw straight. I set the dredger to work on the assumption that the assassin would naturally try to get rid of the revolver, and that the likeliest hiding-place would be this ditch. I reckoned too that he would throw it as far as he could, either one way or the other. And you see we have found it just where I expected. Still, that does not prove that my assumption was right. The thing might have got there in a hundred different ways. Now I think I shall leave you to superintend the dredging while I get back to the Yard and find out what we can from this toy."

Throwing away the dirty sheet of paper, he wrapped the revolver carefully in a clean one and dropped it into his pocket. Then he walked sharply to his run-about.

Harbord found the watching of the dredging rather tedious when he was left alone. Nothing further turned up for some time, and the man had nearly reached the limit set by the inspector when, with an exclamation of contempt, he threw on the road a small object that made a clinking sound as it fell.

Harbord picked it up: a man's watch and chain of the old-fashioned type, discarded now by most men in favour of the wrist-watch.

Harbord took out his handkerchief and rubbed it as clean as he could, noting one significant fact, that the watch had stopped at 12.30. But, when he got all the mud off that was possible, he was disappointed to find no monogram, nothing apparently by which the watch could be identified.

It was getting late in the afternoon when the work that the inspector had ordered was finished, with no further result, and Harbord was just beginning to think that for him it would be possibly a case of sleeping at the Crown Inn – since the nearest station was quite out of walking distance and there was no car to be had in Hughlin – when Stoddart in the run-about came speedily down the track from the Downs and dashed across to the Wood. He stopped the car by Harbord and sprang out.

"Ready?" he asked sharply. "We must get back at once. There is grave news from Porthwick Square. Jump in!"

Still holding the watch, Harbord swung himself over the side of the car. The very sound of Stoddart's voice was enough to show that he was seriously perturbed. But he did not speak until they had left Hughlin's Wood far behind. His lips were firmly compressed, and Harbord knew him too well to be the first to speak. At last, however, they reached a level stretch of ground and he said:

"Ellerby has disappeared!"

"What!" Harbord looked at him in amazement. "How do you mean disappeared – run away?"

"I don't know," Stoddart answered sharply. "All that I can tell you is that he has disappeared from 15 Porthwick Square, apparently in the middle of the night."

"Last night?" Harbord's bewilderment was increasing.

"Last night, of course!" The inspector nodded. "And the fools never thought to inform me of the fact until this afternoon. So that whatever has happened we are twelve hours late on the scene."

"H'm!" Harbord drew in his lips. "Perhaps there was wisdom in this folly. But I thought that 15 Porthwick Square and its inhabitants were all under observation, and that the latter were all shadowed."

"So they are! Flaxman had got the job with as many plain-clothes men as he liked to ask for," the inspector assented. "But their watch does not seem to have been very successful. At any rate, Ellerby has got out, or has been got out of the house without Flaxman and his satellites being any the wiser."

"I can't understand –" Harbord was beginning.

"Don't say that again!" the inspector interrupted him irritably. "I should like to know who does understand any thing about this damned Burslem case. All I can tell you is that Ellerby went to bed as usual, that this morning he was not there and that nobody knows where he is."

"He may only have gone out somewhere on business," Harbord suggested. "If he only went this morning –"

"He apparently went without any clothes," the inspector said grimly, as they neared the suburbs. "It is no use speculating, Harbord. That is all there is to know at present. What there may be behind we have got to find out. We are going straight to Porthwick Square now. I went there at once and locked up Ellerby's box. When we have done we will have a bit of supper at a decent little pub I know of in the mews round the corner. The landlord is by way of being a friend of mine, and he will let us have a room to ourselves and we can discuss some plan of action."

"The watch!" Harbord hazarded tentatively.

"It isn't Sir John's, anyhow," Stoddart said in the same snappy tones. "He had his wrist-watch on. The revolver I have left at Lowson's, the gunsmith's, together with the bullet. I ought to get the report sometime this evening."

They were getting into more traffic now and the inspector had to give all his attention to his steering.

It was seven o'clock when they reached Porthwick Square. The door was opened to them immediately by the butler himself – a fact that spoke volumes for the disorganization of the household.

"Any news?" the inspector questioned sharply.

The butler only shook his head. He was looking oddly white and discomposed.

"We will go to the bedroom first and see what we can ascertain from it. Of course the housemaid had put it tidy, as she calls it, before I heard anything of the disappearance."

"She would have," Harbord nodded as the two turned towards the rooms, the butler merely looking after them in silence.

When they reached the door, Stoddart took out a key and unlocked it.

"Whatever clue there may be after the tidying, which my experience of housemaids tells me is not usually extensive, is still intact."

Ellerby's room was quite a good-sized, comfortable-looking apartment, and the style in which it was furnished was a sign of the esteem in which he was held in the Burslem household.

As Stoddart had said, the housemaid's tidying up had not been extensive. Harbord looked round. The bed had been made. Otherwise probably the room was much as Ellerby had left it. His underclothes, neatly folded up, were on a chair near the bed. A coat and waistcoat were laid on top of the drawers. The trousers were thrown over a chair near the cupboard.

Stoddart rang the bell. The housemaid appeared with a celerity that showed she had been close at hand. Ordinarily a bright, rosy girl, she was pale and nervous-looking.

"Your name, I understand, is Simmonds," the inspector began.

"Yes, sir," the girl said in a frightened tone. "It is – it is Annie Simmonds!"

"Well, Miss Simmonds, will you come over here?" Stoddart went on, going across to the window. "I understand you usually attend to this room."

The girl looked up at him with big, frightened eyes. "Yes, sir!"

"Well, now, don't look alarmed" – the inspector gave her a friendly pat on the shoulder – "we are not going to hurt you. All I want you to do is to answer a few questions. Now, take a good look round the room and tell us if everything this morning was just as you were accustomed to see it when Ellerby had left it."

"Yes, sir, I think so."

The girl looked round vaguely until her glance rested on the bed.

"Except –" She faltered and stopped.

The inspector pricked up his ears.

"Except –" he prompted.

"Except that I didn't see Mr. Ellerby's pyjamas when I did his bed, sir," the maid faltered. "Mr. Ellerby, he generally leaves them on that chair," pointing to the one that now held the underclothing. And then I put them on top of the pillow when I made the bed. But this morning they were not on the chair, nor on the bed, nor anywhere."

"Umph!" The inspector went over to the chest of drawers and took up the coat. "This is the one he wore yesterday?"

"I – I think so." The girl hesitated. "It is the one he generally did wear most days – leastways, he has since Sir John died."

The inspector threw open the cupboard door.

"Now, can you tell us whether anything has gone from here – any clothes, I mean?"

The girl shook her head. "It doesn't look as if there had, sir, but I couldn't say rightly. Perhaps James might know more."

"No boots!" the inspector went on. pointing to a row that stood in the bottom of the cupboard, each pair on its own trees.

"It doesn't look as if any had gone," the maid said, scrutinizing them.

"And the bed was just as usual, not tossed about, nor the bedclothes on the floor or anything?"

"It all looked just the same, sir, just as if Mr. Ellerby had just got out of it."

"Nothing disturbed?" the inspector queried.

"Yes, sir – no, sir." Simmonds hesitated. "Oh, I just call to mind that over that side" – pointing to the door – "the rug was tumbled and tossed in a heap like, almost under the bed."

"And you don't miss anything?" the inspector went on again, going over to the side of the bed she had indicated, and looking down at the carpet on the floor.

The girl glanced round again. "No, sir, I don't. Mr. Ellerby, he never was one to have many things about."

The inspector lifted the lid of a trunk standing near the window.

"Locked!" he said laconically. "Ever seen it locked before?"

"Mr. Ellerby always kept it locked, sir. At least I believe so. Of course I am not in the habit of trying it," she said primly.

"Of course not!" the inspector assented. "Now, Miss Simmonds, I should like a word or two with James. How can I get him here?"

"I will send him, sir." The girl stepped hastily to the door, obviously delighted at this chance of escape.

In a few minutes James appeared. Like the butler, he was looking scared and worried.

"Come in, Mr. Plowman," the inspector said genially. "We shall not keep you long. Just to give us a little bit of help. Now, I want you first of all to look at this coat. Can you tell me if it is the one Ellerby wore yesterday?" the inspector began, taking up the coat and handing it to the man.

James looked at it. "Oh, yes, sir, I can tell that at once. It's the coat he wore yesterday. And the trousers on that chair."

"Now I want you to look in the cupboard, at the suits on the shelves, and the boots – and see if you think anything is missing."

James took his time about complying with this request. He went to the cupboard and spent some ten minutes apparently examining the garments with meticulous care. At last he emerged considerably redder in the face from his exertions.

"There is nothing missing that I can see, sir. Boots, I am sure that they are not. That pair at the end, they were outside the door as usual this morning. They had been cleaned and brought up when I came to see whether there was anything wrong this morning."

The inspector frowned. "Could you tell us anything about the underclothing in the chest of drawers?" James shook his head. "No, sir, I don't know anything about it."

"Then," the inspector said slowly, "so far as you can tell, Ellerby went out of the room in his pyjamas."

"I can't see anything else for it," James said, staring round him. "I believe that there are none of his clothes gone. We can't make it out, none of us."

"I am not surprised at that," the inspector said blandly. "Where do you sleep?"

"Sleep?" the man echoed stupidly. "Oh, I see what you mean – at night. Downstairs in the basement, sir."

"Now, last night, try and remember whether you heard any unusual sound during the night."

"I am sure I didn't. Nobody in the house did. That is what is puzzling us all."

"I suppose you would hear if the front door opened or shut?"

"I don't see how I could help hearing it, sir. Not but what I am a sound sleeper," he added with an obvious desire to be absolutely accurate.

"Then that is all we can do just now, thank you," the inspector said politely. "I may want you a few minutes later on."

When the man had gone the inspector took a curious looking bit of steel out of his pocket.

"I think we must see what there is in this box of Ellerby's."

"Whatever there is is extremely light," Harbord observed, tilting up the edge.

The inspector's skeleton-key opened the lock at once. Then as he flung the lid back both men uttered an exclamation of surprise. Inside was nothing but brown paper, several large sheets, all of which had evidently been used for wrapping up parcels. The inspector's capable fingers turned them over quickly.

"Now, it is a curious thing that none of these papers have anything on them – no label with a shop's name or anything of that kind."

"Is it curious?" Harbord questioned dryly. As he spoke he picked up a small tie-on label from the bottom of the box, from underneath a piece of paper that the inspector had not taken out. "Look at this, inspector."

Stoddart read the name printed at the top – "'Vidame & Green, General Outfitters, Passmore Street, Westminster.'"

"Ah, we must look up Messrs. Vidame & Green."

"Yes, it was a mistake to overlook that," commented Harbord quietly.

The inspector smiled. "It is pretty obvious that a man could not have been overpowered in this room and taken downstairs without anyone in the household hearing or knowing."

"Quite. The impersonation theory frightened him, I fancy." Harbord was examining every scrap of paper with meticulous care.

"It seems probable," the inspector agreed. "And yet there are so many wheels within wheels in this extraordinary case. Ellerby might have been in the way. He might have been got rid of with the connivance of some one in the household. We must not overlook this possibility, remote though it seems. But, even if he were drugged or dead, a man of his weight could not have been got downstairs without anyone hearing."

"Certainly not," Stoddart agreed. "But I am not overlooking the possibility of Ellerby's walking downstairs, and then being overpowered in one of the rooms."

"His clothes?" Harbord suggested.

Stoddart shrugged his shoulders. "I should say it is absolutely impossible for one person to be certain about the state of his wardrobe. Nothing was missing that James remembers having seen. That, I think, is as far as his testimony takes us."

He went over to the narrow bed and stripped it, carefully feeling it all over, even smelling the bed clothes and pillow-cases.

"If Miss Annie Simmonds had kindly left the bed alone we might have known more. As it is, one can only say that there is not the faintest smell of any drugs, no slightest sign of any struggle. The carpet may have been tossed back, but there are no scratches on the paint beneath. No; I feel we may be pretty certain that Ellerby walked out of this room."

"But what happened to him afterwards?"

"We cannot search the house tonight," Harbord said doubtfully.

The inspector drew in his lips. "Plenty of time to get rid of anything that anybody wanted to get rid of, and was able to get rid of, before we came on the scene. Of course now the whole house is under the most rigorous observation and everybody, even the kitchen-maid, is shadowed every time they leave the house. But when the steed is gone, you know. At the present my inner man warns me that supper must be the next thing. First thing to-morrow a visit to Vidame & Green is indicated."

CHAPTER IX

The inspector came into his room at Scotland Yard and threw down his hat with an exclamation of impatience.

Harbord, who had followed him in, looked at him in surprise. It was not often that Stoddart was betrayed into showing any irritation.

"That pistol that was found in the ditch at Hughlin's Wood was not the one with which Burslem was shot."

"Not! But I understood that the bullet fitted."

"So it did – so it does." Stoddart sat down and frowned heavily. "But this new system that they have discovered lately, of examining the bullet through a powerful microscope, which discovers small, almost invisible lines on the bullet, proves positively whether a bullet has been fired from a certain revolver or not, though one shot had been fired from the revolver, mind you, says in this case definitely not. Now we have to begin our search for the weapon used in the Burslem case all over again."

"How then did that revolver with the initials 'J.B.' come in the ditch?" cogitated Harbord. "It must have been Burslem's."

"It may have been – most probably it was," Stoddart corrected. "But so far we have not been able to prove it. None of the men at Porthwick Square identify it; the butler goes so far as to say that he feels sure it is not Sir John's; Ellerby alone could have been certain, and Ellerby has vanished. It is the same with the watch. Henry and James, both of whom occasionally valeted Sir John, do not recognize it. The utmost that I have been able to ascertain from them is that Sir John often wore a watch of that kind, not caring much for a wrist-watch. But the one they both remember is in its case in Sir John's room. Both of them say that they have no recollection of ever seeing the one found in the ditch. So that is as far as our discoveries of yesterday carry us. Heaven knows it is not very far!"

Harbord sat down heavily and leaning his elbows on the table rested his head on his hands.

"It is like a maze," he groaned. "You get what you think is a clue only to find when you begin to follow it that it leads nowhere. To reconstruct the crime seemed fairly easy. The revolver drawn by Sir John to defend himself, seized by the assassin, and turned against its owner, then flung away into the ditch."

"Reconstructing crime is easy enough, but it is a game in which it is possible to make a good many mistakes," the inspector commented dryly.

"And why did that watch stop at 12.30 if it was Sir John's, when he must have been alive until after two o'clock?" Harbord pursued, ignoring Stoddart's interjection.

The inspector stood up suddenly. "I am not here to answer conundrums. You have just come in time to assist me at an interview which may be of interest to both. Harbord, a lady is anxious to claim the reward."

"What lady?" Harbord inquired eagerly.

The inspector shook his head. "I know no more than you. All I can tell you is that I was rung up half an hour ago, and a voice, unmistakably a feminine one, inquired if the speaker could see the gentleman who offered the reward for the discovery of Sir John Burslem's assassin. I told her to come here, and if her information was worth anything the reward would be hers. She replied that she would be round directly, and I am expecting her any minute."

"Where did the call come from?" Harbord inquired.

"Public office," the inspector answered laconically. "Oh, there are not many flies on William Stoddart, my friend. Here she is!" as there was a knock at the door.

A constable in plain clothes ushered in a young woman dressed plainly in black, carrying a fair-sized parcel done up in brown paper.

Both men looked at her with a strange sense of familiarity. Then Stoddart exclaimed:

"It is Lady Burslem's maid!"

The woman's dark eyes glanced at him in an odd, sidelong fashion.

"Yes, I am Lady Burslem's maid, certainly. But my name is Forbes – Eleanor Forbes."

"I am much obliged to you, Miss Forbes," said the inspector setting a chair for her.

Harbord knew by the tone of his voice and the look on his face that much was expected of the coming interview.

"I have come about this reward that is offered," Forbes began. "Who offers it?"

The inspector smiled. "That we are not at liberty to say."

"Well, if you don't tell me that I do not know that it is much use my going on," the maid said in an aggrieved fashion.

The inspector made no reply. He stood looking down at her with an inscrutable expression on his dark face.

Forbes half rose, then sat down again. "Well, perhaps you will answer these two questions – is the reward offered by Lady Burslem?"

The inspector thought things over for a minute. "No," he said, at last, "it is not."

"Is it safe?" Forbes proceeded. "I mean, suppose I give you the information that leads to the discovery of the murderer of Sir John Burslem, shall I be sure to get the thousand pounds offered?"

"Certain," Stoddart assured her. "You need have no doubt about the *bona fides* of the person offering the reward, Miss Forbes. If your information is worth it, you will get the money safe enough."

"That is all I want to know," the maid proceeded. "Well, then, I should like to show you something, but when you have seen it I shall have given the best part of my story away, and you —"

"You will have to trust us," the inspector said more firmly. "The police are not allowed to take rewards, you know, so you have no rivalry to fear from us."

"Oh, well, that is all right then."

Forbes untied the string of her parcel. Then she looked up.

"I am going to show you the frock that Lady Burslem wore on the evening of June 2nd, when she went to Oxley with Sir John."

She tore off the enveloping wrapper and held up to the astonished eyes of the two men the crumpled, stained, torn rag that had once been Sophie Burslem's evening frock.

The inspector put on the glasses he used for examining objects closely.

"You are sure?"

The maid tossed her head. "Of course I am, or I should not have made a fool of myself coming here. There's lots of others that can identify it as well as me if you come to that. I couldn't find it in the morning of June 3rd. And when we heard what had happened to Sir John it sort of took my breath away and then I remembered and began to look for it. At last I found it all crumpled up together, right down at the bottom of the well of the wardrobe and a lot of other things on top of it. I shook it out" – suiting the action to the word – "and I saw the front breadth had been all torn out, or cut out, I should say."

"Cut?" the inspector said, bending over it.

"There is no doubt about that. Anybody can see it has been cut," Forbes said scornfully, "but when I showed it to her ladyship, she said there were a lot of thorns about at Oxley and she must have torn it on them. Pretty green she must have thought me. I racked my brains to think what she had done with the piece she had cut out. Then all at once I remembered that on the morning of June 3rd, when I came to dress her after her bath, she was doing something at her dressing-case, and shut it up very quickly. There is a secret drawer in it, at least she calls it a secret drawer, but the secret of it is not difficult to discover, and of course I opened it, and there I found this."

She took out a small packet that had lain under the frock and unrolled its contents – the long, jagged piece of satin that had once been white, and was now stained, almost all over, an ugly reddish brown.

The inspector took it from her, and placing the frock on the table fitted the strip into it. Then he glanced at Harbord.

Forbes looked at them both. "Well, can I have the thousand pounds?" she demanded.

The inspector smiled. "Not quite so fast, Miss Forbes. This evidence of yours may probably be of great assistance to us, and, if we ultimately trace the murderer through your agency, you may rely upon it the reward will be yours. Is this all you can show us?"

"I should have thought it would have been quite enough," Forbes said. "Can't you see that her ladyship and Sir Charles –"

"No, no!" The inspector interrupted her. "What you may think and what I may surmise is one thing, and a definite proof is another. And you must remember that there is such a thing as a libel action, Miss Forbes. Of course what you say here is privileged; but if you mention names outside –"

"I am not such a fool!" Forbes observed shortly. "And I do not speak without the book as I am going to show you."

The inspector looked at her. "Ah, now you are talking. If you have any further proof –"

"That her ladyship has been carrying on with Sir Charles Stanyard?" the maid said tartly. "What do you think of this?"

She produced another packet from among the folds of brown paper on her knees and unwrapped it. Inside was another packet, of old letters labelled from "C.S." and a photograph: an old photograph, but easily recognizable as that of Stanyard.

The inspector took the packet of letters and glanced at it, turning back the envelopes without untying the string that bound them together.

"These may be from Sir Charles Stanyard, but they were all written before Lady Burslem's marriage. They are addressed to Miss Sophie Carlford."

"Anyway, this was not written before she was married." Forbes brandished a piece of paper from her handbag. "I found this in her ladyship's blotter the other day when Mr. Weldon and Lord Carlford came in and wanted to see her at once, so she went down and left it."

The inspector held out his hand.

Forbes did not look inclined to surrender her find. "I ought to get good money for this. Her ladyship or Sir Charles —"

"Blackmail!" the inspector snapped. "Better stick to the reward, Miss Forbes."

"Um! Well, if I get it," the maid said, putting the paper in his hand with obvious reluctance.

The inspector held it up to the light and beckoned to Harbord. The paper was good, but unstamped and undated. "My own dearest," the letter began in the big, rather childish-looking writing with which the inspector had taken care to familiarize himself with of late as that of Lady Burslem. "I shall hope to see you before long in the place we know. Everything is going on well. There is no suspicion, and the only danger I really fear is that Ellerby may —" There it broke off suddenly. The inspector turned it round and looked at it this way and that; but there was nothing further to be gleaned from it.

"Well," Forbes said impatiently, "what do you say now?"

The inspector went over to his writing-table and sitting down made an entry in his big book of notes. Then he put the piece of notepaper in one of his drawers and shut it up.

"What can I say but that these discoveries of yours will probably be of the greatest assistance to us. As soon as anything definite can be settled I will let you know."

"And the reward?" the maid said blankly.

The inspector looked at her. "Matters are hardly forward enough for us to think of that yet. When they are, well, you may be sure that we will bear you in mind."

"I thought you would give it to me today."

The inspector nearly laughed. "You are rather anticipating matters, Miss Forbes. There is a good deal to be done yet before Sir John Burslem's murderer is found."

Forbes got up with a jerk. "Then I don't see that I have done much good by coming. It seems to me that I might have taken my goods to a better market."

"Oh, come, come!" the inspector said soothingly. "You have done the very best thing you could, Miss Forbes. And you will find that matters will be all right in the end. Only you ladies always do want to hurry matters, don't you? You trust everything to me."

Forbes looked mollified. "Oh, well, if you put it that way –"

"That is the only way to put it," the inspector rejoined. "And you may be sure that I shall do my best for you. I should for any lady, but, Miss Forbes, for you –" He stopped a minute. "Now I wonder whether you could help me a bit about something else?"

"Well, if there is anything I can do –"

"I suppose in the exercise of your duties you saw a good deal of Ellerby, in your position and his in the Burslem household?"

"Yes, of course I saw a good deal of him. In the housekeeper's room, and so on. But he was a man who kept himself to himself."

"Was he really? I had got the idea, but I dare say I was wrong –" The inspector looked at his book again. "Did it occur to you that Ellerby was the sort of man to have – well, shall we say a friendship for any woman other than his wife?"

"My hat! I should think not. I should not think that any woman would look at him if he had. Dried up old fossil! I wonder he ever got married at all. Only I suppose any man can pick up somebody."

"Dear me, do you think so, Miss Forbes? Then there is hope for us all," the inspector remarked politely. "Then I may take it you do not think Ellerby has gone off with any woman? I wonder what you do think has become of him?"

A curiously scared expression crept into Eleanor Forbes's eyes. "I – I don't know. We don't know what to think, any of us."

"If he died in 15 Porthwick Square, his body must be there," the inspector said thoughtfully.

The maid shivered. "Oh, however can you talk like that? I am sure I shall be frightened to go upstairs tonight. There's none of us going to sleep alone. I shall have the head housemaid with me. Nobody will be alone – except her ladyship, and she says she is not frightened at anything. Perhaps she has her reasons," she finished significantly.

"I should have thought that perhaps Miss Burslem –"

"Miss Pamela – not much! She hates her stepmother like poison. She will have her own maid with her."

"You saw and heard nothing the night before last?"

"Nothing – nothing at all. I wish I had," Forbes assured him.

"Well, then, perhaps I had better think things over," the inspector said, standing up. "But I shall want another long talk with you very soon, Miss Forbes, for more reasons than one."

Harbord smiled to himself as he saw how the woman bridled under the inspector's gaze as he escorted her politely to the door.

Stoddart came back when he had seen her safely off the premises.

"Well, what do you think of Miss Forbes?"

"Not much of her personally, but of her story a good deal," Harbord said at once. "She has confirmed me in my – I will not say belief, but my very strong feeling that Sir John Burslem never returned to 15 Porthwick Square – that it was his murderer made up to impersonate him who came back with Lady Burslem and forged the will."

"Ah, the will is a nasty snag in your theory. Experts say it is in Sir John Burslem's writing – hurried, carelessly written, but his unmistakably."

"Don't believe 'em!" Harbord said bluntly. "No, sir, I shall stick to my theory until I hit on a better. Sometimes I have thought you have –"

He looked searchingly at the inspector.

Stoddart frowned. "Theories are no use. If sometimes a faint gossamery suspicion has dawned upon me – well, I don't know that Miss Forbes's discoveries help me much."

CHAPTER X

"We will go right through the Park. I like to have a look at the swells sometimes," Mrs. James Burslem remarked as she said "Home" to the chauffeur.

Pamela was going to pay her promised visit to her aunt by marriage. Somewhat to her surprise her stepmother had made no objection to the plan, and the girl was now on her way to spend the week-end in Mrs. Jimmy's house in Kensington.

The séance, the principal attraction offered to Pamela, was to come off that afternoon. A friend of Mrs. Jimmy's, Winnie Margetson, was to be the medium, and Pamela was in a terrible state of excitement at the prospect of getting into touch with her much-loved father. This had been definitely promised to her by Mrs. Jimmy, who had bidden the girl prepare a list of questions which would be a test of the reality of the communication established with the other world. This Pamela had done, and she now clutched the paper feverishly in her hand as she sat in the car beside her aunt. In the Park, Mrs. Jimmy directed the man to draw up under the trees near Hyde Park Corner.

"Now, I expect we shall soon come across some of your fine friends," she remarked to Pamela.

"I don't know. I have very few friends in town now." Pamela looked inclined to be restive. She was anxious to get on to the séance with as little delay as possible, and at the bottom of her heart she was conscious, in spite of her expressed affection for her new-found relative, of a shrinking from the attention that lady's frequent laugh and loud speech attracted. Rather to Mrs. Jimmy's disappointment, as Pamela could not help recognizing, no acquaintance of the girl's passed for some time, and Mrs. Jimmy was reluctantly agreeing to make a start when a man who had been leaning against the railings lower down raised himself and came towards them. His face brightened as he caught sight of the pair in the car, and he quickened his steps.

"Well, this is luck!" he exclaimed, as he shook hands with Pamela and the girl introduced him as Mr. Richard Leyton to her aunt.

Mrs. Jimmy surveyed him in a puzzled fashion.

"Can we give you a lift?" she inquired at last. "We are on our way to the other side of the Park." The man hesitated and began to refuse; then, catching sight of the pretty, flickering colour of Pamela's cheeks, he rapidly changed his mind, got into the car and seated himself opposite.

"We are on our way to a séance," Pamela said with an excited thrill in her voice.

"A séance!" the man repeated. "What on earth for?"

"I want to get through to my father," Pamela told him. "I want him to tell us who murdered him. And where Ellerby is, and – and several other things."

A pitying look came in the man's eyes.

"I have never known any useful information given at those séances."

"Oh, haven't you?" Mrs. Jimmy interrupted, turning her head. "Well, I can tell you I have. I got some messages through for Lady Burslem, the other day, that surprised her, didn't I, Pam?"

"She – she said so. But I did not hear what they were," the girl said in an unwilling tone.

"Ah, well! Perhaps they were secret," Mrs. Jimmy said with an odd smile. "But I think we shall get something for you today, Pam. I told my friend to concentrate on you."

Pamela clasped her hands. "Oh, how sweet of you, Aunt Kitty!"

The man said nothing as he glanced from one to the other.

He knew a little of Mrs. James Burslem's reputation, and also knew that her husband was popularly supposed to have deliberately chosen ruin hunting in Tibet to the lady's society. He had gathered too from the gossip of the day, which of late had greatly concerned itself with the Burslems and their affairs, that Sir John Burslem and his wife had had little to do with Mrs. Jimmy. It was distinctly a surprise therefore to meet

Pamela in the society of, and apparently on such intimate terms with, her aunt. Mrs. Jimmy looked perturbed and puzzled and there could be no doubt that her expression was one of relief when Mr. Leyton expressed a desire to be set down near the Broad Walk. She turned when the car had started again and looked after the young man's tall figure as he strode along Bayswater Road.

"Well!" she exclaimed, as she threw herself back in her corner. "You seem to know him very well, and you call him Richard Leyton, but if it had not been for you I should have said his name was —"

"What?" Pamela inquired curiously as her aunt stopped.

"Something quite different," that lady answered, closing her mouth with a snap.

They made their way along crowded Notting Hill Gate and Church Street and so to the Royal Borough. Mrs. Jimmy's house was some distance from any of the main streets, in one of those little backwaters which are a survival from the days when Kensington stood miles from the metropolis.

Outside, with its little garden gate, the fastidiously cleaned steps and the green door with its bright brass knocker, there was a conventual air strangely incongruous taken in connexion with Mrs. Jimmy. But inside, as Pamela soon found, everything was quite different. The small lounge into which the door opened was strewn with cushions and papers, debris of all description covered the table, a stray cup and saucer stood on the sofa.

In the midst of it all a flashy-looking maid appeared to be trying to restore some semblance of order.

"Miss Margetson come yet, Marian?" Mrs. Jimmy inquired.

The maid tossed her head.

"Yes, madam. She has, and making herself at home in the drawing-room. Altering the furniture just when I had arranged it. And shutting the windows when I should have thought she would have liked a little fresh air."

"Ah, well, I know what that means." Mrs. Jimmy looked mysterious. "It is all right, Marian. Come along, Pamela." She opened the door at the left.

There was very little light in the drawing-room. Middle of the afternoon though it was, not only were the windows closed as the maid had said, but the dark blinds were closely drawn, and Miss Margetson appeared to be arranging some further sort of covering. She was a small, thin woman with closely cropped hair which evidently owed its blackness to art.

Mrs. Jimmy switched on the light.

"Well, you are doing it all right – properly," she said admiringly.

All the superfluous furniture, of which the room contained a good deal, had been pushed aside, most of it into the back part, which was separated from the front by folding doors and which evidently served the purpose of a dining-room. In the space thus cleared in the front room five wooden chairs were standing in close proximity to a small round table.

"Yes. I guess we are about ready. When are your guests going to arrive?" Miss Margetson inquired, in a voice to which Pamela took an instant dislike.

It was a soft, purring, *false* voice, the girl said to herself, and there was a decided American accent. She had been looking forward to seeing the medium to whom such marvellous powers had been vouchsafed; but now, as Winifred Margetson smiled and shook hands, Pamela felt only a distinct thrill of disappointment. She had seldom seen a face that repelled her more than the medium's. It was sallow and wrinkled, the dark skin everywhere crossed by a network of tiny lines. The mouth, the widest Pamela had ever noticed, was so thin-lipped that lips might have been said to be absent altogether; the even rows of teeth were obviously false and ill-fitting, and probably owing to this fact the corners of the mouth drooped to an extent that gave the whole face an extraordinarily crafty expression. The eyes were big and staring. Possibly open to things not of this earth, they appeared to see nothing close at hand. The sleek, dyed hair was brushed back and cut short, except that a bushy curl was trained over each large ear. The bustless, hipless, waistless figure looked as if two boards had been joined together and clothed in the preposterous garments of the present day.

Winifred Margetson was not the sort of woman in whom Pamela could imagine her fastidious father taking the smallest interest. The thought passed through her mind somewhat profanely that his tastes must have altered in the other world if he made his wishes known through the medium of Miss Margetson.

But the bell outside was tinkling. There were more arrivals.

"Lady Fanyard, Miss Fanyard, Mrs. de Conroy," the pert maid announced.

Mrs. Jimmy introduced Pamela with a wave of her hand.

"My niece, Pamela Burslem." The sound of her name did not excite the interest Pamela had half expected. The new-comers turned lack-lustre eyes upon her; if they had ever heard of the Burslem case it had entirely disappeared from their memory. All three were well dressed and evidently belonged to the moneyed class, but none of them looked particularly intelligent; their chins by one consent appeared to be absent.

Miss Margetson retired apparently to make some last preparations, and after a minute Mrs. Jimmy followed her.

Lady Fanyard turned to Pamela, her eyes upturned, her hands clasped in an ecstasy.

"Isn't she wonderful – our dear Miss Margetson?"

"I dare say she may be, but I do not know anything about her," Pamela said candidly.

"Ah! You are not convinced? You are only an inquirer?" Lady Fanyard brought her eyes down to Pamela's face. "But I could tell you the most marvellous things. Winifred has made life a different thing for me."

She was stopped by the return of Mrs. Jimmy with the wonderful Winifred, clad now in a flowing garment of filmy black, and with something of the expression of the mystic in her great, dark eyes and her small, wrinkled face. She glided to the table, and seating herself leaned back and raised her eyes upwards as if lost in ecstasy.

Mrs. Jimmy beckoned to them to sit round the table, the visitors having removed their hats and gloves. She placed Pamela exactly opposite the medium; then she bade them all place their hands on the table, not touching one another but to spread out every finger separately.

Then suddenly she switched off the light and the room was in absolute pitch darkness. Pamela found out afterwards that there were shutters behind the blinds, which Mrs. Jimmy had managed to close noiselessly. For a minute or two there was silence – silence so dead that Pamela could almost hear herself breathe.

Then the voice of the medium.

"There is a beautiful hymn – 'Lead, kindly light.' That is the first line. We will sing it while the spirits are on their way to us to make our darkness and gloom the perfect light of the next sphere." She stopped.

Then in a quavering voice somebody started the first line of Newman's hymn. The others joined in, more or less distinctly. When the last notes had died away there was silence again.

Then, Pamela told herself that it must be her fancy, but it really did seem to the girl that the darkness was full of moving things. Once she could have fancied a bat-like shape was skimming over the table before her. At last, apparently from a distance, there came a small shrill voice:

"I am Fan-Fan. I want to see – to see –"

"Ah, yes, yes!" the medium spoke, and now her voice had lost some of its purring note; it sounded tired and limp. "Yes, yes, Fan-Fan, who have you come to see?"

"A new lady. Somebody who wants to know." The voice was getting clearer, nearer. "And I bring with me some one who is trying to get to her. He says she must have patience – he is coming – but it is not long since he crossed. He is not sure – it is difficult – but he is trying."

Pamela drew a deep breath. She did not doubt – how could she? – that the words referred to her. She waited, her whole being concentrated in the longing to receive some sign from her father.

Then Fan-Fan spoke again; now her voice had weakened again.

"He is here! But it has been difficult – very difficult! In a minute he will speak. But it cannot be for long. The lady must have patience."

"Yes, yes!" Pamela was beginning, but a low, shocked hush ran round the room.

Then in the silence that followed there came in a man's deep voice the girl's name.

"Pam – child, are you here?"

It sounded like a man's voice, but though the expression "Pam – child" was Sir John's usual way of addressing his daughter, Pamela could not recognize any tone of her father's.

"Yes, I am here," she hesitated. "But, dad –"

"You wanted me – I have come, but it has not been easy and you must not keep me," the voice went on. "Be quick, Pam." "Yes, yes!" the girl said again. It was not easy to speak with all these strangers round, and the voice – the voice that was not her father's voice though it used her father's words –

seemingly floating in the air. She felt half frightened, half doubtful. Yet the much-longed-for opportunity was here. She told herself that she must – she must avail herself of it.

"Are you happy, dad?" she asked in a voice that would quiver in spite of her best efforts.

"It was too soon. They were too quick for me. My work was not done and I want you and Sophie."

Somehow the use of her stepmother's Christian name seemed more convincing to Pamela than anything else.

"Oh, dad," she burst out, "tell me who did it – who shot you."

"No, no! I can't. It is not allowed," the voice began to grow fainter as if the speaker were getting farther away.

"And where is Ellerby?" the girl questioned desperately.

"I don't know. But he is happy – he is helping those he loves." There was another pause, then the voice went on. "I – I must go. They are calling me away. Be good, Pam – child. Sophie will help you, and be kind to Aunt Kitty. She has done more for me than anyone since I came over."

"I will, I will!" the girl promised. "But – but, dad, can't you help me – tell me –"

"No, not now. I cannot stay. Only remember I am watching you, Pam. Good-bye!" There was a sound as if some one was blowing a kiss, then silence.

"Oh, dad, come back!" Pam cried desperately.

But there came no answer – only that dense, impenetrable darkness.

CHAPTER XI

"Vidame and Green! Here we are!"

Inspector Stoddart was the speaker. He and Harbord got out of a bus at Victoria and had walked down Witwick Street.

Vidame & Green's was quite a small shop; a stock of hosiery in the windows looked as though it was seldom altered.

Nevertheless it was obviously fairly well frequented, and there were several customers in the shop when the detectives entered. Two assistants were serving, and a dapper-looking little man in spectacles came forward.

"Mr. Vidame?" the inspector said inquiringly.

The little man coughed. "There is no Mr. Vidame, sir. My name is Mercier. I married Mr. Green's daughter, and I am the only representative of the firm in the business, though I am glad to say Mr. Green is still living at Hampstead. But anything I can do for you, gentlemen? I may say that our goods are among the most reliable in London."

Inspector Stoddart handed him a card. "If you could spare me a few minutes, Mr Mercier –"

Mr. Mercier's colour visibly altered as he saw the name.

"Certainly, inspector. Will you come to my office?" He led the way to a small room at the rear of the shop. "Now, gentlemen, I am at your service, though I am at a loss to understand –"

Stoddart took out of his pocket the tie-on label that had been found in Ellerby's room at Porthwick Square and which had on it Messrs. Vidame & Green's name. He handed it to Mr. Mercier.

"I presume this had been used for some purchase made in your shop? The figures 25/6/2 represent no doubt the date when the article, whatever it was, was bought. This number on the other side – 5 – I take it refers to the assistant who served your customer?"

"Exactly, inspector," Mr. Mercier said. "These labels are put on every parcel which is made up on the premises. I insist on it, as in the case of any dissatisfaction it is necessary to know all the details."

"Can we see the assistant who made up the parcel to which this label was attached?"

"Certainly you can." Mr. Mercier took up the speaking-tube which stood on his desk and spoke down it. Then he went to the door and returned with a tall, reedy-looking youth. "This is our Mr. Thompson, inspector. I am sure that any information he can give you –"

"Our Mr. Thompson" looked distinctly scared as he turned his prominent, light eyes on the detectives.

Mr. Mercier held out the label. "You served this customer?"

Mr. Thompson looked at the label, rather as if he thought it might bite. "Yes, sir, I did."

"You can remember the transaction?"

There was a pause while Mr. Thompson tentatively touched the label and apparently racked his brains, then he said:

"Yes, sir. I do. More especially as the customer made several purchases and I had seen him in the shop before."

"Have you seen him in the shop since?" Stoddart inquired.

Mr. Thompson began to look worried. "I can't call to mind that I have, sir. I have not seen him this last week, I am sure. But then I might not have noticed him if one of the other assistants had been attending to him."

The inspector took out his notebook. "Now, can you give me any sort of description of this customer of yours?"

"I do not know that I could, sir." Mr. Thompson hesitated and stammered. "He was not, so to speak, anything particular to look at."

"Old or young?" the inspector questioned.

"Oh, not to say old, sir. Nor yet young. Oh, not young by any means."

"Middle-aged, perhaps you would say," Stoddart suggested.

Mr. Thompson looked relieved. "Yes, sir. That's right. Middle-aged I should call him."

"Now about his hair, was he fair or dark?" the inspector pursued.

Mr. Thompson's bewilderment apparently increased.

"I am sure I couldn't say, sir. I can't call to mind that I ever saw his hair. He was clean-shaven, I know."

"Should you recognize him if you saw him again?"

"Oh, yes, sir!" This time Mr. Thompson had no doubts.

The inspector took a case from his pocket and held out the photograph it contained.

"Is this like your customer?"

Mr. Thompson took the card in his hand gingerly. He stared at it, he held it in different positions, and apparently studied it with meticulous care. At last he looked up at the inspector.

"I don't know. I couldn't say. I never saw him laughing like that – and without his hat," he said despairingly. "It might be him and then again it might not."

"Um! Not very illuminating," the inspector said, retrieving the photograph and replacing it in its case. "Well, Mr. Thompson, with regard to this customer of yours, can you tell us how many times you served him – approximately, of course – and anything with regard to his purchases?"

The assistant took a notebook from his pocket and glanced at it, then his face brightened.

"Yes, sir, I can. I remember perfectly now. I have served this same gentleman on three occasions. And each time the purchase has been the same – a dozen day shirts and three pyjama suits. The thing that has struck me as peculiar about it, and that has fixed it in my mind, is that each time the gentleman mentioned the fact that they were for himself, and yet each time they were different sizes."

"Different sizes!" echoed the inspector. "That seems curious. I could understand a man making a mistake once – got a little thinner or a little stouter, maybe – but it seems odd he should do it twice."

"Perhaps he was not so much thinner or stouter as he had expected," Harbord suggested. "He did not ask you to change them, then" – returning to Mr. Thompson – "or I take it for granted you would have done so."

"Certainly, sir. No, he never made any such suggestion."

"And he never had parcels sent to his address, I suppose?"

Mr. Thompson shook his head. "Not when I served him. I offered to send them, of course; they made such a big parcel for him to carry. But he refused. He had not far to go, he said, and he always preferred to be independent. But once I noticed he got into a taxi outside."

"I can understand that," Harbord murmured. "What sort of class – social class, I mean – should you say this customer of yours belonged, Mr. Thompson? Seeing as many people as you do, I take it you would size up a man pretty quickly."

Mr. Thompson looked flattered. "As quickly as most, sir. I should say this customer – well, he would not belong to the real higher classes, so to speak, though he was a well-spoken chap. But I should have taken him for a tradesman, or it might be a gentleman's servant."

"Ah!" the inspector drew a long breath. "You are a man of observation, Mr. Thompson. Well, we may have to see you again later, but that is all for today, I think."

With a word of thanks to Mr. Mercier, they departed, leaving that gentleman and his assistant looking after them with wondering and somewhat discomfited faces.

Outside Harbord looked at his superior. "Well, we are not much farther, sir."

"Don't you think so?" the inspector questioned, a far-away look in his eyes. "Well, perhaps not. But it all fits in – it all fits in."

"And yet I suppose in one way we are," Harbord went on dreamily. "For I think Ellerby's purchases make it certain he did a bunk – that no harm happened to him."

"Do you think so?" the inspector coughed. "Well, the room had been carefully stage-managed, I admit. From the first moment I entered it I felt certain that Ellerby walked out of it, probably alone, certainly of his own free-will. But afterwards – I would give a good deal to know what happened afterwards."

"But what could happen afterwards?" Harbord cogitated.

The inspector shrugged his shoulders.

"How can one tell? The only thing we know is that he was in some one's way. You remember that letter. All was going well. The only danger to be feared was from Ellerby."

"Lady Burslem's letter. Yes, I remember," Harbord said thoughtfully. "But she –"

"The fragment of a letter that Forbes brought in," Stoddart corrected. "It looked like Lady Burslem's writing certainly. But –"

Harbord looked surprised. "You think it is not."

"I don't think," the inspector returned mendaciously. "But if that hastily written will was not really in Sir John's writing this also may be a forgery – to put us off the scent."

"At any rate," Harbord went on, "as far as I can see there is no doubt that Lady Burslem is in it up to the hilt."

"No doubt," the inspector assented. Then after a pause, "No doubt at all that she is in it up to the hilt, as you say, or that some one is trying – has been trying all along – to make us think she is." He smiled as he saw the mystified expression on Harbord's face. Then he hurried forward. "Here, from this corner we can get a bus to Battersea. There is one coming now."

"To Battersea!" Harbord repeated reflectively. "You mean —"

"I think it is time we had a look at Mrs. Ellerby's abode," the inspector said as they got in. "The corner of Vine Street will be our nearest stopping place, I think."

From Vine Street to Dorrimer Street, where Mrs. Ellerby's house was situated, was but a step, as the inspector remarked.

The street was one of those melancholy ones beloved of the modern builder, in which every house is a facsimile of its fellows. No. 80 only differed from the others in that instead of an aspidistra in its front window the place of honour was occupied by a small table on which at the present moment a large black cat was lying, blinking lazily at the passers-by as it basked in the sun.

The inspector rang the bell and sounded the brass knocker.

The door was opened almost immediately by a tall, faded-looking elderly woman in a black dress and wearing a large, white apron.

"Mrs. Ellerby?" the inspector said inquiringly.

"Yes, sir. But if it is about rooms, I have none to let just now."

"I am glad to hear that," the inspector said politely. "It shows that business is good. But I have not come about rooms. It is just on a matter of business that I want a few words with you, if you will allow me." He handed her his card. "I rang you up this morning you remember – from Scotland Yard."

"From Scotland Yard! Oh!" A very scared look flashed into the woman's faded eyes. "But I haven't anything to tell you, gentlemen. I told you over the phone I had not. I know no more than the dead –"

"I think we will come in just for a minute nevertheless, if you will allow us," the inspector said, stepping forward.

Mrs. Ellerby perforce gave way and silently pushed open the door of the front room. Stoddart and Harbord walked in.

"As I said, Mrs. Ellerby," the inspector began, "we shall not keep you long. And it is really in your own interests that I want you to answer a few questions. I am sure that you are as anxious as we are that your husband, Mr. Robert Ellerby, should be found and –"

"As anxious!" Mrs. Ellerby interrupted him. "As anxious – my God! What can your anxiety be to mine? Day or night I haven't rested since I heard he couldn't be found. Your anxiety? What is that to mine – his wife's?"

"What indeed?" the inspector echoed, his keen eyes roving round the room. "I suppose I may take it for granted that you have heard nothing of your husband since the night before last when he left 15 Porthwick Square?"

"Left Porthwick Square?" the woman echoed. "Is that what you like to call it? Since he was murdered, like Sir John before him – because he knew too much, I should say."

"Murdered in 15 Porthwick Square?" the inspector said gravely, regarding her fixedly. "Do you realize the serious nature of the charge you are making, Mrs. Ellerby?"

The woman nodded, drawing her thin, bloodless lips together.

"I know. And I do not mind telling you what is the talk of London today – that, if it had been in a poor woman's house that my husband had been made away with, something would have been found out before now. It is money – money, that is making the Burslem Mystery, as they call it. Not much of a mystery either. Ask her ladyship who signed the will they call Sir John's that left poor Miss Pamela without a penny. It was not Sir John that would have treated his own flesh and blood like that. And ask her ladyship what she was doing wandering about the house, night before last, when all decent people were abed. Oh, there is no doubt that Ellerby knew too much for them."

The inspector vainly tried to stem the torrent of words.

"Mrs. Ellerby," he said, when at last he could get a word in, "you're making very serious accusations without, so far as I can see, one iota of proof in support of them."

"Proof – ugh!" Mrs. Ellerby's sallow cheeks were dyed a dusky red now. "There's plenty of proof to be had by those that know where to look for it," she observed enigmatically. "Ask Elsie Spencer what she saw in 15 Porthwick Square the night before last."

A look that Harbord knew well dawned in Stoddart's eyes.

"Elsie Spencer!" he repeated. "Ah, one of the maids, isn't she?"

"Yes. She is one of the maids," Mrs. Ellerby mimicked. "She is the second housemaid. And if she keeps her wits about her she will not be a housemaid much longer, I say."

The inspector raised his eyebrows. "When did you last see your husband, Mrs. Ellerby?"

"Alive, do you mean?" The woman's lips began to quiver, some of the fury which had upheld her had departed.

"Alive, certainly," the inspector assented. "Do you mean that you –"

"He was here the afternoon before they did him in. I had written to ask him to come, for I had had trouble with one of my lodgers – I couldn't get the money for my back rent and I was short of the ready, for I was let down pretty badly over Peep o' Day. So Robert he came over and gave my lodger a talking to and left me a bit that I was to put in the bank if I didn't want it. Which I did – put it in the bank I mean, for Ellerby had put the fear of God into my lodger and he paid up."

"How much did your husband give you?" Stoddart questioned.

For a moment Mrs. Ellerby looked mutinous, then something in the inflexible face of the man before her compelled obedience.

"It was fifty pounds," she said sulkily.

The inspector raised his eyebrows. "Doesn't that look to you as if your husband knew he would be away some time? Fifty pounds is a large sum, you know."

"I know it doesn't go far in these days," Mrs. Ellerby said defiantly. "You would know that if you had to see to a houseful of lodgers and meals to provide and getting the money from them as bad as pulling their teeth. Your wife would –"

"Haven't got one," the inspector said shortly. "Now, Mrs. Ellerby, I want a look at the room in which your husband generally sat when he was at home."

"And that would be difficult to show you," Mrs. Ellerby went on in the same injured tone. "It just depended on what rooms were let. When we had one empty Ellerby and I would sit there and he would read his paper. But it wasn't often we did sit down, either of us, we had too much to do. Ellerby often didn't do more, for weeks together, than just look in and pass the time of day. Perhaps he'd have a bit of a snack if there was anything going, and that was all I would see of him. Might just as well not have had a husband I used to say."

"Yet I understood from the servants in Porthwick Square that Ellerby always slept at home once a week, and frequently more often."

"That's right," the woman acknowledged grudgingly.

"But it was late when he came generally – time for bed when he had had his supper – and up again early in the morning to get back in time for Sir John."

"I see." The inspector nodded. "Now, Mrs. Ellerby, I want to have a look at your husband's bedroom."

"Which is mine, too. We do not go in for any newfangled ways," Mrs. Ellerby remarked scathingly. "Not that that makes any difference. My rooms are always so that anyone can go in them. I may not be grand but I am clean."

"I am sure of that, Mrs. Ellerby," the inspector agreed politely. "Now, if you please –"

Mrs. Ellerby led the way upstairs to a fair-sized apartment on the third floor. The big, wooden bedstead in the middle took up most of the room, but there was a wardrobe and a chest of drawers, that apparently did duty as a dressing-table, and a large washstand. Over this hung three photographs, one of Sir John Burslem, one of Pamela as a child with long hair, and one of a woman of middle age with a happy, smiling face. Mrs. Ellerby pointed to this last.

"Sir John's first wife, and a good deal better-looking than his second, if you ask me."

"Well, I am inclined to agree with you there, Mrs. Ellerby," the inspector said diplomatically. "Or shall we put it that Sir John had a pretty taste in wives?"

Mrs. Ellerby tossed her head. "I am sure I don't know. Pretty is as pretty does, I say. Well, I will leave you to look round if you feel like it, gentlemen. Not that you will find anything. I am sure of that. The top drawer is Ellerby's and the left-hand little one. But there is not much in them."

"One moment," said the inspector, detaining her. "Had your husband any relatives that he was friendly with?"

"He had a brother, William, in Cumberland that he used to stay with in the holidays. But William doesn't know anything of him now. I wired at once and got his answer."

"I should like to see it," the inspector said.

"Well, you can't," Mrs. Ellerby said snappily, "for I put it straight in the fire. And that is the only kin that Ellerby had that I know of except a sister that went wrong years ago and lives somewhere in the East End."

"I should like her address."

Mrs. Ellerby tossed her head. "I don't know it. And I don't believe Ellerby did, either. She was not the sort we should care to keep up with – either of us. So if that is   all –"

"Only one more question," the inspector said with a glance at Harbord. "Can you give me the name of any tradesman with whom your husband dealt? Tailor or outfitter?"

Mrs. Ellerby shook her head.

"I don't know that he went anywhere regular. Picked things up where he fancied them I should say."

"Vidame & Green's?" the inspector suggested.

"I don't know. He may have done," Mrs. Ellerby said carelessly. "I seem to have heard the name."

"Shop down Victoria way," the inspector told her.

But she made no further remark as she banged down a bunch of keys on the washing-stand.

"There, you will be able to get into everything with them."

"Thank you." The inspector looked at Harbord when she had gone. "Nice sort of lady. Ellerby would be justified in keeping out of her way."

Harbord shrugged his shoulders. "Doesn't make one feel in love with matrimony – some of the wives one meets. I wonder whether she knows more than she says, sir."

The inspector had opened the wardrobe and was going over the contents carefully. For the most part they seemed to be garments of Mrs. Ellerby's, but an old suit of Ellerby's, neatly folded, was on one of the shelves and a hat-box held a well brushed silk hat. But there did not seem to be much to help them with their investigation, and at the end of the first half hour the detectives were about to confess themselves beaten when the inspector's quick eyes caught sight of a small box pushed right up against the wall beneath the chest of drawers. It was made of drab cardboard, almost the same colour as the painted skirting-board against which it stood. The inspector went down on his knees and managed to poke it out with the handle of an umbrella he found in the wardrobe.

It held some curious-looking articles, Harbord thought, as he took off the lid, and together they looked at the contents of the box. Tubes, lumps of what looked like coloured chalks, and black and coloured pencils – what observation in restaurants and omnibuses had taught both detectives to recognize as lip-stick and boxes of powder, white, red and brown. Various dirty bits of rag were tucked about and among them. Then at the bottom were tiny tweezers, and different shaped knives. The inspector took up one or two of the tubes and squeezed them gingerly, smelt the contents, smeared them on his hand and then wiped the mark off again. At last he glanced at Harbord.

"What do you make of this?"

Harbord's expression was very doubtful. "Well, I suppose it is a paintbox. Though I never heard that Ellerby was anything of an artist."

"I am beginning to think he is an artist of a kind," the inspector said with a curious smile. "I see you do not realize the significance of this, Alfred," tapping the box as he spoke. "These are grease paints. Part of an actor's make up. Our friend Ellerby may have used them or he may not. But I think we will say nothing of our discovery to the dear lady downstairs for the present."

He replaced the contents as much as possible as they were and pushed the box back against the wall.

CHAPTER XII

It was Elsie Spencer's day out. She was looking very forlorn and miserable as she stood at the corner of the street waiting for her bus. She was going down to Stoke Newington to see her sister, but she was not feeling particularly happy. Her young man had given her the chuck, as she phrased it, the week before, and going down to tea at Stoke Newington without a young man was a dull affair indeed in pretty Elsie's opinion.

For Elsie was a very pretty girl looked at either way – with the dimples peeping out and her little white teeth showing, or, as today, with the corners of her mouth drooping pathetically and her big blue eyes looking as if she had been crying for hours. She was well-dressed too. Her powder-blue frock barely reached her knees and her grey silk stockings and suede shoes, as well as the little pull-on hat that matched her frock had been recommended by Lady Duff Gordon in the *Daily Graphic*, so that Elsie knew that her garments at any rate were unexceptionable. She was just thinking that her bus was a long time coming when a young man who seemed to be waiting for the same bus looked at her rather closely.

His face seemed faintly familiar to Elsie. She flushed red as he raised his hat.

"Miss Elsie Spencer?"

"Yes, that's right," the girl said shyly. "But I don't know –"

The man smiled.

"You have forgotten. My name is Harbord, and I saw you when I came to 15 Porthwick Square."

"Ah, the detective!" Elsie's pretty colour faded and a frightened look came in her eyes.

"Yes, the junior detective," the man confirmed. "But detectives have eyes like other men, Miss Spencer. And hearing it was your day out, and such a lovely day too, I wondered if I could persuade you to come for a drive with me down to Richmond or somewhere. Then we could have a cup of tea and drive home by moonlight. What do you say?"

Elsie thought it sounded very attractive. She was not quite sure that she ought to accept. But she told herself that it was not as if she knew nothing of Harbord, and the feeling of naughtiness would lend a spice of adventure to it all.

While she was hesitating Harbord beckoned to a passing taxi.

"We will have it open," he said to the driver. "Come, Miss Spencer, it will be ever so much nicer than the top of the bus this dusty day."

Elsie thought it would too as she let him help her in.

But Harbord found as they bowled off towards Richmond that he would have his work cut out for him. Elsie was not one of those talkative girls from whom it is easy to extract information. She was very quiet and shy, and sheered off at once from any mention of 15 Porthwick Square or its mysteries. He told himself that he must wait and see whether tea would loosen her tongue, and devoted himself during the drive to trying to make her feel at home with him. In this he was so far successful that by the time they reached Richmond the dimples were in full play again and Elsie was beginning to chatter.

They put up at an old-fashioned hostelry that Harbord had discovered rather off the main track, and had tea in a pretty, quaint, little pleasance sloping down to the river. Harbord ordered a luxurious tea, sandwiches of various kinds, dainty little cakes and fruit, and they both did justice to it after their drive. Then Harbord produced cigarettes and Elsie confessed to a weakness for a good smoke.

By now they felt almost like old friends. Harbord talked of his work and its difficulties and, in some cases, dangers. Elsie listened with increasing interest, and when at last he managed to introduce the Burslem Mystery, though he fancied she grew a shade paler, she made no attempt to check him. For a few moments he confined himself to Sir John Burslem's death and to the tremendous loss to small punters caused by the scratching of Peep o' Day. Elsie acknowledged to having put most of her savings on the colt, and also to having persuaded her young man to do the same, thus laying the foundation of the estrangement between them.

Harbord listened and sympathized. Then he skilfully turned the conversation to Ellerby and his disappearance. Here Elsie was inclined to become restive, but Harbord seemed so unconscious of any disinclination on her part and talked on so placidly that she soon quieted down.

"I have often remarked to a friend of mine," the young detective said at last, "that I thought it was uncommonly plucky of young girls like yourself to remain in 15 Porthwick Square after all that has happened, or is said to have happened, there."

There was no mistaking Elsie's pallor now.

"Oh, I wish I need not," she breathed, clasping her hands. "But we were all told that wherever we went we had to keep the police informed of our whereabouts and hold ourselves in readiness to obey any summons at any time. I couldn't get another job, not a good one, if I told folks that, and I can't afford to live at home. So I just stay on at 15 Porthwick Square until things are settled up, and then I shall be jolly glad to get away – jolly glad."

"I am sure you will," Harbord's voice was very sympathetic. "I don't know that I should care to stay in the house myself – I don't believe I should sleep at night."

"That is just how I feel," Elsie breathed. "I used to sleep that sound I was off the moment my head touched the pillow. But now I lie awake and think and wonder. It has been dreadful, dreadful – ever since Mr. Ellerby went away. There's none of us will sleep alone."

"I don't wonder at that. And you may well say went away. I wonder where he did go," Harbord said speculatively. "I wonder whether you have any notion, Miss Spencer?"

"Me – any notion?" repeated Elsie, shuddering. "I should think I have not. Do you think he did go – out of the house, Mr. Harbord?"

Harbord shook his head. "I would give a good deal to be able to answer that question. There's only one thing I do think – and that is that some one in the house must have known what has become of Ellerby and how he went – if go he did."

"I don't believe there is anybody that knows anything about it – not on the staff, anyhow," Elsie contradicted. "If anyone does – it is her ladyship."

"Now I wonder why you should say that?" Harbord questioned. "Though I have heard the theory put forward before, mind you. But how should Lady Burslem know anything of the valet's disappearance? I cannot imagine. What makes you say so anyhow?"

Elsie shivered. "I don't suppose it is anything really, and – of course it isn't. But – but her ladyship was walking about the house that night."

"She was!" Harbord could not prevent a note of triumph from creeping into his voice. "But how do you know, Miss Spencer?"

Elsie began to look thoroughly frightened. "I wish I hadn't said anything about it. But you – you wheedled it out of me somehow. And now – I don't know what to do." Her blue eyes were swimming in tears.

Harbord just touched her hand.

"Now don't you trouble yourself, Miss Spencer. You have done the wisest thing in trusting me. What you tell me goes no farther. And you must tell somebody. I can see it is making you quite ill, the keeping it to yourself."

"Yes, that's right!" Elsie said tearfully. "Well, I will tell you. If it gets me into trouble, I can't help it. It will be a comfort to have it off my chest." She stopped and gazed round. "There's nobody can hear us here, can they?" pointing to a couple at a table on a line with them.

"Not a bit of it!" Harbord said reassuringly. "Now put the matter in a nutshell. How do you know that Lady Burslem was up and about the house on the night of Ellerby's disappearance?"

"Because I saw her," Elsie said in a whisper.

Harbord drew a deep breath.

"I expected as much. Now just tell me exactly what you saw and heard."

"It – it wasn't much anyway," Elsie said, tears vibrating in her voice. "But I was sleeping with Clara Hill, the kitchenmaid, in a room at the back of the house on the third floor. And I got the toothache something cruel. I had some very good stuff for toothache that my sister gave me and I had lent it to Mary Clarke, the head housemaid. She sleeps in a room at the end of our passage, so I made up my mind I would go along and get it. Clara Hill was awake too, and she came with me. I wouldn't have dared to go by myself since Sir John died – we none of us would. Well, right at the end of the passage there is a green baize swing-door that opens on to the corridor that runs along the front of the house. Just as we got up to Mary's room we saw a streak of light under the green baize door. We wondered whether it had been forgotten, for when Sir John was alive he was most particular about all the lights being out, and then we thought of burglars and got real scared. At last we just pushed the door very gently and peeped through. Some one – a woman – was coming down the passage carrying an electric torch in one hand and a parcel – a good-sized parcel – in the other. We couldn't make out at first who it was, then as she came nearer we saw that it was her ladyship."

"You are sure?" Harbord questioned half incredulously.

The girl nodded emphatically. "Certain! We saw her face quite plain – me and Clara both. At first we thought she was walking in her sleep, but then she would not have brought the torch or the parcel, would she?"

Harbord shook his head. "No, I should say that is out of the question. What else did you see, Miss Spencer? Where did she go?"

"I – I think downstairs," Elsie faltered. "But we didn't wait any longer, me and Clara. We were too much afraid of getting into trouble if we were caught,' so we just hurried back to bed, and I never got the toothache mixture after all; for the seeing her ladyship put everything else out of my head. And the tooth stopped aching just as if by magic. So I kept it warm in bed till morning."

"Ah, I have heard that a fright often takes toothache away," Harbord said thoughtfully. "What time was this, should you say?"

"Just before three," said Elsie. "For I heard it strike directly after I got back into bed. Clara made the remark that she wondered what her ladyship could be doing. Then the next day we heard that Mr. Ellerby could not be found, and we have wondered and wondered did the one who was about the house see anything, or know anything, or – or do anything," her voice dropping to the merest whisper. Harbord had to lean forward to catch it. His face was grave as he sat still, his eyes fixed upon the tiny ripples on the river's surface. He did not speak.

After one glance at him, big tears welled up in Elsie's eyes, and rolled miserably down her cheeks.

"We have been too frightened even to speak of it to one another. I did just say a word to Mrs. Ellerby when she came to ask about her husband, and I have been sorry ever since I spoke," she said, her voice shaking. "And now I have been and told you all about it. And – and I don't suppose I shall ever hear the last of it. Clara will never forgive me."

"There is no need she should know anything about it that I see," Harbord said, rousing himself. "Or anyone else for that matter. What you saw does not affect the Burslem Mystery one way or the other, as far as I can judge, unless it adds a minor one. You I say her ladyship was alone?"

"Oh, yes. There was nobody else about then."

"How was she dressed? I mean, for going out, or in indoor things."

"Oh, indoor," Elsie said quickly. "I mean she looked as if she had just thrown on some sort of loose, dark dressing-gown. She hadn't got a hat or anything on her head, for her hair just caught the torchlight as she came along."

"It is a strange thing, and I don't see what she could be doing. Was she helping Ellerby get away or was she –"

"Trying to prevent him getting away?" Elsie whispered. "Mrs. Ellerby she makes sure she was – she might be afraid he would talk, Mrs. Ellerby says. And – and we don't know how much he knew or – or guessed."

Harbord could not forbear a slight smile.

"My dear Miss Spencer, with the best will in the world, I don't think a slight, rather delicate woman like Lady Burslem could do away with a strong man like Ellerby, or even prevent him getting away from the house, for that matter."

"He – he might have been shot or – or poisoned," Elsie said in the same scared whisper.

"What became of the body, then?" Harbord questioned, his smile deepening.

Elsie was not looking at him now.

"She – she was carrying a parcel. I have asked myself sometimes what could have been in it."

"Well, hardly Ellerby, dead or alive, I presume." A hint of amusement Harbord could not help feeling was creeping into his voice now.

"No, of course not!" Elsie began indignantly; then the frightened note came into her voice again. "Not – not whole," she whispered.

This time Harbord really could not repress a laugh. "Oh, my dear girl, what have you been doing? Having a course of the 'Mysteries of the Rue Morgue' or something of that kind? Come, I am going to take you for a walk by the river. And then we will have a drive round and home. That will sweep all the cobwebs away. And you will be all the better for having spoken of your fears to somebody – somebody who is quite safe, moreover. And, believe me, you can put all those same fears away – you are conjuring up an impossibility."

CHAPTER XIII

We understand that Peep o' Day, the late Sir John Burslem's wonder colt, who was scratched for the Derby at the last moment owing to the owner's lamented death, has finished his racing career. He has been sold by Lady Burslem to Señor Ramon da Villistara, one of the biggest breeders in Argentina, for £45,000. Peep o' Day will leave by an early boat and on reaching La Plata will proceed at once to the Ramon da Villistara stud-farm, which with the adjacent *estancia* stands some distance north of Rosario da Santa Fe. It is rumoured that Señor da Villistara has decided that Peep o' Day shall serve only his home mares. Enormous fees are said to have been offered by other owners and to have been refused by the Señor, who possesses some of the finest brood mares in the world. The breeding of Argentine racehorses is Señor Ramon da Villistara's great hobby, and it is for the furtherance of this and the introduction of the best English strain that Peep o' Day has been purchased.

"Is there any truth in this paragraph?" inquired Mrs. Aubrey Dolphin, tapping the *Daily Wire* smartly with the cigarette she was about to light.

The two sisters – she and Lady Burslem – were sitting in the latter's sitting-room at 15 Porthwick Square. To the general surprise Sophie Burslem had persisted in staying in town all through the summer, even when the exigencies of the inquest would have allowed of a visit to the country.

For the inquest had formally concluded now, in a very unsatisfactory fashion, since the verdict that Sir John Burslem had been shot but that by whom the shot had been fired there was no evidence to show.

"Most unsatisfactory verdict," the public called it and raised a great outcry about the supineness of the police and the deficiencies of the C.I.D. These sentiments were coupled with adverse comments on the non-discovery of Sir John Burslem's murderer and scornful inquiries as to what had become of his valet, Robert Ellerby. It spoke volumes for the failure of our police system that a house and its inmates should be under police observation and that a man should absolutely disappear from that house and that the C.I.D. should find no trace of him, dead or alive.

But these scathing comments of the public, like the police investigations, produced no result, and the whereabouts of Robert Ellerby, like the question of the murderer of Sir John Burslem, remained a mystery.

The widowed Lady Burslem remained in seclusion and grew thinner and more shadowy looking day by day. The tragic look in her eyes went to the hearts of those who loved her. But she spoke of her excellent health and invited no sympathy. So far as Inspector Stoddart had been able to ascertain, there had been no attempt at communication either on her side or Sir Charles Stanyard's. And the inspector's thoughts were more often busy with the person to whom the half letter of Lady Burslem's that Forbes had brought to him had been addressed than he would have cared to confess.

Mrs. Dolphin rapped the paper again and repeated her question:

"Is there any truth in this paragraph?"

Lady Burslem glanced at the paper listlessly.

"About Peep o' Day? Oh, yes, he is sold to Villistara."

"You got a good price for him," Mrs. Dolphin remarked. "But I wonder whether Sir John would have liked him to go to Argentina? He was so proud of Peep o' Day, and so anxious that English racing should prosper always."

"Ah, he quite approved," Lady Burslem said at once. "He – you know I get into communication with him through Kitty, Mrs. Jimmy Burslem. She has séances at her house nearly every week, and they almost always manage to get through to him."

"Really, Sophie." Mrs. Dolphin sat back in her I chair and crossing her legs gazed at her sister in amazement as she lighted her cigarette – "how you can talk such arrant nonsense amazes me! Is it likely that John, who detested Mrs. Jimmy in his life, should spend his time in communication with her after his death?"

Lady Burslem's lips quivered slightly. "Death alters everything. Heaven forbid that we should take our enmities and dislikes into the next world. And John lets me know his wishes through Mrs. Jimmy."

"I expect his wishes mostly concern Mrs. Jimmy's," said Mrs. Dolphin sceptically. "Give poor Kitty a tenner or something of that sort, probably. I suppose you will be told to give her a good piece of Peep o' Day's price."

"I don't think so," Lady Burslem dissented. "A good deal of that will be invested in Argentina. John had a great belief in the future lying before that country when its resources are fully developed."

"Had he really?" Clare Dolphin's tone was not convinced. "Did he say so in his lifetime? Or did he communicate this belief of his through Mrs. Jimmy?"

"Oh, I have heard him say so heaps of times," Lady Burslem said decidedly. "And I don't think you should scoff at communication with the dead, Clare. Look at all the clever people who do believe in it: Oliver Lodge and – and heaps of others."

"I was not scoffing at communication with the dead," Clare Dolphin said, regarding her sister with pitying eyes. Heaven forbid that I should. But I don't imagine that Sir Oliver Lodge has much to do with Mrs. Jimmy's little game. What I object to is her exploitation of you for her own ends."

Lady Burslem drew her lips together in an obstinate line with which her sister was only too familiar. "I don't agree with you at all. I am getting quite fond of her. She has done everything she could to help me since John's death."

"And that is precious little, I expect," Mrs. Dolphin remarked. "Well, Sophie, I am sorry you have taken this quite extraordinary liking to Mrs. Jimmy. But we cannot all think alike. I want to know where you are going abroad and when. Now that this tiresome business is over I suppose you can go when you like."

"I suppose so," Sophie said languidly. "Oh, yes, of course I can. But there is a lot of business to be done in connexion with John's affairs. Still I must have a change. Forbes is going next week and I have engaged a new maid, an Italian. So I think I shall go to the Italian lakes first, then work round to Biarritz and perhaps go on to Madrid. I have always wanted to see the Escorial."

"I don't think that is at all the kind of change you want," Clare Dolphin said decidedly. "Racing about like that! And who are you going to take with you, may I ask? I am sure you are not fit to go by yourself, and I could not possibly manage it. I must go to Scotland with Aubrey. He will not hear of anything else. If you would come with us –"

Lady Burslem shook her head. "You are very kind, but I couldn't," she said decidedly. "I was there, you know, last year, with him – John. I must go somewhere I have never been before – somewhere I can try to forget."

Mrs. Dolphin shrugged her shoulders. "Well, if that is how you feel I can do nothing. But you will take Pam."

Sophie smiled faintly. "How we should both hate it! No, Pam will go to her friends, the Stanmore- Greens, probably yachting. I shall be all right."

"You cannot go with only a maid – a strange maid too!" Mrs. Dolphin's eyes were wide with amazement.

Lady Burslem's smile deepened, though there was little enough of real amusement in her eyes.

"Why not? You seem to forget that I shall be alone – always – now." Her voice dropped to a whisper.

"Do not be a sentimental idiot, Sophie!" reproved her sister, delicately flicking her cigarette ash into the tray. "You have had your time of mourning for John Burslem – quite long enough in my opinion – and now it is your duty for your own sake and that of your relatives to pull yourself together and buck up. And as for being alone always – rot! You may have been fond of your husband, no doubt you were – a great deal fonder than I ever gave you credit for being, for that matter – but you are young, you have your life before you. As for being alone always – well, I expect you will tell a very different tale this time next year. Of course you will marry again and have children of your own, and –"

"Clare!" Lady Burslem sat up, her cheeks flushing, her eyes sparkling with anger. "Once for all, I shall never marry again. Please to understand that. It is wicked of you – wicked to suggest such a thing." Mrs. Dolphin regarded her sister with unmixed amazement.

"Very well. Do not excite yourself, my dear girl. For the future the subject shall be strictly taboo. But we shall see."

Two little vertical lines that were new, and yet were rapidly becoming habitual to Sophie's brow, deepened now.

"You certainly will," she said coldly. "But now, Clare, I have to see Mr. Burrows on urgent business. He rang me up just before you came."

"And who in the world is Mr. Burrows?" Clare Dolphin inquired, staring at her sister.

"The manager in the City," Sophie said quietly. "At least the manager of one of the departments. John himself was his own general manager of course. And he gave me so many lessons that so far I have got on fairly well. But I shall have to look out for another manager soon. It is almost too much for me."

Clare Dolphin drew a long breath.

"I should jolly well think it was. I am sorry for John's business if you are going to have much to do with it. I remember what a mess you always made of your accounts when we were girls and had to manage our own allowances."

"This is a very different matter," Lady Burslem said listlessly. "John always said I was the best pupil he ever had, and I have had the most complicated papers sometimes to go through. They say down at the office I am quite wonderful."

"So I should imagine!" her sister said dryly. "I wonder how many more surprises you have in store for us, Sophie."

"I don't know," Sophie said carelessly. "But I must see Mr. Burrows. You can stay in the room if you like. It is something about some minerals that are only to be found in the Urals.

We must get the sole rights if it is possible to come to any permanent agreement with the Russian Soviet Government."

Clare Dolphin's eyes opened wider than ever.

"I shall certainly stay in the room and hear your conversation with this Mr. Burrows," she said decidedly. "Urals – and minerals and Soviet governments! I shall find it most intriguing, I am sure."

They waited a few minutes in silence until Mr. Burrows was shown in. He carried a portfolio of papers and looked what he was, a prosperous business man. Lady Burslem introduced him to her sister and then drew her chair up to a small table. Mr. Burrows placed his papers upon it and began to make his explanations in a low voice. To Mrs. Dolphin all that she could hear appeared to be so much Greek. She was amazed to find her sister, though speaking little, making her few observations in a thoroughly capable, intelligent fashion, evidently meeting with Mr. Burrows's entire approval.

At last he rose and gathered his papers together. Lady Burslem laid her hand upon them.

"You must leave them with me for a few days, Mr. Burrows. I never seem to grasp things until I have gone into them by myself."

Mr. Burrows bowed. "It is, of course, important that you should perfectly understand both what we want and the concessions and securities that we are prepared to offer, and to accept from the Soviet Government. You will see –"

Clare Dolphin could contain herself no longer.

"Really, Sophie, how did you get to know anything of the Soviet Government or – or concessions or anything?" she burst out.

"I told you John taught me," Lady Burslem said simply.

The manager turned to Mrs. Dolphin. "Lady Burslem is a marvellous woman. Her grip and insight into business affairs is simply wonderful. And when it comes to international complications Sir John himself could not have had a clearer vision. Really, I say sometimes it is like what they say in the Bible – the mantle of Elijah hath fallen upon Elisha. Certainly the spirit of Sir John seems to speak through Lady Burslem. She makes rough notes on the margin that might have been written by Sir John himself. Sometimes it seems to me that even her writing is getting like his. Last time when the deed came back, if I had not known, I should have said one of the side notes had been written by Sir John himself. It was just his turn of the 's'."

"H'm! Well, it becomes more and more astonishing," said Mrs. Dolphin, getting up. "She never could write for nuts. You know the awful scrawl you used to perpetrate, Sophie."

CHAPTER XIV

"Now," said Inspector Stoddart, "we shall have things our own way, and if there is anything to be found in 15 Porthwick Square we shall find it." He rang a loud peal at the door of Sir John Burslem's town house as he spoke.

Lady Burslem had been as good as her word. She had departed for Italy with only her maid and a courier. The household staff had been given an indefinite holiday with wages and board wages. And though, as Elsie Spencer had said, all the servants had been warned that they must keep in touch with the police, they had departed to their several destinations well pleased at the prospect of leaving 15 Porthwick Square and its gruesome secrets behind. The house was now in the hands of caretakers. Rumour had it that before long it would be put up for sale, as Lady Burslem had been heard to say that she could not stand the prospect of living in it alone. As soon as the inhabitants were well out of the way Inspector Stoddart had applied for a search-warrant and obtained it, and he and Harbord were now on their way to put it into execution.

The door was opened after a delay which raised the inspector's ire, and a woman in a rusty black gown appeared. Inspector Stoddart recognized her at once as of the old-fashioned caretaker type. He stepped inside, Harbord following.

"It is our duty to go through this house. We shall disturb you as little as possible."

The woman looked thoroughly taken aback and tried to put herself in the way.

"It is more than my place is worth, sir, to let you in. It is her ladyship's orders that no strangers are to be allowed in the house at all while she is away." Inspector Stoddart held out his card.

"Inspector Stoddart of Scotland Yard, and we hold a search-warrant for this house. You have no choice but to stand aside; you cannot obstruct the police in the discharge of their duty."

The woman stared at him for a moment, then with an extraordinary sound between a howl and a sob she threw her apron over her face.

"I wish I hadn't come here," she wailed. "If I hadn't heard that all the fuss with the police about Sir John was over I wouldn't. But it was good money and my husband said we could not afford to refuse. But now – now –"

"Now, no harm will come to you if you are a sensible woman and keep a still tongue in your head," the inspector told her. "Now, I think we will begin with one of the rooms on the first floor." He looked at Harbord. "And then we will have a look at the basement. I shall want all the keys of the kitchens and the cellars, please."

The caretaker threw out her hands. "I haven't got them. You don't think that their grand butler would trust me with his keys."

"I am sure they could not have been in better hands," the inspector said politely. "But we shall manage without them, I dare say."

He stepped sharply across the hall and up the stair-case, followed by Harbord and pursued by a volley of exclamations from the caretaker.

"Here we are," he said, turning to Lady Burslem's sitting-room. The door was unlocked. The inspector raised his eyebrows. "We shall not find much here. They will have taken care of that. But one never knows what may have been overlooked or" – he paused a moment – "put ready for us to find."

Lady Burslem's delicate furniture was all enshrouded in brown holland; the curtains and the tapestry had been taken down, and the carpet rolled up. The writing-table and the bookcase alone were uncovered. The inspector went over to the former and tried the drawer, pinching in his lips as though about to whistle when he found it open. Inside there was nothing but a mother-of-pearl blotter. He opened it and held it out to Harbord with a slight smile. The blotting- paper was clean and untouched.

"Knows a thing or two, doesn't she?"

Harbord made some inarticulate answer. He was on his knees before the small bookshelf taking out each book and shaking it in turn. Presently he spoke:

"There are several books here about Argentina and its exports and imports. One about South America, taken more as a whole; another on shooting in the southern Andes and – yes, still another about Santa Fe. What can they have been wanted for?"

"Ah, there you are!" There was a curious expression on the inspector's face as he gazed at his young confrere. "Peep o' Day was sold to an Argentine, you must remember," he added.

"Yes. But these books will not give much information about Peep o' Day." Harbord fetched one of them out and opened it. "Pretty well read too, I should say."

The inspector took it from him.

"Yes. Well, Argentina is a good place to start from, if you want a hiding-place."

"They fetched Jabez Balfour back," Harbord reminded him.

"I said to start from," the inspector remarked, turning over the pages of the book he held. "Chili and Peru and Bolivia. Lots of little places, scarcely heard of here, in Brazil, and the Pampas themselves give plenty of scope. This fits in very well with a little discovery I made the other day. Lady Burslem is gradually investing large sums of money in different South American securities."

"The price of Peep o' Day," Harbord suggested.

"Pish!" the inspector said contemptuously. "Peep o' Day's price would be a flea-bite to what I have heard. Even if Señor da Villistara has paid up yet, which I doubt – Spaniards are notoriously dilatory. *Mañana* is probably all Peep o' Day has brought in at present."

"H'm!"

Harbord again applied himself to his task of shaking books, and the inspector strolled round the room. Presently he turned to the door.

"We shall not find anything more here, I think. We will go to the cellars now. They have intrigued me considerably ever since Ellerby – went away."

"You do not think –" Harbord began; then he checked himself and followed his superior in silence.

Right at the back of the entrance hall a green baize swing-door opened into a wide passage. The inspector looked round. To the right the passage evidently ran by the dining-room, with the kitchens beyond. To the left lay the housekeeper's room and the butler's pantry, then past the servants' hall the passage narrowed and they came to a low, nail-studded door. The inspector tried it.

"Ah! Locked, of course. Now we shall see."

He took a curious looking steel implement from his pocket and with a few dexterous manipulations the door swung back. The short flight of steps before them led down to what was evidently the wine-cellar, the one probably in general use.

"Makes one feel thirsty to look at the bottles," Stoddart remarked jocularly as he unfastened the door at the farther end. "Curious, rambling cellars these houses in Porthwick Square have. And some of them are very old." And then he said what in Harbord's ears had an odd and very sinister significance, "I should not ask for a better hiding-place."

The second cellar was pretty much like the first, save that down one side ran long, brick thralls with huge barrels on them held in place by wooden logs, and further, in some cases, chained to staples in the wall behind.

The inspector tapped one of them. "Empty! Umph! Well, we shall have to try them all. And maybe find out what is in some of them."

The first two cellars had been lighted dimly enough by gratings high in the wall, probably communicating in some way with the old paved court at the back of the house. The next one into which they penetrated was pitch-dark; yet that there was some sort of opening was proved by the fact that the air was not vitiated beyond endurance.

The inspector turned on his electric torch. This cellar was rather smaller than the preceding ones and seemed to contain nothing of importance – a few bottles, a cask standing on one end in the corner. There were two small, arched doors at one side. The inspector's sharp eyes turned to them at once.

"Notice anything particular about these cellars, Harbord?"

"Vaults, I should call 'em," his subordinate answered, sniffing about him. "Well, first I notice that they are not as stuffy as they might be. Secondly, visitors have been here before us."

"And how do you deduce that?"

"Well, there are some cobwebs about," Harbord said thoughtfully, "but not as many as there would have been if some one had not been in in the last few months. Then the dust of the floor has been disturbed."

"The butler may have come in, you know," Stoddart reassured him. "Quite in the way of legitimate business."

"H'm! Yes, he might," Harbord acquiesced. "But this was not the butler. It was a woman."

"How do you know that?" inquired the inspector. "Not" – with a grin – "from her skirts trailing on the ground, I presume?"

Harbord grinned responsively. "Hardly! A fool of a woman told me the other day her staircase was haunted. She always felt her skirts caught by unseen hands when she went up it. 'My dear girl,' I said, 'it must be a clever spook to get hold of your skirts!'"

"Quite!" the inspector agreed. "But what made you feel sure it was a woman, then?"

"The footprints. The shoes that made them were small and narrow-soled and pointed, with high heels."

"Well done," was the inspector's comment. "You have your head screwed on the right way, Alfred. I will say that for you. Now did you notice anything else?"

"No, I can't say I did," Harbord answered, looking at him. "Was there anything else?"

"Well, in the second cellar something had been dragged or laid down. There was a big, confused mark near the wall on which the casks were chained. Still, as I said a moment ago, it may have been done by the butler, though judging from the state of things I should not think that worthy pays these farther cellars many visits. Now for those two small doors. As far as I can judge from the look of them, they have not been opened for years. But appearances are deceptive so here goes." He applied himself to the lock of the nearest, which was very stiff and was moved with great difficulty. "Heard once of a place like this," the inspector said as he pushed the door open. "New servants going into the house found a quantity of bones supposed to belong to the skeleton of a young woman. The last tenant was an old lady who had lived there for fifty years. They never found anything out about the skeleton."

"Well, there is nothing of that kind here," Harbord observed as the electric torch disclosed a small, vaultlike apartment apparently quite empty and with the floor deep in dust, which looked as if it had lain undisturbed for centuries.

"Not to be found at sight," the inspector said, as he went on to the second door.

This was not so difficult to open as the first, and inside, though there were no very distinct footmarks, it did look as if the dust had been disturbed in some way; otherwise the small, rather damp-smelling apartment was a facsimile of the first.

The inspector rubbed his nose reflectively. "Now, where shall we begin? Every bit of these floors will have to be sounded. But we haven't got the wherewithal to-day."

"The dust is a pretty good guarantee that the floors have not been troubled," Harbord remarked.

"In these last two it is," the inspector assented. "But in the first three it is not. One can see that somebody has been in, and that is about all. And I am not taking any risks. We are up against no common criminal, you must remember. The scattering of dust or the laying of false trails is no very difficult matter. But I think – I think, for to-day, we will begin with the second cellar, the one with the casks. I have a feeling, a very strong feeling that if we find anything it will be there."

They went back, leaving the doors open, and taking care not to disturb any traces of other visitors.

The second cellar, the one upon which the inspector's suspicion had fixed, was quite as large as the first, and differed from it only in having the brick thralls on the one side. In front of the big chained barrels there was a quantity of dust mixed with sawdust, and it was here that the traces of disturbance were most apparent.

The inspector attacked the barrels first. He tapped them, examined them through his glass, even managed with Harbord's help to move them a little.

At last he gave a dissatisfied grunt. "Nothing there! The barrels have not been interfered with. I scarcely expected to find that they had."

Harbord began to poke about under the thrall.

"Plenty of room beneath here," he said as he passed one of the supports. "And, by Jove, there is something!"

The inspector knelt down beside him, turning on his electric torch as he did so.

"You are right," he said quietly. "But it looks like a roll of dark cloth or something of that kind."

"You remember the parcel Lady Burslem carried on the night of Ellerby's disappearance," Harbord suggested.

The inspector nodded. "She never came down here by herself that night, though. She could not have got the keys and come down here without being heard."

"Perhaps those who heard kept their own counsel," Harbord observed significantly, poking more energetically with a stick he had brought down. "It is coming now, sir. There, if you could catch that end –"

The inspector caught and pulled. The thing, whatever it was, was closely wedged up at the back of the thrall. A short, rather thick bale of drab cloth, very dirty, it looked to be as the inspector pulled it forward.

"What on earth –" he began, as he started to unroll it. Then he uttered a sharp exclamation as he held up a man's light overcoat – an overcoat that, crumpled and begrimed though it was, plainly showed large, ominous, dark stains down the front. The inspector touched them with his finger; he smelt them. Then he glanced at Harbord. "Don't want a microscope to say what they are."

"No," Harbord assented. He looked at the collar. "One of the best tailors in Savile Row," he said. "The pockets, sir?"

The inspector was already feeling in them. He held up a fine, white handkerchief also with those sinister stains upon it, and pointed first to that and then to the initials at the corner – J.V.B. He put in his hand again and brought out a crocodile cigarette-case mounted in gold and enamelled with a monogram – J.V.B.

The inspector stood up and shook the coat.

"Nothing more. But enough for our purpose perhaps. Do you realize what this is, Harbord?"

"It is, I should say, one of Sir John Burslem's coats," the younger detective responded.

"Right! But it is more than that," the inspector said quietly as he felt the lining over. "It is the one in which he started out on that fatal 2nd of June, which he carried over his arm when he came back with Lady Burslem; and which we have never been able to trace since; for you remember the attendant at the parking ground said the man who brought in Sir John Burslem's car, and whom he identified from a photograph as Sir John Burslem himself, wore a dark overcoat."

Harbord had been poking again under the thrall. He got up now and dusted his trousers down.

"How in the world did that coat get here after he was murdered?"

"Yes," said the inspector. "That's the puzzle."

CHAPTER XV

Amelia Burslem was staying with the Stanmore-Greens at their place in Perthshire. The Stanmore-Greens were very rich, at least Mrs. Stanmore-Green was. She was an American, the daughter of Woodruffe B. Larnack, sometimes quoted as among the six greatest multi-millionaires of the world. She was very young, very pretty and very smart, and had taken an instant fancy to Pamela Burslem when she had met her as the schoolgirl friend of her younger sister. The liking had been mutual. A long visit to the Stanmore-Greens' Highland home had been owing since the preceding year, and the Burslem Mystery had given Pamela an added charm in Mrs. Stanmore-Green's eyes.

Pamela had decided weeks ago that nothing should induce her to go abroad with her stepmother. Nevertheless she had been conscious of a distinct feeling of pique when it became apparent that Lady Burslem in no wise desired her society. The only point upon which Lady Burslem had insisted was that Pamela should take with her Wilmer, who had been maid to the first Lady Burslem, and after her death Pamela's personal attendant.

Fond as Pamela was of Wilmer, she was inclined to think that the woman was old-fashioned, and that she would have preferred some one more modern as her maid at the Stanmore-Greens'. Lady Burslem, however, had been adamant on the point, and Pamela had been compelled to yield. And now that she was at Fallock Castle, as the Stanmore-Greens' place was called, after a day among a big house-party every member of which was entirely unknown to her, Pamela was conscious of a feeling of warmth and gladness when she found Wilmer waiting for her, all her things laid out just as she liked them, and the maid anxious to pet and cosset her just as she had done in her childish days.

But Pamela had been a week at Fallock now, and she was beginning to feel quite at home. To-night Mrs. Green was giving what she called a small dance, but which seemed to include not only everybody in the immediate neighbourhood but everybody within motoring distance. Pamela was looking forward to it enormously. Her pleasures had necessarily been circumscribed since her father's terrible death. She had all a healthy young girl's love of dancing and pleasure, and the natural reaction from the long period of doubt and fear through which she had passed in 15 Porthwick Square.

She was wearing a lovely frock to-night, one that she had chosen at a great man dressmaker's just before leaving town. It was of white crepe covered almost all over with the most exquisite embroidery in seed pearls and silver. It came just below her knee; white silk stockings had replaced the nude, and the silver shoes had buckles of real diamonds. Her silver girdle was caught up on one side with a bunch of silver flowers and in the heart of each one, like a dewdrop, there was set a tiny brilliant. Her only ornament was a great rope of pearls which had been her father's last birthday present.

Wilmer had set her shingled hair perfectly; and one of Pamela's charms was the beautiful poise of her small head on her long neck like the stem of a flower. It would not have been in a girl's nature not to feel a touch of gratification as, on entering the ballroom, she caught sight of her full-length reflection in a long mirror in the wall opposite.

Mrs. Green caught her hand.

"I am a little worried – how sweet you look, darling! – but the most awkward contretemps has happened. Do tell me you won't mind."

Pamela laughed. "I am sure I shall not," she said gaily. "Don't look so upset, Sadie dear. What has happened?"

"Just the last thing in the world I should have thought possible," Mrs. Green declared dramatically. "You know I asked the Mackintoshes to bring their house party to-night?"

"Yes, I think so," Pamela said doubtfully. "You have told me such a lot of people were coming, you know, Sadie darling, that I am a little muddled. Do you mean that the Mackintoshes have cried off?"

"Cried off! No, indeed, I wish they had! You – you really won't mind, Pam?" Mrs. Green caught Pamela's hand and gazed up in her face, with an imploring expression that made the girl laugh. "It is some one they are bringing with them."

"Of course I shall not mind," Pamela said comfortingly. "Do you mean that they are bringing someone who is not quite – quite –"

"Oh, heavens, no! It isn't that. What should I care – what would anybody care about that? And it is not a her – or a she – I don't know which you call it at all. It is a man."

"A man!" Pamela's face was a blank. "Why should I mind meeting a man? What has he done – broken the seventh commandment or the tenth?"

"No, no. It is worse than that. It is –"

Mrs. Stanmore-Green paused and gazed round as if for inspiration. "It is no use beating about the bush," she said at last. "It is Sir Charles Stanyard. There it is out, and you can say what you like to me."

"I don't want to say anything," Pamela turned rather white. "It is unfortunate, for us both. But it cannot be helped. And of course it is not your fault. I expect I was bound to meet him some day. Now that I know he will be here I can keep out of his way."

They had no time for more. Mr. Stanmore-Green was claiming his wife's attention and their guests were beginning to arrive.

Pamela was claimed for the first dance by Tom Murray, a young man staying in the house with whom she had struck up a great friendship. Large as the ballroom was it was soon full, for Mrs. Green had been catholic in her invitation and the neighbourhood was quite ready for a little gaiety.

More than once Pamela looked round, wondering whether her arch-enemy, as she called Sir Charles Stanyard to herself, was present. She had no idea what he was like, but after some doubt she pitched upon a tall, thin young man with a dark, saturnine face as being the most like her idea of Stanyard. Young Murray found her distraite and almost dull, quite unlike his previous experience of her. He began to chaff her upon her inattention, but got little response, and was almost regretting his choice of a partner when the band struck up "Paul Jones", and for a minute they were separated.

As Pamela danced round in the circle she saw that the dark, saturnine man was getting quite near her, and made up her mind that at all hazards she must be prevented from falling to his lot. Then she glanced farther on, and she almost stood still in her amazement. Surely it was Dick Leyton dancing round and almost obviously trying to manoeuvre himself opposite her. Gladly Pamela did her little best to help, and was rewarded by finding herself in his arms for the waltz.

But the circle was going round again and the moment with Leyton was over. Pamela's pallor had gone.

She had not the faintest idea as yet what the feeling was that dyed her cheeks red and made her eyes bright and shining, and she told herself it was only because she was anxious to frustrate Stanyard's designs that she determined to find herself opposite Leyton again. When the band stopped he smiled down at her.

"Luck has favoured me enormously to-night."

"Has it?" Pamela was suddenly tongue-tied.

"Has it?" he mimicked. "I should rather think it has. Now, how many dances are you going to give me? The next?"

"No. I am engaged," Pamela murmured. "I – I am engaged for all the dances."

"Then we will have some extras and you shall give them all to me," he said audaciously. "But first of all I have a confession to make to you. Will you promise me absolution beforehand?"

"Yes, I think I will. I don't fancy you would do anything very bad," Pamela said with an adorable upward smile.

His face suddenly became grave.

"What will you say when I tell you that I am frightened, very frightened?"

Pamela's smile deepened. "I shall say –"

She was interrupted by the dark, saturnine man who had come up to them and was shaking hands with her companion.

"Stanyard, my dear fellow, will you introduce me?"

Stanyard!" Pamela stared at her escort, whose face had distinctly deepened in hue beneath its tan. Her newly gained colour faded.

"You – you are Sir Charles Stanyard!" she gasped. "Not – not him?"

"Not me, certainly," said the dark one cheerfully. "I shouldn't mind if I was Stanyard at the present moment."

"I think you would be rather sorry for yourself if you were," the real Charles Stanyard said grimly. "Miss Burslem, this is Lord Corder, the greatest ass I know. Now, be off with you, Corder! You have done as much harm as you can for one evening." He turned Lord Corder round as he spoke.

That young man extricated himself from Stanyard's grasp with an injured air.

"I haven't a notion what you are talking about, old thing. I wanted to ask Miss Burslem to give me a dance. I thought –"

"Well, you can't. So be off and ask some one else," Stanyard said with a sudden accession of heat, as Pamela began to show distinct signs of attempting to escape from them both. "Can't you see when you are not wanted, you fool?"

"I beg your pardon." Lord Corder disappeared with an air of offended dignity.

Stanyard turned to Pamela. "Will you ever forgive me – now that you know?"

"Why did you tell me your name was Leyton?"

Pamela inquired icily. "Not" – with a contemptuous laugh – "that I am surprised that you do not want to own to being Sir Charles Stanyard. I think in your place I should be ashamed of it too."

"I am not in the least ashamed of it," the man declared, holding his head high. "And my name is Richard Leyton. Charles Richard Leyton Stanyard. You must let me tell you how it was. I did not know your name either that morning we met in the Park. But I was just about to tell you mine when you suddenly blurted out that Charles Stanyard was the man you hated most on earth. Then, I must own it to you, I was a coward. I thought I would try and make you like me before I told you I was Stanyard. You don't know how much I had thought and dreamed of you since our first meeting. And I felt sure that if I told you I was Charles Stanyard then you would turn me down – you would have no more to do with me. And – and I could not face that."

"You need not have told me lies," Pamela said coldly. "But still it is of no consequence; it does not matter a bit. Only I don't think I want to talk to you any more – you – you who – I cannot bear it." Her voice quivered and she turned away.

In a second Stanyard was beside her.

"You cannot go like this, Pam," he said hoarsely. "The worst criminals have a right to be heard in their own defence.

Give me five minutes – no more. Let me tell you my story myself."

Pamela hardened her heart against the anxious misery in his eyes, the pleading in his voice. She was shaking from head to foot with anger; her eyes were blazing with wrath as she faced him defiantly.

"What do you want to tell me – how you murdered my father?"

"No!" the man thundered. He caught her hands and crushed them in his grasp. "Now, by Heaven, you shall listen to me. I never hurt a hair of your father's head – Heaven knows I am a poor sort of a chap and I have never done any particular good in the world; but I have drawn the line at murder. Now, do you accept my word?"

Pamela hesitated; but her own heart was playing the traitor. Her hands that had been struggling fiercely quieted down and lay quivering in his.

"You wanted Perlyon to win the Derby."

In spite of his anger Stanyard laughed aloud.

"Much good it would have done me, if I had been hanged for murdering your father! Besides, anyhow Perlyon would have won the Derby. The colt could have given Peep o' Day pounds and won. No, Perlyon was the certainty. I know it and his trainer knew it."

Pamela's resolution was fading under the influence of Stanyard's smile, his words.

"My stepmother," she faltered.

"Ah, yes, I dare say. I believe that people were good enough to hint that I murdered Sir John Burslem in order to marry his widow. As if I should be such a fool, as if any johnny would be such a blinkin' fool as to hang about after a girl that had given him the chuck once. And Sophie Burslem would be about the last woman I should want to marry. People must take me for a darned ass. But you know better,

Pam" – holding her hands firmly in his he pressed them to his heart – "you know what woman I want to marry, don't you?"

With a sudden wrench Pamela tore her hands away. "No, I don't. How should I?"

Stanyard gave her a little push that sent her into the seat behind.

"Let me tell you, Pam. You shall listen –"

"No, I will not!" The girl put her fingers in her ears. "I will not listen to anything. I will not think of anything until my father's murderer is found."

"Poor little girl!" The man looked down at her with eyes that were now only gravely compassionate. "Is that how you feel? But suppose the secret remains a secret to the end? Isn't it better for you to think of your father as at rest than to waste your young life dreaming of a revenge that perhaps he would not wish you to take?"

Pamela looked at him. "You know who is guilty?"

"Indeed I do not!"

Something in his tone carried conviction to Pamela, but her eyes were still fixed on his face.

"Then – then you suspect?"

Now the man looked away and there was a subtle change in his tone. "I have no reason to suspect anyone. And if a vague, formless fancy does cross my mind sometimes – why, it counts for nothing, it means nothing."

"You were there at Hughlin's Wood – that night," Pamela pursued, her eyes searching his face as though they would read his very soul. "You passed when he was – there."

"If I did, I didn't know it," Stanyard said steadily. "I spoke to no one after I left Epsom until I got back to town, except a woman who spoke to me when I was lying under my old bus tinkering away at her. How my handkerchief got in Sir John's car, or how his cigarette-case got in mine I have no more idea than the dead."

He was interrupted, the door was opened and Mrs. Green's pretty head was poked in.

"Pamela! I have been looking for you everywhere. Your partner is distracted. Sir Charles Stanyard!"

CHAPTER XVI

A smart-looking car had stopped before the door of Mrs. Jimmy's house. That lady looked out. She was seated at the window of her small lounge. She was dressed for walking and at the moment occupied with a letter that had just arrived from Scotland.

A man who had got out of the car, and was occupying himself momentarily with looking over one of the brakes, turned to the door. Mrs. Jimmy's eyes grew round. She uttered an exclamation.

"My! Who would have thought of this?"

At the same moment the man came up the steps and sounded the bell and knocker. He was a man of middle size garbed in a well-fitting motoring suit. To initiated eyes, in spite of the difference in dress and a certain indefinable change that seemed to have passed over the face, he would have borne a distinct resemblance to Inspector Stoddart.

Mrs. Jimmy hurried to the door and opened it.

"Well, to think of seeing you again," she exclaimed as the man raised his hat with a bright smile.

He held out a small parcel carefully done up in tissue paper.

"I have come to restore some of your property. Won't you ask me in?"

"Why, of course I will," Mrs. Jimmy responded, throwing the door hospitably open. "I shall be real glad to see some one to talk to, for all my friends are out of town just now."

"Then that is a pretty considerable stroke of luck for me," the man said as he stepped inside and looked round the lounge, a little tidier now than when Pamela saw it. "You have a real, cosy-looking little nest here, Mrs. Burslem; a sight to make the mouth of a lone bachelor like myself water. But, after all, it is only what I expected. A man knows a real home-maker when he sees one."

Mrs. Jimmy was almost purring under this flattery and, seating herself on the sofa, invited her visitor to take a seat near. Then she glanced at the parcel she still held.

"Oh, my Indian vanity bag that poor Jimmy gave me! I thought it had gone west. I rang up the box-office first thing this morning to see if I had left it at the theatre, and they said it hadn't been brought in, so I had given it up."

The man smiled, fixing his eyes boldly on Mrs. Jimmy's face. Here was a woman who would swallow any amount of flattery, he told himself. Aloud he said:

"Ah, I am to blame for that. But, when I saw this pretty trifle lying on the floor just where you had been sitting, I yielded to the temptation to pick it up and put it in my pocket. It will at least give me a chance of seeing her again, I thought to myself."

Mrs. Jimmy smiled, well pleased, while she aimed a playful blow at his arm with a paper that lay beside her.

"You are a very naughty man, I am afraid. But how did you know where to find me? The bag did not tell you that."

The man's smile broadened into a laugh, then he pretended to flinch from her feigned wrath. "It is to be a real confession then. I looked in the bag and found a card-case; I ventured a little further and found a card with your name and this address. Then it was all plain sailing. I couldn't want a better excuse than I had got. So you see I came along the first minute I had."

"I don't know what to say to you," Mrs. Jimmy said, glancing at him coyly. "You deserve a good scolding, you know."

"I shall not mind that if you give it me," the man said daringly. "But now, Mrs. Burslem, I have a favour to ask you."

"Well, I don't say I shall grant it," Mrs. Jimmy said, bridling. "But first, you have got an unfair advantage; you call me Mrs. Burslem and Mrs. Jimmy as pat, as you please, but I haven't got a notion what your name is."

"My name," said the man, "why, William, called by my friends Billy – or sometimes Sweet William. You can take your choice."

"Now! Now!" Mrs. Jimmy aimed another blow at his arm. "This is worse than ever. You know what I mean right enough. Your surname of course."

"And that is William too," the man said, laughing. "Leastways, Williams. William Evan Williams is my name, to be exact. Welsh, my mother was, though I am English enough, being born in Camden Town. Still I always say 'Good old Wales.' Many a pleasant holiday I have spent at Harlech, which is just close to my mother's old home."

"That is real interesting," Mrs. Jimmy remarked, without apparently having any intention of reciprocating these autobiographical details. "But now, Mr. Williams, I feel that you deserve some reward for bringing my bag back. It would have broken my heart to lose it. What do you say to a cocktail?"

"A cocktail is never unacceptable," Mr. Williams said accommodatingly. "Not that I want any reward. At least I have got all the reward I want." His glance pointed his words.

Mrs. Jimmy would have blushed had such a feat been possible. She got up and rang the bell. A maid appeared – not the one who had been there on Pamela's visit. Mrs. Jimmy never kept her domestics long. She brought in a tray with two long, narrow tumblers, a dish of ice and seltzer-water siphon. Evidently Mrs. Jimmy possessed the morning cocktail habit. From a little cupboard containing a tantalus she produced the other ingredients.

"Do you like to take your drinks through a straw?" she asked abruptly. "I hate it myself – making a fool of your mouth I call it – but lots of folks seem to like it."

Mr. Williams tossed off the contents of his glass at a swallow.

"I agree with you, Mrs. Burslem. That was something like a cocktail! You are the sort that knows how to make a man comfortable. A real home-maker, that's what you are. And do you know what you are beginning to make me do?"

Mrs. Jimmy shook her head. "Unless you want another cocktail?" she suggested.

"Well, no! My head won't stand too many, and that's a fact. No, Mrs. Burslem, what you are making me do is break the tenth commandment!"

"The tenth commandment – I wonder what that is," Mrs. Jimmy said with a broad smile that displayed all her purchased teeth. "I believe I learnt all the commandments when I was a kiddie, but I have forgotten all about them now. And it is no good looking them up, for they tell me everything will be altered in the new Prayer Book."

"Well, you look this up anyhow. The tenth, don't you forget. And if they do alter it I can tell you I shall not mind," Mr. Williams said daringly. "Is that a portrait of Mr. Burslem I see over there?" pointing to a large photograph in a frame of beaten copper that stood on the mantelshelf.

Mrs. Jimmy nodded. "Though it isn't much like him as he has been of late years. That was taken about the time we were married."

"Was it now?" Mr. Williams got up and looked at it more closely. "A good-looking young man too. Not much like his brother Sir John, was he? Though there is a certain resemblance."

"Did you know Sir John?" Mrs. Jimmy inquired with a slight change of tone.

"Lord bless you, no!" Mr. Williams said easily. "But the papers were full of likenesses of him a little time back. Terrible thing that was – I little thought what an interest I should be taking before long in one member of the family when I was reading about the Burslem case in the papers."

Mrs. Jimmy smiled, then her face clouded over.

"I was hoping folks were beginning to forget that. There has not been anything about it for so long."

"Everybody suspected Lady Burslem knew more than she said," Mr. Williams rejoined. "But some people went rather beyond the limit in hinting at her. At least so it seemed to me."

"It was disgraceful!" Mrs. Jimmy said, drawing herself up. "Poor Sophie! She had nothing to do with her husband's death, I am certain. She is the only one of the family I like, to tell the truth."

"Oh, well, if you like her, then I am sure I should," Mr. Williams said. "But, if she doesn't know anything about her husband's death, who does?"

Mrs. Jimmy tossed her head. "I don't know, and, what's more, I don't care. I never liked John Burslem, and he is not much loss anyway. But if you want to talk about John Burslem and his death you mustn't come to me, Mr. Williams. You will understand it is not a subject that we Burslems are fond of discussing."

"Me want to discuss it!" exclaimed Mr. Williams. "Bless you! Murders and such-like do not interest me a bit. It was only to hear you talk that I mentioned the subject. Anything else would do as well as long as you took to it. And all the while I was only putting off time in order to gather up my courage, for above all things I want to ask you to do me a favour."

"Well, you may be sure I will if I can." Mrs. Jimmy settled herself back in her seat and crossed her legs, exhibiting a generous amount of nude silk stocking, clothing a pair of remarkably thick legs and two fat knees. "I shouldn't have taken you to be the sort of man who would be backward at asking for what you wanted," she added with a coy glance as she drew her cigarette-case to him. "Help yourself."

"Thanks!" He took one and held it unlighted in his hand. "No, I suppose you wouldn't call me a shy man naturally. But when one thinks one may lose even the little one has got by asking for more, why, it is enough to make any man pause."

"Bless my life, what is the man aiming at?" ejaculated Mrs. Jimmy, taking her cigarette out of her mouth and staring at him. "What is it you want – a subscription? Because if it is, get it off your chest and be done with it. I hate hints!"

"Subscription!" echoed Mr. Williams scornfully. "Do I look like the sort of man who would come and ask you for a subscription? No, the favour I want you to grant is this. I have bought a new car – there she is outside. Now, I want you to come and look at her. You told me the other night you were interested in cars – then if you think well enough of her, I want you to come for a spin in her and have lunch somewhere in the country. I can't tell you how grateful I should be if you would."

"Why, of course I will, and jolly glad to get the chance," said Mrs. Jimmy jumping up. "Give me a minute and I'll be ready. Go on with the cigarettes and there is the *Daily Wire* to look at while I am away."

"Oh, I shall not want that," Mr. Williams rejoined, with a knowing glance. "I shall have plenty to think about."

Well pleased, Mrs. Jimmy waved her hand to him as she hurried across to the stairs. She was distinctly too canny to go out to look at the car without a hat. Hair, however carefully treated, was apt to show traces of its treatment in the sunlight, she knew.

Left alone, Mr. Williams's demeanour underwent a remarkable change. He hurried over to the portrait of James Burslem and gazed at it intently. Then he turned swiftly to the drawing-room, of which he could catch a glimpse through the half-open door. Untidy it was, as Mrs. Jimmy's drawing-room was sure to be; the quick eye of the man looking in wandered over the disorder, glanced sharply at the various knick-knacks scattered about everywhere, finally focused themselves on a framed photograph standing on a distant table. In a couple of strides he was across the room and had caught up the photograph; that of a couple – a very smiling man and woman, both from their pose and expression suggesting the idea that they were accustomed to facing the camera.

"Mr. and Mrs. James Burslem photographed on their wedding morn," he murmured.

Then he slipped the photograph, frame and all, into his pocket and tiptoed hurriedly back to the hall, where sounds of Mrs. Jimmy on the landing above could plainly be heard now. He went to the door and opened it. The fresh morning air and the warm sunshine were a welcome change after the scented, vitiated atmosphere of Mrs. Jimmy's rooms. But the lady was coming downstairs now and he turned to meet her.

"Now, what do you think of my car?" he said as they went down the steps. "I don't pretend to be an expert motorist like yourself, but I think she is a real beauty."

Truth to tell, Mrs. Jimmy's opinion of the car was by no means as high as its owner's; but she was inclined to think a few rides in it with that same owner would be very pleasant, so she temporized.

"One cannot tell much about it until one has really tried it," she said. "I should like to drive it myself."

"So you shall when once we are out of the traffic," the man promised her. "But I can't let you touch the wheel until we are well out of London. Precious things must be taken care of, you know." He glanced at her in almost an affectionate manner as he helped her in and settled the rug round her. "It is a bit cold when we meet the wind," he remarked, as he deftly transferred the purloined photograph to the back locker.

Mrs. Jimmy laughed as he got in beside her. Mr. Williams was an adept at the style of conversation she understood and enjoyed. She had put on her fur coat and a black pull-on hat which came low down over her forehead, but on the small portion of her countenance which could be seen she had bestowed a liberal portion of paint and powder. Mr. Williams found her in an accommodating mood. They took a long drive into Kent, lunching at an old inn on the borders of Sussex, and when at last they turned homeward they were chatting together like old friends.

"At last!" Mrs. Jimmy said as they drove up to her door. "My maid will have been thinking I am lost."

"I wish you were – with me," Mr. Williams said tenderly. "To-day has been just like a bit of heaven to me. I am a lonesome sort of man and don't make friends easily. When will you take pity on me and come out with me again?"

"Oh, any day you like," Mrs. Jimmy said carelessly. "We have had a ripping time. And you talk of being lonely – what about me, a poor little grass widow?"

"A grass widow!" Mr. Williams echoed. "You will be cross with me if I say what is in my mind, Mrs. Burslem. But I think I shall risk it."

"I should," said Mrs. Jimmy comfortingly. "It would take a deal to make me angry with you – after to-day."

"It is this, then," Mr. Williams said boldly, "I wish there was not that little word 'grass' before the widow."

Mrs. Jimmy grew very red. "What is the good of wishing that?"

"No good at all!" the man said, in a disconsolate tone. "That is the worst of it."

CHAPTER XVII

"This looks just the sort of place for lunch,' Charles Standard said, slowing down. "What do you think now?"

"Ripping," Pamela said laconically.

She was looking her best to-day in a long motoring coat over a petunia two-piece frock, and with a smart hat of the same colour pulled low over her eyes, her sunny hair just peeped out at the sides, and her bright colour, enhanced by the wind, flickered under Stanyard's ardent gaze.

The two were great friends. Amongst their own immediate circle their engagement was an acknowledged fact, but Pamela had refused to allow it to be announced until at least six months after her father's death. It was but a very few weeks to wait now; Stanyard, however, had a very great difficulty in concealing his impatience. Lady Burslem was still abroad, Pamela had written to her, to inform her of her impending engagement, not to ask her consent, since the girl absolutely refused to recognize her authority as guardian. She had received a vaguely worded note in reply expressing neither approval nor regret, but speaking of the engagement as a thing that must stand over until the writer returned to England and had time to look into things.

Anything better calculated to make Pamela take the matter into her own hands could hardly have been devised. The girl, with' Wilmer as her maid, was staying in Harker Place with some old friends of her father's – the Hetherington Smiths.

Mr. Hetherington Smith was in some sense a partner in Burslem's, since he had a small interest in the mine in South

Africa, which had laid the foundation of Sir John Burslem's fortune. Mrs. Hetherington Smith was Pamela's godmother, and since her father's second marriage the girl had spent much of her time with her. Being wealthy and childless Mrs. Hetherington Smith had become almost as fond of the girl as if she had been her own child, and she had eagerly welcomed the prospect of a long visit from Pamela while Lady Burslem was recuperating abroad.

Mrs. Hetherington Smith had not, however, reckoned on Sir Charles Stanyard's almost constant presence in her house, and had at first been inclined to resent his friendship with Pamela. But her prejudice, born of gossip and the common feeling against Stanyard, had melted under the influence of the young man's charm and pleasant manners. Her faith in Stanyard's entire innocence of any complicity in Sir John Burslem's death was now as strong as Pamela's own, and she was looking forward to the announcement of their engagement almost as eagerly as the young couple themselves.

One thing Pamela had never been able to bring herself to do, and that was even to simulate an interest in Stanyard's racing-stable. She shrank from even the mention of Perlyon. Stanyard, for his part, was very patient with her. He never mentioned his stables or his horses to her, and only through the papers did she learn that he had a couple of "leppers" in training for the Grand National.

Pamela never rode now, but she had developed a passion for motoring. She was looking out for a car of her own, and in the meantime Stanyard was giving her lessons. To-day they had been for a long drive into Berkshire, keeping, as far as possible, from the beaten track. Stanyard had seen an old, black-raftered farmhouse back from the road. A card on the gate had borne the legend, "Meals for Motorists – Parking Ground." Inside, it did not quite come up to their expectations. The rooms were charmingly arranged, but it was evidently more of a regular resort for motorists than Stanyard had imagined. However, he managed to get a private room on the first floor with a little balcony overlooking the veranda, on which a party was already ensconced eating with great relish enormous platefuls of ham and eggs.

Stanyard ordered omelettes and coffee, with cream and whatever fruit was available. While she was waiting, Pamela took a chair by the open window and lighted a cigarette. Down below some of the party were smoking too. Scraps of their conversation floated up to the girl above. At first Pamela took little notice. The long drive in the keen air had tired her, and Stanyard, after ordering their meal, had gone back to the car to look at a screw that he fancied was defective. Suddenly the sound of her own name roused the girl's attention.

"Pamela Burslem! She must be a queer sort of girl. They say she is as good as engaged to Stanyard, the sporting baronet, and goodness knows how much he had to do with her father's death."

"That may be all talk!" The second speaker was a man. "I thought Stanyard was in love with Lady Burslem and that that was supposed to be the motive –"

"Oh, that's all off!" the first speaker rejoined. "The Gwenders have been staying in Spain and they were motoring from Madrid to some place far away among the mountains, when their car broke down and they had to put up in some little, unknown hostelry. There, to their amazement, they came across Lady Burslem, who was staying there with her maid and secretary. They knew her fairly well, meeting her in society and so on, so they made tracks for her at once. But her ladyship was not having any. She showed them plainly enough that she wanted to be alone. But the point of this is, that the people there all thought she was going to marry the secretary."

"Good Lord!" the man interjected. "Do you suppose she knew him before, or has she picked him up over there?"

"That is just what the Gwenders wondered. He was a foreigner, they said. Couldn't speak a word of English. An Argentine, they thought. Jolly outside sort of rotter, old Gwender said. Anyway, I'm surprised at Sophie Burslem's taste."

"Never was over particular I should say, chucking over a decent chap like Stanyard."

"Oh, well, it was Burslem's money she was after. Jolly sick she must have been of the old beggar too. But if she helped him off for the sake of this ancient Argentine, I should say it will be a case of out of the frying-pan into the fire."

"I say, old thing, you will have to be careful or you will be getting pulled up for libel," the man's voice said jokingly, yet with a note of warning in it.

The woman laughed carelessly. "Not a bit of it. I guess Sophie Burslem would have something to do if she brought libel actions against everybody who talks about her. Besides, I'm only telling you what Olga Gwender told me. It was taken as an accepted thing among the people with whom they were staying. She said that the landlady at the hotel told her that the pretty English senora, who was a heretic, was going to marry the big, ugly Argentino, who was an atheist."

"Is that so? Oh. By Jove! I suppose it is just my fancy, because we have been talking about him, but I really thought I saw Stanyard coming up that way from the parking ground just then."

"What is that you say?" a third voice interrupted. "Thought you saw Stanyard. Dare say you did. He and Miss Burslem drove up half an hour ago; I believe they are lunching in the room over this."

"I hope they have not got the window open or we shall be in the soup," the first speaker remarked.

Dead silence followed for a moment. Then the scraping of chairs and a hubbub of conversation showed that the party was breaking up.

The fact that she had overheard a conversation evidently not intended for her did not trouble Pamela much. The substance of it amazed her too much. True, she had always expected that her stepmother would marry again, but that such an event should be talked about already came upon her as a shock. She was astonished, too, by the mention of the man apparently chosen as her father's successor. She had been amazed at the sale of Peep o' Day to the Argentine; it seemed to her now that there must be some link between this and her stepmother's Argentine secretary, but it was not easy to find.

She was still puzzling over the problem when Stanyard entered the room. He noticed the signs of perturbation on her face at once.

"What's the matter, Pam? Anybody been here?"

"No." The girl hesitated a moment. Hitherto, she had avoided the mention of her stepmother to Stanyard, but to-day it seemed inevitable. She poured out the story she had overheard to him.

Stanyard's face was grave as he listened. He hesitated a minute or two before he spoke. He was well aware of the general opinion that Lady Burslem had in some mysterious fashion managed to rid herself of her elderly husband in order to marry some secret lover. Only too well was he aware also that at one time his own name had been freely mentioned in this connexion. But this was the first he had heard of the Argentine, and, like the rest of the world, he had marvelled at the sale of Peep o' Day, and, like Pamela, he was inclined to think there must be some connexion between this and the foreign secretary.

"Asses those johnnies must be to talk where anybody could overhear what they said," he remarked at last. "But I should not take any notice of the footlin' sort of stuff they talked, Pam. Sophie Carlford was always a little duffer at writin', and that sort of thing. I suppose she has picked up this blighter because he was the only chap at hand, and she havin' a lot of writin' to do, bein' executrix to your father, and all that."

"But Lady Burslem isn't by any means a duffer at writing," Pamela said, staring at him. "And she has had an awful lot to do since Dad died. Mr. Hetherington Smith says she's quite wonderful."

"Well, if she had any head for figures she kept it dark when I knew her. She was a jolly, good-lookin' girl, Sophie. And I was a fool about her at the time. But it was a bit of calf love on both sides, I fancy. Anyhow, she soon gave me the chuck when your father came along."

"Oh, yes, for the sake of his money," Pamela said scornfully.

"No, there I think you wrong her," Stanyard said thoughtfully. "I always fancied myself that, though the money might have somethin' to do with it – gilding the gingerbread so to speak – Sophie took a bit of a fancy to Sir John. Makes me feel small when I look back, but there you are."

"I don't believe she did," Pamela said obstinately. "Anyhow, if ever she liked Dad she got over it pretty soon to help on his – his –"

"Now don't say it, Pam," Stanyard advised with a touch of real feeling in his voice. "I knew Sophie Carlford pretty well all through, and there was nothin' of that sort about her. Give you my word – Sophie don't know anythin' about your father's death."

"Then who does?" Pamela inquired, her mouth setting in grim lines.

"I don't know," Stanyard confessed. "I think about it sometimes till I can't get to sleep or anythin', don't you know.

Till I could almost fancy I did it myself so that Perlyon should win the Derby."

"I don't believe Dad had an enemy," Pamela cogitated. "Do you think it might be Ellerby?"

"No, I don't," Stanyard said sturdily. "Decent sort of a chap, Ellerby. Though what made the old chap do a bunk like that, or how he managed to get away with it I can't think."

"Lots of people think he has been murdered too," Pamela went on.

"Lots of people think all sorts of footlin' things," Stanyard said. "Stands to sense, dear thing, that a man couldn't be killed and his body done away with in a house that was being watched by the police, as 15 Porthwick Square was. No, Ellerby scooted right enough. Though why he did it and where he has got to only Heaven knows."

A diversion was caused now by the entry of a waiter with their lunch.

"Ah, this is the sort of thing I want," Stanyard said approvingly. "Light as love, those omelettes, and I have been telling the landlord how I like my coffee made, like I used to have it in my student days. I have taught my man; he is a dab hand at it. Come, Pam, let us begin before those things have a chance of gettin' stale."

Pamela found that she was really very hungry when she began to eat, and Stanyard succeeded in persuading her to eat a good meal, and also in diverting her thoughts from the mysteries of Porthwick Square.

He was thankful that, so far, no hint of the latest rumour had reached her, for he knew that it had been freely bruited about that some strange discovery had been made by the police in searching the house after Lady Burslem's departure. As to what it was, public opinion was divided, but it was generally taken for granted that it was something that showed definitely that Sophie Burslem had some guilty knowledge of her husband's death. Stanyard himself was inclined to think that the discovery had been exaggerated if not invented, and that the gossip would soon die out if nothing occurred to revive it.

He was the more disappointed therefore when, on their arrival at Hothmar Place, they were met in the hall by Mr. Hetherington Smith, with the announcement:

"Your stepmother is in town!"

"Lady Burslem!" Pamela stared at him. "She can't be. I passed through Porthwick Square this morning and the house was not opened up."

"Oh, she isn't there!" Mr. Hetherington Smith said quietly. "She is staying with her maid at Stormount's. She rung me up just now. She told me to ask you to go there either to dinner or later on this evening and to take Wilmer with you, as she has some news for her too."

"Dear me! How frightfully early Victorian I shall look, taking a maid with me. But I had better ring her up," Pamela said, turning to the telephone. "Stormount's, please. What in the world has brought her back?"

"Business!" Mr. Hetherington Smith answered shortly. "This Bolivian concession is not going through as it was hoped it would. And Lady Burslem had to be on the spot. She couldn't pull the wires from Spain."

"Nor in town, I should say," Stanyard laughed. "I don't fancy it makes much difference where her ladyship is."

"Oh, but indeed it does," Mr. Hetherington Smith corrected. "Lady Burslem has one of the clearest heads and is one of the best business women I know."

"Well, then, she has altered since the days when she couldn't make her bridge score tally with anyone else's," Charles Stanyard rejoined.

CHAPTER XVIII

Tormount's was perhaps the largest of England's palatial hotels. It was managed on American lines with a staff that was distinctly cosmopolitan. Pamela was not a shy person, but she felt quite small and lonely when she entered the vast lounge, which looked big enough to house a small army. Following her instructions, she had brought Wilmer with her. As she glanced round, to her surprise the first person she saw was Mrs. Jimmy coming across to meet her in a fearsome evening frock of voyant mauve.

"Hallo, Pam!" she began in her cheerful strident tones. "How are you? Here you are! I told Sophie I would come and meet you. I thought you might be shy without your young man." She linked her arm in the girl's with a laugh that made every one within hearing turn and look at them.

"Sophie is doing it in style, you know," she went on. "Got a private suite of rooms; no dining at the public tables for her, if you please."

"Are you staying here with her?" Pamela questioned as they got in the lift.

"Me! Bless your young life, no! She rang me up this afternoon and I just dropped in to see her. And then as she was rather pressing I stayed to dinner with her and the secretary man, Señor Jaime da Dominiguez."

The lift had stopped now and they got out. As they walked down the luxuriously carpeted corridor, Mrs. Jimmy, who had not loosed her hold of the girl's arm, gave it a pinch.

"I hope you are prepared for something happening there. Pam, you will be having a step-papa before you know where you are."

Pamela freed her arm with a jerk. "I simply could not have such a relative, Aunt Kitty. If Lady Burslem marries again, her second husband will be no connexion of mine. But I can hardly believe, even of her, that she is thinking of replacing my father so soon, and by such a man."

"Why, you have not seen him yet," Mrs. Jimmy said, her voice a little subdued as they stopped and she sounded an electric bell, and a smartly dressed maid appeared. "Just like a private flat, isn't it?" she whispered, as they were conducted to Lady Burslem's sitting-room.

Sophie was alone, sitting at a little table near the fireplace, a couple of great ledger-like looking volumes open before her, into which she was rapidly making businesslike looking entries from a small notebook at her side. Of Señor Jaime da Dominiguez there was no sign.

Lady Burslem got up as they came in. "Oh, Pam, I am glad to see you!" she cried, kissing the girl's cheek.

Pamela did not respond in any way. "I was amazed to hear that you were in town again," she said stiffly. "You didn't even mention coming home when you wrote."

Lady Burslem's arm, which she had placed affectionately on the girl's shoulder, dropped by her side. She stood quite still, her eyes, in which there lay now a hint of tragedy, gazing at Pamela's face mournfully. "I had no thought of returning when I wrote. It was this Bolivian trouble that compelled me to come. I don't expect to be in town more than a few days. But I hoped you would have been a little glad to see me, Pam."

Pamela ignored the attempt at conciliation. "Mr. Hetherington Smith said you wanted to see me particularly, so I came!"

"I see you did," Lady Burslem said in a tired voice. "I thought I should like to talk things over with you. But if you would rather not – well, they can be left a little longer."

"As far as I know there is nothing to talk over," Pamela said coolly.

Lady Burslem sighed. "Well, if you feel like that. But I asked you to bring Wilmer; I have some good news for her. Where is she?"

"She walked up. She is always so frightened at lifts. But of course she would wait outside," Pamela said, looking round.

Lady Burslem turned to the door. "Poor Wilmer: I expect my maid has taken her to my dressing-room. She generally does her sewing there. Shall we go and find her? Kitty, will you come too. I expect Marie has been looking out those patterns you wanted." "I am sure I hope she has," responded Mrs. Jimmy. "I will come at once, of course. I should like to see Wilmer too. I have heard a lot about her."

"Aunt Kitty," Pamela said suddenly, "hasn't Uncle James come home yet?"

"Well, no, he hasn't, and that's a fact," Mrs. Jimmy said cheerfully.

"Do you know when he will come?" Pamela pursued.

"No, that I don't. I never know when he will do anything. But I have heard on good authority that he will turn up when I least expect him. Isn't that so, Sophie?" with a playful pinch of the arm.

Lady Burslem's face was white. She shook off Mrs. Jimmy's hand with a shiver. "I suppose so – I mean, I don't know anything about it."

"Well, we none of us do, if you come to that. Jimmy is rather an unknown quantity, especially lately," Mrs. Jimmy remarked with a jolly laugh. "Come along, Pam. They have given Sophie an awfully decent bedroom, don't you think so. And she has a bathroom of her own, silver taps and all complete."

"Quite decent," Pamela echoed, without a glance in the direction in which Mrs. Jimmy was pointing. "Don't you think it is strange that Uncle James has not written to me since Dad died, Aunt Kitty?"

"No, I don't," said Mrs. Jimmy bluntly. "And you wouldn't if you knew the sort of place he is in. They haven't post offices round the corner. Besides, he has really seen very little of you. And he didn't get on with your father, you know."

"Still, he was his only brother," Pamela argued. "One would have thought —"

"Oh, Pam, you give me the hump worrying about Jimmy." Mrs. Jimmy turned her shoulder deliberately to the girl. "I suppose he will write when he wants to and gets the chance."

Pamela looked injured. "Well, I think it is very strange of him," she persisted. "And Mr. Hetherington Smith told me a friend of his said he felt sure he saw Uncle James in town some time after Dad's funeral."

"Well, if he was, he didn't let me know," Mrs. Jimmy said shortly. "And I don't believe he was, either. But do quit talking of Jimmy, Pam. He isn't a subject I'm fond of, and I want to have a gossip about frocks to-day. Come along, child." Lady Burslem had already passed into the dressing-room. They could hear her talking to Wilmer.

"It was just a memorandum in Sir John's writing, Wilmer," they heard her say. "But it showed he meant to leave you an annuity of £80 a year. His wishes are sacred to me, so I am taking steps to buy an annuity in one of the great approved benevolent societies for you. Then you will be quite safe."

"Oh, my lady, it is too much. I don't know what to say." And indeed poor Wilmer looked quite overcome.

Mrs. Jimmy went on to the maid, who was busy mending some old lace. "Got my patterns, Marie? I want to get the frocks in hand."

The maid, a diminutive looking Frenchwoman, got up.

"But yes, my lady — yes, madame. They are all quite ready and I have cut them to Madame's size."

"That is a good thing," Mrs. Jimmy smiled. "For I guess it would not be much good me trying to get into her ladyship's."

The maid smiled too. "No, madame, I think that also."

Mrs. Jimmy took up an end of the lace shawl the maid held. "How beautifully you are doing this. Look, Pam, isn't it wonderful?"

"It is really," the girl said admiringly. "Her ladyship has such a lot of lace too, she will be glad to have some one to keep it in order. But I expect you know all about that, Marie."

"But no," the girl said, lifting her hands in energetic protest; "for two days I have had time to do very little. For it is only one day in France that I come to Milady and one day here. That is not much."

"Of course it is not," Pamela assented. "I quite thought you had been with Milady all the time she was away."

"Ah, no, mademoiselle. Only the one day. It is a sad story –"

"What is a sad story?" Lady Burslem inquired. "What are you telling Mademoiselle, Marie?"

"Only that I come to Milady only a day or two before she come home. And Mademoiselle she is quite surprised. She tink I have been wiz Milady many months."

"Ah, yes! Didn't I tell you, Pam?" Lady Burslem turned to her stepdaughter. "Emilia was taken ill and I had to send her to a clinic. I was very fortunate in being able to replace her so quickly; and Marie is very capable."

Lady Burslem spoke easily enough. But Pamela wondered whether it was only her fancy or did her stepmother look for one moment discomposed. Another fancy of hers, that Lady Burslem glanced quickly as if for help to Mrs. Jimmy, Pamela dismissed as absurd.

"Milady, it was the good fortune for me –"

Marie was beginning when there came a cry from Wilmer:

"Miss Pamela, you had your pearls on when we started. And now they are gone!"

"Gone?" Pamela put her hands to her throat. "They – they have dropped off." She thrust her hand into the front of her frock. "No, they have not dropped down. What *can* have become of them. Dad's last present to me!"

"I told you I thought the snap was a bit defective when you were putting them on yesterday, Miss Pamela," Wilmer said, her eyes searching round, "But you wouldn't let me have them."

"No, I wanted to wear them. But I meant to call at Laycock's and get it seen to."

"Never mind, they can't be far away if you had them on when you started," Lady Burslem said sensibly. "They must be either in the hotel or the car. The odds are a million to one against your dropping them when you crossed the pavement, either getting in at the Smiths' or out here."

Pamela rushed into the bedroom. "If they dropped off in the lounge they mightn't be much safer than in the street. I must go down and ask about them." She hurried off. Lady Burslem and Mrs. Jimmy followed her. The two maids were left alone.

"Ah, but she is careless, this mademoiselle," Marie said, as she shook out the lace. "She does not know where she has lost her pearls. Dey may be in de lift or outside in what you call de corridor. But we too must find."

Downstairs Pamela found the management extremely anxious to recover the pearls, but quite evidently displeased at the insinuation that they must be in the hotel, and very much inclined to say that Miss Burslem must have lost them on the way there. At this suggestion Pamela rang up the Smiths to inquire if anything had been heard of them, and to ask if they would send the carriage back at once in case they had fallen off into the rug.

Then it suddenly occurred to her that when she threw off her cloak in her stepmother's sitting-room the pearls might have caught in the lining.

Leaving Lady Burslem and Mrs. Jimmy to superintend operations downstairs, she hurried back to the former's suite.

The lift offered no opportunity of concealment if she had lost them there, but the lift-boy told her that he had gone over the interior inch by inch.

As they entered Lady Burslem's suite, to her amazement, Pamela caught the sound of a woman sobbing. It seemed to come from the sitting-room. She pushed open the door and looked in.

Wilmer was sitting on a chair in the middle of the room, apparently in violent hysterics. Over her the French maid was bending, evidently trying to console her.

Pamela went up and laid her hand on one of those that were trembling so pitifully. "What in the world is the matter, Wilmer? Surely you aren't worrying yourself to this extent about the pearls. It was my own fault, you know – not the least little bit of it yours."

Wilmer raised her face. It was absolutely white. Every bit of colour seemed to have been washed out of it by the tears that were rolling miserably down her cheeks.

"It isn't the pearls, Miss Pamela. It is that I have seen what I never thought to see while I am a living, breathing woman."

"Zat is it," the French maid interposed; "zat is what she say all the time she have seen a *revenant* – a spirit."

"I have seen a ghost, Miss Pamela. A ghost Heaven help us all. Ah, Heaven, I wish I had died before this day."

"A ghost!" Pamela felt excessively provoked.

"Don't be so foolish, Wilmer," she rebuked. "I thought you had more sense! Whose ghost, pray?" Wilmer burst into something like a howl. "Heaven help me, I don't know – I can't tell you. Miss Pamela."

"Hoity-toity! What's all this about?" Mrs. Jimmy had come up behind them unobserved. "What is that you say, Wilmer – seen a ghost! Well, there is nothing to make such a disturbance about if you have. The dead will not hurt you. If you lived in constant communion with them as I do –"

"A–h! I would rather die," Wilmer sobbed.

"Then you would be a bally ghost yourself!" Mrs. Jimmy informed her breezily. "Don't be a fool, Wilmer. Probably it was one of her ladyship's frocks hanging on a chair, or something of that kind you saw. You took it for a ghost. I have done the same thing myself. We have found your pearls, Pam."

"Oh, where, Aunt Kitty?" Pamela cried, while

Wilmer kept up a sort of chorus. "Oh, no! It wasn't that! It wasn't that."

"In the car," Mrs. Jimmy went on, "the likeliest place of all. They couldn't be seen until we shook the fur rug. However, all's well that ends well!"

CHAPTER XIX

"Just in time. I am expecting a visitor this morning," Inspector Stoddart said, as Harbord entered his room at Scotland Yard. "Mr. Gregg of Gregg & Cook, pawnbrokers of East Foreham Street, Bow. Some things of Sir John Burslem's, notably a brown coat, have been put in pawn with them. I heard from them last night. Here is the letter." He tossed a typewritten sheet over to his subordinate. Harbord picked it up.

"To the Director of Criminal Investigation, New Scotland Yard" was typed across; Messrs. Gregg and Cook's address beneath.

Then the note began:

SIR,

It is my duty to inform you that a coat which appears to have belonged to the late Sir John Burslem came into our hands in the way of business last week. I hasten to let you know in case you should consider the matter of any importance. Awaiting the favour of your reply,

I remain, Sir

Your obedient servant,

J.W. GREGG

(For Messrs. Gregg & Cook)

"On receipt of this letter by first post this morning, I rang up Gregg & Cook," the inspector pursued, "and requested that the coat should be sent to us without delay. In reply, Gregg volunteered to bring it up himself. He may be here any minute now."

"A coat that appears to have belonged to the late Sir John Burslem," Harbord cogitated. "I wonder what that means exactly. Was it marked? And I don't see what possible bearing this coat of Sir John's can have on the Burslem mystery. He was wearing his dress clothes."

"No." The inspector stroked his chin, eyeing Harbord's puzzled face thoughtfully the while. "There are two mysteries you must remember," he went on at last – "the murder of Sir John Burslem and the disappearance of Ellerby. If this coat has no bearing upon one it may have upon the other."

Harbord's bewilderment apparently increased. "I don't see how –"

"Well, we must ascertain when and by whom the coat was pawned," the inspector said. "A discarded coat would naturally become the valet's perquisite. Should he have pawned it after the date of his disappearance from Porthwick Square it would show us that the worst of the fears with regard to his fate was without foundation. Anyhow, we shall soon know something about it, for, if I am not mistaken, here comes our friend, Mr. Gregg," as there was a knock at the door.

The inspector got up and answered it in person.

"Mr. J. W. Gregg, I presume," he said to a smooth-faced, pleasant-looking, little man, escorted by a constable in plain clothes.

The little man bowed. "At your service, sir. I have brought the coat, as you requested."

As he spoke he put down the brown paper parcel he carried on the table beside the inspector.

"Thank you very much, Mr. Gregg. We will have a look at it directly; but first sit down and tell us how this came into your possession."

The inspector put a chair forward and Mr. Gregg sat down, breathing rather heavily as he put one hand on each knee.

"It was brought to us, inspector, by a man named Halliday, whom we may call a pretty regular customer of ours. Leastways, he is round with something or other most weeks."

"Oh, by a man you know?" The inspector's face betrayed some of the disappointment he was feeling.

"Well, just in the way of business," Mr. Gregg qualified, with what appeared to be a favourite phrase of his.

"What is he like?" the inspector questioned abruptly.

"Like? Halliday?" Mr. Gregg said vaguely. "Well, he is an oldish man and perhaps one would say middle-sized. He has reddish hair, what there is of it, and a ragged, reddish moustache."

"At all like this?" The inspector produced his snapshot of Ellerby.

Mr. Gregg just glanced at it. "Oh, Lord, no! About as unlike that as he well could be, I should think."

"Well, let us have a look at the coat.'" The inspector returned Ellerby's portrait to the pigeonhole in his desk.

Mr. Gregg, economically untying the string of his parcel, held up a short, brown coat.

"We lent five shillings on it. It is good stuff and not in a bad condition."

The inspector took it from him and looked for the maker's name. It had been neatly cut out. Then he turned it over.

"I am wondering how you came to the conclusion that this was Sir John Burslem's coat."

Mr. Gregg smiled. "They were cute enough to take the maker's name out, inspector, but they overlooked this."

From his own pocket he drew a small gold pencil case with an amethyst set in the top forming a seal. He pointed to the sides of the pencil – "John Burslem, 15 Porthwick Square." It was engraved in tiny characters on a shield.

The inspector took it and examined it minutely. "Yes, that is Burslem's right enough. Where was this found, Mr. Gregg?"

"There was a bit of the seam in the right-hand pocket that had come undone; this pencil must have slipped through. When the coat was hanging up I caught it in passing, felt the pencil and then discovered the defective lining. It really might have been done on purpose, inspector."

"Yes, and overlooked on purpose." the inspector assented. "It is really extraordinary how things of this kind happen. Well, now we must see Halliday with as little delay as possible. You have his address, of course, Mr. Gregg?"

"We have an address, of course," the pawnbroker said slowly. "But you know, inspector, how very often it turns out that the address in the books is a purely fictitious one."

The inspector nodded. "Still, we must risk it. Did you bring it with you?"

"Yes." Mr. Gregg pulled out a piece of paper from his waistcoat pocket. "And I left directions that if Halliday came in he was to be detained as you told me on the phone. This is the address. He has always given the same as far as I remember, Barford Street, Bow, and the street is a real one, so perhaps we shall find the gentleman."

"We will have a good try, anyhow," the inspector said, getting up. "I am much obliged to you, Mr. Gregg, for your promptness and courtesy. You may have helped us more than any of us realize at present."

"All in the way of business – it is all in the way of business, inspector."

As the sound of his footsteps on the stone-paved passage died away, Harbord looked at the inspector.

"Well, sir, what next?"

"What next?" the inspector echoed. "Well, the next thing I think is to interview Mr. Halliday and see what we can ascertain from him with regard to this coat. Let us see – Bow. We can get a bus most of the way, and a blow on the top, if we can find an uncovered one, will take our cobwebs away."

Harbord was rather silent as they made their way to Charing Cross, but a glance at his face with its knit brow told the inspector that his mind was busy with the many complicated problems of the Burslem case.

They were fortunate enough to get an uncovered omnibus and also to obtain a front seat. Then at last Harbord glanced at the inspector.

"I see you have formed some theory, sir."

The inspector shrugged his shoulders. "Nothing so definite. From the very first a vague suspicion has been floating hazily in my mind. Utterly unjustifiable, you would have said – anybody would have said. And, yet, sometimes it seems to me that, as straws show which way the wind blows, so various trifling bits of evidence do point to my shadowy fancy being right. Still, nothing is certain except that it is always the unexpected that happens. A few more steps forward, which may be taken to-day, and we shall know everything."

Harbord pondered over the inspector's words without speaking for a few minutes, then he glanced keenly at his superior officer's inscrutable face.

"Even if Ellerby is only in hiding, sir, it is impossible that it could be he who shot Sir John Burslem. It stands on the testimony of the other men that he went to bed rather earlier than usual and that one of the footmen, Henry, I think, saw him there."

"Did he stay in his room when he got there?" the inspector questioned with a curious, sidelong look.

Harbord paused. "He was there, at any rate, when the other man went to call him to witness Sir John's will."

"Naturally he was," the inspector assented.

"Then, he could not have impersonated Sir John."

"I never imagined for one moment that he had!" There was an odd note in the inspector's voice that was puzzling Harbord, as nothing about the inspector had ever puzzled him before.

"Think it over, my boy," Stoddart went on. "If some day you stumbled on the same idea as I have done, I shall know that I am justified."

Barford Road, Bow, proved to be one of those melancholy side-streets that, once respectable and residential, have now sunk to the level of the tenement house. No. 39 was in no way superior to its neighbours. The basement held a quantity of broken bottles, a small black cat, a mangy looking terrier, a fat baby sitting on a rag heap in the middle and crowing alternately at the kitten and the passers-by who looked over the railings, while brandishing in one hand the neck of a broken whisky bottle.

"No 1 Basement," the inspector read out. "Well, there is nothing for it but the area steps. Come along, Harbord."

The chuckling infant gazed at them in open-eyed amazement. Evidently it was not used to visitors, and for a moment they thought it was going to howl; then it changed its mind and broke into a wide smile, holding its bottle-neck out to them in the friendliest fashion.

"That kid will give itself a bad cut in a minute. The glass thing ought to be taken from it," said Harbord, turning to the child to put his words into action.

As if divining his intention, the baby clutched its plaything in both hands and set up an ear-piercing yell. At the same moment a young woman appeared at the open door; her sleeves were rolled up and she was wiping the soap-suds from her arms with her sacking apron.

"Why, whatever's the matter?" she began. "Oh what can I do for you, gentlemen?" as she became aware of the two strangers.

Stoddart stepped forward, removing his hat politely.

"We are looking for a Mr. Halliday, ma'am, I think he lives here."

"That's right!" said the woman, making a grab at the baby and throwing its dangerous plaything on the ground. "That's enough, Mary Ann!" she said warningly. "You be quiet or your mammy will give you a spanking!"

Young as the child was, it seemed to understand, and subsided into silence. Its mother looked at the detectives.

"Halliday, that's Father, sir. He's somewhere about if you will just step into the kitchen."

The kitchen was fairly bright and tidy for a London slum. The window was clean enough to allow the light to pass through, the floor looked as if it was, at any rate, occasionally scrubbed, and on the table, near the window, at a zinc bath, the lady with the baby was evidently engaged in performing operations on the family washing. She moved forward two apologies for chairs, one with a broken back, the other with the seat caved in.

"If you will sit down, gentlemen, I will look for Dad."

After one glance at the chairs both men decided that they preferred standing. They had not long to wait. In a couple of minutes the mother of Mary Ann returned with an undersized man, with a ginger moustache and a bald head, following in her wake.

He touched his forehead awkwardly to the detectives. "If there should be any work you want doing, gentlemen, I'll bet Dick Halliday will do your job as quickly and as cheaply as anyone else."

"It isn't work exactly that we have come about, though it may lead to it," the inspector said diplomatically. "It's about this coat," opening the parcel out on the table and displaying the brown coat. "I have received this" – tapping it with his forefinger – "from Messrs Gregg & Cook of East Foreham Street, Bow. I believe that it was taken there by you." Halliday's face fell. "Yes, it was. But that is my business and nobody else's," he said truculently.

"Not exactly," the inspector differed, and his tone was mild. "We have reason to think that this coat belonged to Sir John Burslem."

Mr. Halliday looked at them and scratched his head. "Don't know nothin' about him," he said sullenly. "Not unless" – a gleam of animation lighting up his heavy face – "you mean the bloke what was done in – him as Peep o' Day belonged to."

The inspector nodded. "That's the man. And, if you can tell us where you got that coat, you may help to catch the scoundrel that murdered Sir John and stopped Peep o' Day running."

"That's right, guv'nor. I would do a good lot to get hold of him, blast him, but I don't know as I –" he paused reflectively – "can do anything," he finished. "That there coat was given to my missus, and when I felt down in the mouth and wanted a drink I took it round to Gregg & Cook's. Five shillin' was all they would allow on it. But they give that and I had a good glass of spirits before I come home."

The inspector was not inclined to doubt the truth of this statement.

"The rest of it, what there was over, I brought home to Liz here," Mr. Halliday pursued. "But about this 'ere Burslem, I don't know nuffin'. Nor yet my missus didn't. 'Twas she that give me that coat; 'It'll keep you warm in the winter, Tom,' she says. But I've had a lot of expense and it had to go. Maybe I should have got it back, though."

"I expect you would," the inspector agreed politely. "But have you no idea where Mrs. Halliday got this coat from?"

"Well, I have and I haven't." Mr. Halliday took a good stare round. "I know as she must have got it from one of her places. She hadn't a regular job, if you understand, but there was a good many ladies as she obliged at times. It was one of them gave it to her. I mind when she come in she says 'Tom,' she says, 'Mrs. Somebody-or-Other gave me this.' But the name, what it was, 'as clean gone. I never gave it another thought, you might say."

"No," the inspector said slowly. "I'm afraid that I must see Mrs. Halliday herself, though. When should I find her at home?"

"You won't find her here no more," Mr. Halliday said, pulling out a grimy rag of a handkerchief and blowing his nose noisily. "She's gone for good, she 'as."

The inspector looked rather blank. This was somewhat of a facer. "Well, if she has gone away perhaps you could give me some information that would enable me to trace her," he said at last.

Halliday shook his head. "No, that I can't, nor nobody else," he said roughly. "She's a wearin' a white gown and singing up above now – leastways that's what they used to teach me in the Sunday School I went to when I was a kid. Or, as she never thought much of music, and never could keep her aprons clean anyhow, maybe it's the other place she has gone to. Anyway, wherever she is I 'opes I shall go to the same. She was a good wife to me."

"Dead!" The inspector found himself up against an unexpected deadlock now. This contingency had never occurred to him. "I am very sorry to hear this," he said truthfully.

Mr. Halliday wagged his head from side to side like a reflective mandarin.

"Ay, that's what I said myself. Took with the 'flu she were and gone in a twinkling, as you might say."

"But perhaps you could give me a list of the places where she used to work," the inspector went on.

"No, that's just what I can't," Halliday went on. "She 'adn't got none as I know of."

"But surely she put down the addresses on something when she went out," the inspector argued, "in case any of you were ill or anything."

"Yes, maybe she did sometimes," Mr. Halliday acknowledged. "I've seen her stick a bit of paper on the mantelpiece over there with some writing on it. But I never looked to read it. She were a deal better scholard than me – poor wife was."

"Would your daughter know more perhaps?" the inspector suggested.

"Dunno, I'm sure." Mr. Halliday went to the door. Liz and her offspring had retired to the area. He called out, "Liz, these here gents want to know about them places where your poor Ma went to oblige."

Liz looked amazed. "Which places?"

"That is the awkward part of it," the inspector explained, stepping forward. "What we really want to discover is where this brown coat came from. Did you by any chance hear your mother say?"

"That brown coat," Liz repeated, staring at it as it lay on the table. "Why Mother brought it home last day but one she went out. She said – Let's see who did she say had given it to her?"

"Ah, now, if you could remember that, we might be able to do something," the inspector said vaguely.

"It was her day for Fountain Street," Liz said thoughtfully.

She wrinkled up her brows and stuck her fingers in her mouth. From outside came the delighted cries of Mary Ann, and a low growl from the puppy whom she had captured by his tail. At last Liz said slowly:

"She had three or four places as she went to – Mother had. I can't say as I mind them all, but I think, I do think she said Mrs. Hall gave her that coat, or was it Mrs. Beach? I can't be sure which, but I think it was one of them two. If not, it was some one in Fountain Street. That I'm pretty sure of. She didn't go anywhere else that day. Fountain Street day she used to call it, Friday. Three or four of 'em she used to do and come home as tired as a dog."

The inspector was scribbling something hurriedly in his notebook. "Hall, or Beach, I think you said the name was. Well, we must toddle along there and see what we can find. I am much obliged to you, and to you, Mr. Halliday. And it may be that I shall have a job in a day or two's time. If so, I will think of you."

"Thank you, sir. A job, that would put fresh heart into me – that would."

"You shall have the first that comes, anyway," the inspector promised.

He stepped outside, politely raising his hat to Liz as he did so. In the area he stopped to slip half a crown into Mary

Anne's hand. The friendly baby received it with a chuckle and attempted to swallow it, a proceeding that Liz had to frustrate.

Arrived on the street level once more, the inspector took off his hat and stood bareheaded for a minute or two in the road taking deep breaths.

"How these poor folks in London live and rear their families in these dismal underground dungeons beats me. And Halliday's is a mansion compared with some of them. Well, now for Fountain Street. It is a ten minutes' walk from here, and there doesn't seem to be any bus that would help us. So we shall have to foot it, for I should imagine that taxis are an unattainable luxury here. This will be our best way, I think."

The inspector dived down a narrow street on the opposite side to the Hallidays'.

"I fancy we cut off a bit this way," he said. "But I have an appointment at the Yard in half an hour's time" – as a clock close at hand struck the hour – "and that does not leave me much margin. I think I shall have to leave the inquiries in Fountain Street to you for to-day, Harbord. It isn't a difficult place to find. The third turning on the left takes you into Broadmoor Road, and then you just keep straight on until you come to a post office. Turn down by that, and the second on the right is Fountain Street.

"Hall, or Beach, is the name, she thinks, Nos. 14 or 16. If they both deny any knowledge of the brown coat, then you will have to go down the street till you find the right one by the process of elimination."

"Yes, sir. But that will be a longish job." Harbord looked at his watch. "I doubt whether I shall manage it to-day. For they don't welcome you very warmly in this sort of place when the menfolk come home from work."

"Well, do all you can, and leave the rest until to-morrow," the inspector said, catching sight of a passing taxi and hailing it.

CHAPTER XX

"Ready, Mrs. Jimmy? If there is one quality I like better than another, it is punctuality. And you never keep a man waiting – you are always ready on the tick."

Mr. William Williams was the speaker. He had just driven up to Mrs. Jimmy's house in a most luxuriously appointed car, to find her waiting for him in the hall. He glanced admiringly at her as he spoke.

Mrs. Jimmy was in evening dress – a new frock that had been sent home that very day from Madame Benoine. It was fashioned of white ring velvet in the latest style – that is to say there was as little of it as possible, sleeveless and practically backless, it appeared to be slung from her shoulders by two strings of crystal beads. It was very short; when she was standing it almost reached her fat knees; seated they were unashamedly visible. The white silk stockings and the satin shoes with their crystal buckles were all that fashion demanded. But magnificent as the gown undoubtedly was, anything less becoming to Mrs. Jimmy's ample form could hardly have been devised. The pure white, too, showed up her brick-red skin and the make-up which she had been indulging in very freely.

Mr. Williams took her white evening cloak from her arm and wrapped it round her reverentially. Then he escorted her to the waiting car and helped her in with a tender deference that she found very attractive.

"I have the chauffeur to-night," he said as he got in and seated himself beside her. "I thought it would be more convenient – leave my hands free," with an arch glance that was not lost on Mrs. Jimmy.

She gave him a playful blow on the arm – a blow that left a streak of white powder.

"I am ashamed of you. I hope you are going to behave this evening."

Mr. Williams heaved a mock sigh. "It is so difficult to behave when I am in your company. Mrs. – No, may it not be Kitty for this one evening?" he said imploringly.

Mrs. Jimmy shook her fat forefinger at him.

"You know you will do what you like whether I say yes or no."

"No, that is slander," Mr. Williams said, regarding her affectionately. "I would not do anything to annoy you for the world – Kitty."

"There, what did I say?" Mrs. Jimmy said archly. "I knew you wouldn't wait till I said you might."

Mr. Williams squeezed himself as near her as the car allowed.

"Would you ever have said I might?"

Mrs. Jimmy did not withdraw herself.

"Well, perhaps some time. I am a bit of a fool where you are concerned."

Mr. Williams bit his lip. The lady was distinctly forthcoming to-night, but his objective was far from being attained. He had to persevere.

"You don't know how happy it makes me to hear you say that." He lowered his voice to a caressing whisper. "Ah, if only there were no Mr. Jimmy!"

"Well!" Her face wore quite a different expression now as far as the man could see it by the uncertain light of the car. Her eyes looked determined, defiant; yet, as she glanced at him, her lips quivered into a smile. "Perhaps – there – isn't," she said slowly.

Mr. Williams stared at her.

"Perhaps there isn't – what?"

Mrs. Jimmy hesitated a moment.

"Well I had private information some time ago that my husband had died – had been killed in –"

"In Tibet, was it?" the man asked, his voice gravely sympathetic now.

"In Tibet," she confirmed, her eyelids flickering for one instant. "It – it isn't certain yet, Mr. Williams, you know, and perhaps it never may be, but there it is –"

"But that is awfully hard on you," the man exclaimed. "You will be wasting your youth and your sweetness on the – on the desert air."

No flattery was too much for Mrs. Jimmy. "Oh, but I shall not," she exclaimed. "No desert air for me, thank you. If I don't hear from Jimmy in a reasonable time – well, isn't there such a thing as presuming your husband's death? I'm sure I have heard of it."

"Yes, I believe I have," Mr. Williams said slowly. "But – but that would be a bit risky, wouldn't it?"

Mrs. Jimmy pouted. "I never thought you would say that. I fancied you would have said you would have taken any –"

"Me?" Mr. Williams opened his eyes as far as they would go. "Bless my life! You can't imagine I was thinking of myself! It was you that was first in my thoughts, as you always are." He placed his hand over hers. "It was the risk for you I was thinking of. But I think we will chance it. What do you say, Kitty?"

As he said the last word, the car stopped before the Langford, the fashionable restaurant at which he was entertaining Mrs. Jimmy at dinner. She gave him a coy glance as the commissionaire opened the door.

"Now, you will not be able to talk any more nonsense for a bit."

"Shan't I?" Mr. Williams's laughter shone in his eyes as he sprang out. "I have arranged with the head waiter, who is a bit of a pal of mine, to have a nice little table in an alcove. There won't be anybody within ear-shot. I have seen to that."

"Well, upon my word, you are a caution!" Mrs. Jimmy said with a giggle as he helped her out. "I never know where I am with you."

"You will some day," Mr. Williams rejoined enigmatically.

The Langford was very smart – so smart that there was little chance of Mr. Williams or Mrs. Jimmy recognizing any acquaintances.

But the head waiter had been as good as his word. A small round table for two had been arranged in an alcove that commanded a good view of the room and of the dancing, while those who sat at the table could withdraw themselves from sight as much as they wished.

Mrs. Jimmy looked round with approval. "This is a real tip-top place and no mistake. The band is first-rate."

"Yes. It is a pity I am no dancer," Mr. Williams said regretfully.

"Ah, well, I am not frightfully keen about it, and I don't care about mixing it with my dinner."

"After dinner sit a while," Mr. Williams quoted. "Well, to go back to what we were talking about. I hear Lady Burslem is reported to be going to set you a good example. And Miss Pamela too."

A slight shade of uneasiness crept into Mrs. Jimmy's voice.

"Who is going to set me a good example, Lady Burslem or Pam? I don't quite understand."

"Both of 'em are," the man told her succinctly. "Miss Pamela is going to marry Stanyard – that is an open secret. And isn't it pretty much the same about Lady Burslem? She is going to marry her foreign secretary, isn't she?" He watched Mrs. Jimmy's face keenly as he spoke.

She fidgeted under his gaze. "What an old gossip you are! And don't believe everything you hear about Sophie Burslem, you take it from me. She is a real good sort, is Sophie."

"I am sure she is if you say so," Mr. Williams responded with his usual gallantry. "But does that mean that what they are saying isn't true?"

Mrs. Jimmy tossed her head. "I don't know whether it is true or not. If it is, I suppose I shall hear of it from Sophie in good time. And let me tell you, Mr. Williams, if she does get married again, I shall back her up for all I'm worth. Guess she was pretty well bullied and kept under the first time. The Burslems are like that. And why shouldn't she please herself the second time? That secretary is a decent sort of fellow – for a foreigner. So that's that! And, as for Pam, if she likes to marry Stanyard it is nobody else's business. I never believed he killed her father. Why should he? He didn't want to marry Sophie, as he has shown plainly enough. And, as for Perlyon and Peep o' Day, from all I can make out his colt was as good as the other. Besides, a man don't get hanged to win the Derby. Anything else you want to know, Mr. Inquisitive?" Her eyes were sparkling and her tone was not altogether pleasant.

Mr. Williams leaned forward, his arm on the table, his hand hovering dangerously near Mrs. Jimmy's.

"Do I care who Lady Burslem marries or her stepdaughter either? I have enough to do, hoping and planning that I shall be able to persuade one of the family to marry me."

Mrs. Jimmy would have blushed if the state of her skin would have allowed it.

"Oh, you want to know too much!"

A waiter was standing at Mr. Williams's elbow. That gentleman looked at Mrs. Jimmy.

"Will you choose, or shall I order for you?"

"Oh, I leave it to you. You pay the piper so you must call the tune," she responded politely.

Mr. Williams's choice made her mouth water. A *crème de menthe* frappé, cold soup, a *sole blanche*, a chicken, Russian salad, *côtelettes aux petits pois*, *pêche Melba*, black coffee and a bottle of Pommeray.

"You know how to do yourself well," Mrs. Jimmy laughed as the man departed.

"Naturally I want to do my best when you honour me," Mr. Williams responded. "Now, how soon will you be prepared to risk it?"

"To risk what?" she inquired innocently.

Mr. Williams's eyes smiled down at her. "You know – Kitty. Risk what you have just told me being true, and marry me."

Mrs. Jimmy gave an affected little shriek. "Here now, what are you talking about? I haven't even thought of such a thing! And you say when am I going to do it! I declare you are a cool customer!"

"I don't know about that. But when I want a thing I do not mean to lose it for the sake of asking," Mr. Williams responded as the cocktails arrived. "Now, when you have had one of these, maybe you will feel a little more kindly disposed towards your humble servant. You may be willing to take a certain amount of risk. After all, nobody can get death certificates from Tibet!"

"Well, not when folks die right in the interior," Mrs. Jimmy qualified, wrinkling up her brow. "I don't think there is much risk in taking it for granted that poor Jimmy is gone. The first I heard of it was at a séance, you know."

"A séance! Oh, good Lord!" Mr. Williams's dismay was almost ludicrous. "You don't mean that that is all you have to go upon?"

"Of course not! I had private information from some fellow-explorers." Mrs. Jimmy finished her cocktail and sat back. "They sent me two or three of his personal belongings –

things that I know Jimmy would not have parted with if he had been alive."

"That sounds more like," Mr. Williams commented as their dinner arrived. "We shall have to be careful, though. For though I don't mind taking any risks for myself – glory in them, for your sake – I shouldn't be willing to put you in any danger. It isn't nice punishment for bigamy."

Mrs. Jimmy shivered. "No, no! I shan't run any risk of that. My proof of Jimmy's death is too definite. He will never come back to trouble me, Mr. Williams."

"Mr. Williams! There you go! I have a Christian name as well as you. It will sound like music from your lips."

"Oh, dear! What a man it is!" She sighed, noting with satisfaction that her glass was filled to the brim. "Now, how am I to know what your name is?"

"Oh, you know well enough," Mr. Williams said fondly. "William it is – called Billy by some. One friend I had, gone now, used to call me Willie. I have a fancy I should like to hear you do the same."

"Well, perhaps you shall – some day," Mrs. Jimmy responded, with a would-be girlish giggle. "If you are good, that is to say."

"I always am good," Mr. Williams assured her. "Particularly to-night, so you can begin right away, Kitty."

Mrs. Jimmy was a bit of a gourmand. She thoroughly enjoyed her dinner, and towards the end began to wax affectionate; but, communicative as she seemed, Mr. Williams found that she sheered off at any further mention of her sister-in-law and her contemplated second marriage. With regard to the possibility of her own, she was distinctly more communicative, but Mr. Williams failed to extract any more than a vague promise to show him her proof "some day."

By the end of dinner the man was getting a little tired. His respect for Mrs. Jimmy's powers of conversational fencing grew and strengthened. He began to feel that matters must be left for a time at any rate. He made an imperceptible sign to a passing waiter, and presently the man reappeared with a telegram on a salver.

With a murmured apology Mr. Williams opened it. Then he uttered a sharp exclamation.

"Who was to think of this coming to-night?"

"What is it?" she questioned, her tone somewhat alarmed.

"It – it concerns an investment I made a few weeks ago. I was a little uncertain about it at the time," Mr. Williams said, his eyes still fixed on the telegram. "Mines are always risky in my opinion. And now it seems water has got into it from an old working. Will you forgive me? This must be seen to without delay."

"Of course it must," Mrs. Jimmy assented amiably. "You just see me to a taxi, and then you can go off about it as soon as ever you like."

"I do like a woman that sees reason," Mr. Williams said with an air of relief. "The car shall take you back, and I will take a taxi. Yes, I insist. We might fix up a theatre for to-morrow perhaps if I can get this business of the mine finished. Anyway, I will ring you up first thing in the morning."

When he had seen Mrs. Jimmy safely off in the car he went back to pay his bill, casting a rueful glance at the total. Then he went out and boarded a passing omnibus that was bound for Highbury Station. From there it was but a couple of minutes' walk to his rooms. He let himself in with his latchkey, and turned into the front room to the right of the door. Somewhat to his surprise Harbord sat by the table writing busily. Before him lay the brown coat, freed from its encasing brown paper.

Harbord jumped up.

"I thought I had better write in case you were not back before I had to go. But what a swell you are, sir!" with an amused glance at the other's evening clothes.

Stoddart tossed off his light overcoat. "I have been courting, and it is hard work," he said grimly. "And thirsty work. I think a long drink is indicated." He went to the rather rickety looking sideboard and produced a bottle of whisky and a siphon of soda-water.

"Help yourself," he said as he set a couple of glasses on the tray.

Harbord declined. "I have had a couple of pegs already to-day," he observed. "And that is more than my usual allowance."

"I don't go in for allowances," the inspector grinned as he poured himself out a liberal tot. "And I'm pretty well pumped out to-day. However, everything comes to an end sometime and this Burslem case isn't going to be any exception."

"Isn't it?" Harbord questioned dubiously. "Don't see any way out of the tangle myself."

"Nevertheless there are indications." Stoddart took a long pull at his whisky and soda, then he pointed to the brown coat. "Have you found out anything?"

"Well, I have not been altogether unsuccessful," Harbord said with modest pride. "I worked Fountain Street and Mrs. Halliday for all I was worth, beginning at Mrs. Hall and Mrs. Beach, as you advised. Both of them disclaimed any knowledge of the brown coat. At last by the process of elimination I arrived at a certain Mrs. Johnson. She swore she hadn't seen the coat and knew nothing about it. Mrs. Halliday had only worked for her just lately and she hadn't given her any presents she vowed. She had just done a few days' odd jobs and that was all she knew of Mrs. Halliday. But I didn't take to Mrs. Johnson from the first. There was something fishy about her I thought. She had asked me into the sitting-room before she knew my business, and I took the opportunity of looking round. Then, suddenly there came a knock at the front door. Mrs. Johnson looked scared as if she was expecting bad news and thought it had come. I heard her talking to some one in the hall, but, try as I would, I couldn't make out what it was about. At last they went upstairs and I caught sight of a waste-paper basket poked away under a table. I went over to it; there were several bits of paper there and I was rewarded by finding among them – this."

He held out an empty envelope that had been through the post. It was addressed to "Mr. Ellerby, 56 Lorraine St., Northlands Square, Bow, E."

The inspector raised his eyebrows as he read it.

"A find, indeed. You have done well, Harbord."

"Wait a bit, sir, I am all at sea still," his subordinate observed. "I was just looking about to see what else there was to be seen when an untidy little slavey came in and said her missus was very sorry but that she would not be able to spare me any more time, and she did not know nothin' about the brown coat. I thought this was a bit of unexpected luck, so I showed her the envelope. 'Is this gentleman here now?' 'No, he hasn't been here for ever so long, but the missus she keeps taking his letters in. He is her brother, you see.' Well, that did give me a start, I must say, but I hadn't much time to spare, so I just showed her the brown coat. 'Ever seen this before, miss?' I said. Her eyes grew round with amazement. 'Why – I believe – I do believe it is one as used to hang in Mrs. Ellerby's room, but I never saw him wearing it.' 'When did you last see Mr. Ellerby himself?' I said. She looked at me. 'I come here in middle of August. He were 'ere sometime after that. Beginning of September it would be when he went away I should think.' 'Where did he go?' I asked her. She fidgeted with the corner of her apron. 'I dunno. Missus, I heard her say somethink about foreign parts, but I don't rightly know where.'"

"Well done, Harbord! Now we really have something to go upon." The very sound of the inspector's voice told that he was well pleased. "Ellerby disappeared from 15 Porthwick Square on June 30th. If he was staying with his sister in Fountain Street in September, that at any rate makes it certain that no harm happened to him – that he merely ran away. And why – that is what we want to know. We must set all our wits to work to find Ellerby and make him explain himself."

"Yes, sir. But it isn't all such plain sailing as it sounds," Harbord said slowly. "I thought of the snapshot of Ellerby that we both have. Of course I had mine in my pocket. I fetched it out and showed it to her. 'Is this a good likeness of Mr. Ellerby?' I asked her. She stared at it. 'No! That it ain't. So 'elp me, I never saw anybody like this gent.' Rather a facer, wasn't it, sir?"

"It was undoubtedly." Stoddart's face had altered. He was frowning, biting the end of the pencil with which he had been making notes of what Harbord told him. "Did you ask her any more?"

"Yes. I questioned her as to what the Mr. Ellerby who had stayed there was like. But I didn't get much out of her. She said he looked older than the Ellerby of the photograph, older and whiter – not a bit like him anyway."

"Older and whiter," the inspector repeated staring at Harbord in a puzzled fashion. "Still, people do alter, you know."

"But the girl was very positive that this was not, could not have been, their Ellerby, whom she described as more or less of an invalid, rarely going out."

"Did she really?" the inspector drummed with his fingers on the table. "Well, I think I will have another tot while I think matters over. Can you get hold of this child again?"

Harbord smiled. "I thought of that. She is only a day girl, but she has to be at Mrs. Johnson's by eight o'clock in the morning and she stays there till eight o'clock or after at night. She gets an hour or two off on a Sunday afternoon, and that is her only recreation, poor kid."

The inspector rose and took a turn or two up and down.

"Well, there is nothing else to be done; you will have to meet this girl going to work to-morrow morning."

"To-morrow morning? That won't be losing much time."

"No, and there isn't much to be lost," the inspector said with a curious glance at the young man's face. "I will give you another photograph and you must see whether she can recognize it."

"She was so very definite about this one that really I don't think it is much use trying her with another," Harbord said doubtfully.

"No," assented the inspector. "But suppose – just suppose – that it is not a photograph of the same man!"

CHAPTER XXI

"It is inevitable!" Inspector Stoddart said, and there was no faintest shadow of yielding in his tone.

The manager of Stormount's stood a minute staring at the inspector's card. At last he looked up.

"It is extremely awkward. I don't see how it is to be managed in the circumstances."

"It must be managed," the inspector said emphatically. "Surely you frequently engage fresh waiters?"

"Naturally. But our waiters don't get much chance of seeing Señor Jaime da Dominiguez. His meals are served in the dining-room of Lady Burslem's suite; and he, as well as Lady Burslem when she takes her meals there, is waited upon by Lady Burslem's own maid."

"Isn't that rather extraordinary?" Stoddart questioned.

The manager shrugged his shoulders.

"It may be; we are used to all sorts of eccentricities on the part of our guests. I don't know that I have given it a second thought."

"Lady Burslem herself dines downstairs in the public room, I think you said?"

"Sometimes – not always. I made inquiries, as you desired, and find that Lady Burslem has not dined out since coming to the hotel. Either she has remained in her own rooms or dined at the table d'hôte. She has received no visitors that I have been able to trace, except her father Lord Carlford, Miss Burslem, Mrs. Aubrey Dolphin twice, and Mrs. James Burslem. The last-named lady comes most days. Of course there have been other people connected with the late Sir John's business."

"And Lady Burslem does not go out." Stoddart frowned.

"Her ladyship's instructions when she came were that she was only in town for a few days on important business, and that nobody was to be admitted to her without an appointment. Every day of course, as you probably know, she goes down to Sir John's business place."

The inspector pricked up his ears.

"What time does she go?"

"Almost always, but not invariably, in the morning. Occasionally she goes down after lunch as well."

"And the secretary remains upstairs, dealing with her correspondence?" the inspector said incredulously.

"He remains upstairs certainly," the manager assented. "According to her ladyship's maid, 'He write – write all day.' This piece of information she gave to one of the chambermaids and I happened quite accidentally to overhear it."

The inspector thought for a moment. "As far as I can see the waiter is the best plan I can think of. He must make a mistake and get into the room."

The manager looked distinctly opposed to this suggestion.

"I really don't think I can allow –"

The inspector held up his hand. "The responsibility is mine, not yours. As for not allowing, that card" – pointing to the one in the manager's hand – "is your authority."

The other man took a few steps up and down as far as the narrow confines of his office would permit.

"I understand that fully, and also that I have no choice in the matter. But this and similar hotels in Paris and Brussels are the property of a syndicate. I hope you will speak for me should my conduct come up before my committee."

"I don't think it is likely to do so," Stoddart observed comfortingly. "But, should anything be said to me, I will of course bear testimony to your complete innocence in the matter."

The manager did not look satisfied, but he perforce had to remain silent.

The inspector took his leave with a promise to return in the morning – a promise which the manager received with a suppressed groan.

The rest of the evening passed in making a few changes in the inspector's appearance and in a chat with Harbord, who called for the photograph he was to show to Mrs. Johnson's slavey in the morning.

The inspector made him sit down. There was a light of suppressed triumph in his eyes that his subordinates knew well.

"I fancy I shall want you to-morrow for special duty. Report at the Yard on your return from Fountain Street, and wait there until you receive my instructions."

Harbord looked surprised and extremely curious.

"Any fresh discoveries, sir?"

"Nothing but trifles corroborating what I have suspected all along," the inspector said slowly. "Straws that show how the wind blows."

Harbord sat up, his folded arms on the table and gazed at his superior. The inspector looked back at him, the suggestion of a smile on his closely folded lips.

"I have always felt that you had some very definite suspicion with regard to the murderer in the Burslem case," Harbord said at last. "But though the Burslem Mystery has intrigued me more than any case I have ever heard of, though I have puzzled over it by day and dreamed of it by night, I haven't been able to think of any explanation that seems at once natural and feasible."

"No, I suppose not." The inspector sat back in his chair and leaned his head on the top, his elbows supported on the arms of his chair, his fingers joined together at the tips. "Have you ever gone over the data on which you had to work right from the beginning, putting each fact in its proper place and giving each happening, however small, its own significance?"

"Well, I don't know," Harbord said, his gaze still fixed on the inspector. "Put like that, perhaps I haven't. Not in words anyhow. Though, upon my word, I don't see how the veriest trifle can have escaped me. The only theory I have ever formed is that of impersonation, and that you –"

"Meaning?" the inspector interjected. "Put it into words, lad."

Harbord hesitated a moment.

"Well, roughly speaking, I have asked myself whether it could be possible that some man, some lover of Lady

Burslem's – not, I think, Stanyard – met the Burslem car by arrangement with Lady Burslem at Hughlin's Wood, that Sir John was shot and thrown into the ditch, and that his murderer, who had previously been made up to resemble his victim, came back with Lady Burslem, signed the will, or produced one already signed, managed to deceive the servants and then possibly thinking that at the garage he might be recognized and asked inconvenient questions took the car to that parking ground near the river.

"What became of him afterwards?" the inspector questioned abruptly.

Harbord shrugged his shoulders. "I don't know. I suppose – the only thing I can think of is that he is keeping dark until a decent interval has elapsed and he can marry the widow."

"And Ellerby?" Stoddart snapped out.

"I suppose he knew too much and was got rid of," Harbord hazarded.

There followed a pause. Both men sat silent for a minute or two. Then Stoddart leaned forward and clapped Harbord on the shoulder.

"Good for you, my boy! But utterly untenable from start to finish. In the first place, the most rigorous inquiry has failed to discover the slightest trace of any old lover of Lady Burslem's except Stanyard. And he was not disguised when he left Epsom. I should say it would have to be a very clever chap who could so disguise himself – sitting in his car – that he could deceive Sir John's servants, even his trusted valet Ellerby."

"But don't you see that that is the point?" Harbord interrupted. "I don't think Ellerby was deceived. I fancy he either pretended to be just at the time or else he was in the plot at the beginning."

"Wrong, wrong all through. Though, mind you, the theory is well reasoned out, and does you credit. But, now, let us look at the facts." The inspector fidgeted about among his notebooks. "We will begin with what we know – surmises can follow later. Sir John and Lady Burslem, to all appearances the best of friends, start out after dinner in a two-seater driven by Sir John himself to Epsom, to Harker's stables to see Sir John's colt Peep o' Day, which is expected to win the Derby the next day. They leave the car some little distance from the stables, why, I don't know, and appear to have met several acquaintances and talked to them. They leave Epsom about half-past twelve, and we know nothing more definite about their movements until they reach 15 Porthwick Square just after two o'clock.

"They leave the car outside, and come into the house, Sir John carrying his light overcoat over his arm. James is sent to summon Ellerby, finding him in his room, you observe. The two men then witness Sir John's extraordinary will. Sir John goes out to the car and now wears a dark overcoat. Her ladyship, according to James, remains in the library with Ellerby. James himself goes to bed. But Sir John doesn't take the car to the garage. Instead he, or some one singularly like him, drives it to a parking ground in South London. Another car driven by a woman is brought on next. This woman is observed by the parking ground attendant suspiciously near the Burslem car, and she then bustles away after Sir John. Nothing more is known of Sir John or his movements. But about 7.30 a message is received at 15 Porthwick Square saying that Sir John is believed to have met with an accident at Hughlin's Wood. I am also summoned, being informed that a body believed to be that of Sir John Burslem has been found in a ditch at Hughlin's Wood.

"We are on the scene before Ellerby, and I identify the dead man as, to the best of my belief, Sir John Burslem, with whom I am slightly acquainted. Ellerby's identification is more positive and is followed by that of Sir John's doctor and solicitor. The body is in evening-dress, everything marked with Sir John's initials, but the body, mark this, wears no overcoat, and at the time no trace of either dark or light overcoat can be found. Two questions confront us now: what made Sir John go back to Hughlin's Wood, and who put the light overcoat, stained with blood, under the thrall in the cellar at 15 Porthwick Square?"

"It seems to me that both questions are answered by my theory of impersonation," Harbord broke in eagerly. "If Sir John had been murdered and his impersonator returned to Porthwick Square carrying his overcoat and after he had gone, finding it marked with blood, it was hidden where we found it later, by Lady Burslem or the impersonator."

The inspector got up, and leaning against the mantelpiece regarded Harbord fixedly for a minute or two. Then he said:

"Good for you, my lad. But remember this – nothing is more fatal than a preconceived theory. You will find yourself trying to make every happening fit into it; instead, take your happenings and form your theory to fit them. For instance, that will of Sir John's was written in his own handwriting, as is testified to by his solicitor, his friends and, last but not least, the experts. The writing may be a little hurried, but otherwise it is in his handwriting. That is a bit of a snag for you, Alfred."

Harbord looked crest-fallen, but he was not inclined to give way at once.

"Handwriting may be forged," he said quietly.

The inspector raised his eyebrows. "Your impersonator must be a pretty cool customer if after having committed a particularly cold-blooded murder he could make himself up to represent his victim, drive back to town and then have his hand steady enough to forge that will. Not only the signature, mind, but the body of the will was all in the same writing."

"I know," Harbord said, his tone growing more mystified. "But if I had any idea what you were working on, sir —"

"You shall have very soon," the inspector promised. "Shall I tell you something, Harbord? To-morrow — yes, I think I may say to-morrow afternoon I shall want your help to arrest the murderer in the Burslem case."

"The — the murderer?" Harbord stammered. "Inspector, I have no idea who —"

Stoddart put his hand on the younger man's shoulder.

"I know you have not, my boy, and I know you feel aggrieved that I have not taken you into my confidence before; but it is one of those cases in which the veriest breath may blow away in a moment everything one has been trying to build up. Even now tomorrow's arrest is only a possibility, not a certainty. A great deal depends upon you."

"Upon me!" Harbord echoed in amazed accents.

"Upon you," Stoddart confirmed. He took a sealed envelope from his breast pocket and handed it to his subordinate. "Take that with you to Fountain Street when you go to meet your slavey friend tomorrow. I trust to your honour not to break the seal until then. You will find that it contains the photograph I promised you. Just ask her whether it is a photograph of the man she knew as Mr. Ellerby, Mrs. Johnson's brother."

Harbord drew a long breath as he put the photograph carefully in his pocket-book.

"Yes, sir. And then —"

"And then," said the inspector with his slight, curious smile, "make your way back to the Yard as soon as you can and wait for me and for developments."

CHAPTER XXII

The new waiter at Stormount's was a smartlooking man. The head waiter gazed at him curiously as he reported after breakfast. But the new-comer appeared to be in no way anxious to avoid his duties and proved himself quite an adept in the art of clearing away, balancing trays and plates and dishes with the skill of a professional juggler. He was making remarkably good progress from the waiter's point of view, when the manager made an unexpected appearance. He did not glance at any of the astonished faces as he passed, but stopped momentarily beside the new man.

"The car is ordered in a quarter of an hour to take her ladyship to the city."

"Right, sir." The man went on with his clearing up, but in a minute or two he slipped quietly and unobtrusively away, and one of the others, looking round for the new waiter, stared in bewilderment when he found that he had apparently disappeared.

Stoddart went upstairs in the lift and reached the corridor into which Lady Burslem's suite opened, just as she came out. He stood aside with an absolutely impassive face and she passed him without a glance.

He waited until she had entered the lift and then went on and tried the door. It opened at once, but as he stepped in the French maid came down the passage dangling the key in her hand.

"Vot are you doing 'ere?" she began. "Milady, she is all of most particular zat no one shall come in her apartments wizout sounding ze bell. And 'ere I find you walking as if vot is it you say – all de place belong to you."

Marie's dark grey eyes made very effective play under her black lashes as she spoke.

The inspector gazed at her admiringly.

"Her ladyship could not keep your admirers out if they knew you were here."

"My admirers!" Marie repeated with a giggle. "But I 'ave not such t'ings – me!"

The inspector laid his hand on his heart. "You have one anyway." he said gallantly. "But you will get me into trouble with the manager, mademoiselle, if your beautiful eyes keep me from my work. The manager has sent me –"

"My beautiful eyes!" interjected Marie. "But you are ze bad man, monsieur."

"It is you that are making me so then," the waiter responded. "But now, mademoiselle, there is something wrong with the electric light. I have got to test all the switches and so I must be getting on. See you again when I come out, mademoiselle."

"Oh, vell, I do not know," Marie said with a pout as he passed her. "I do not wait *pour les messieurs – moi.*" She tossed her head as she went on and locked the door. "Now you will 'ave to say to me ven you want to go out," she said apostrophizing Stoddart's back as he went into Lady Burslem's sitting-room. "He is not young, zat one," she said to herself, "but he is brave homme and he has ze gay 'eart – ze very gay 'eart."

Meanwhile Stoddart found Lady Burslem's sitting-room empty, but there was a door on the opposite side by which he entered, and he knew that it opened into the room Lady Burslem used for her work and where she gave instructions to her secretary. He turned the handle. The door was latched, but not locked or bolted.

He pushed it open and entered, then stopped as if surprised when he saw the room was tenanted. A dark, foreign-looking man was sitting at the writing-table immediately opposite the door. He looked up as he heard the sound.

"This room is private," he said quietly. "No one at all is allowed to come in."

"I am very sorry, sare." And now it was noticeable that the new waiter spoke with a distinctly foreign accent. But his keen eyes were taking in every detail of the foreign secretary's appearance – the dark, abundant hair, the dark eyes of which he got just one glimpse before Señor da Dominiguez put on a pair of horn-rimmed spectacles that were lying on the table beside him, the dark beard streaked with grey and the regular features that looked as if they had been refined and pointed by illness.

"It ees ze manager zat is to blame," the intruder went on volubly. "It ees he who sent me, de lights" – pointing to the electric globes – "went all what you call wrong last night. And because dat ees what you call my job, I have to go round every room in ze hotel, and see dat it ees right."

"It is quite right here," the secretary said, regarding the waiter fixedly. "That is all, I presume. Have you seen what you want?" with a wave of his hand to the open door.

"Yes, sare. Thank you, sare." The new waiter retired, bowing and muttering confused, inaudible thanks.

He did not attempt to look at the electric light in the other room, not even that in which Marie was eagerly awaiting him, but using his keys he opened the door into the corridor, and turning away from the lift he spoke a few hurried words to a man, apparently a workman, who was engaged in attending to the sashline of the nearest window.

Downstairs Stoddart went straight to the manager's room, where he found that functionary awaiting him, anxious, perturbed and more than a little wrathful.

"I hope you are satisfied, inspector?" he began.

Stoddart looked him gravely in the face.

"Satisfied that matters are as I thought. I understand that her ladyship will be home to lunch?"

"Usually she is, not invariably."

The manager's face had whitened visibly.

"Well, we must have patience an hour or two longer if she is not. You have seen to it that the private telephone is disconnected. And the men will be stationed as I have directed. All of them will show my red check."

"Yes, yes. All your instructions will be carried out. But, once more, I must appeal to you. Is it really necessary that this – this" – he paused as if searching for a word – "this affair should take place here?"

The inspector looked at him.

"Absolutely. Can't you see for yourself that no other course is possible? I must ring up the Yard without delay; but perhaps I had better go to a public office. In the meantime, no one but Lady Burslem and anybody with her is to enter her rooms. Should any callers come, they all – including Mrs. James Burslem and Miss Burslem – are to be told that Lady Burslem is not receiving to-day. After Lady Burslem has returned no one is to be allowed to leave her suite until you hear from me. My men will see to this, but it will be necessary for you to give the orders to your own staff. You understand that the hotel is surrounded and every exit guarded. The front door into the lounge is the only one through which visitors will be allowed to pass unquestioned. So it will probably be as well to make certain that the others are not used."

The manager groaned. "It is terrible, terrible. I rely upon you, inspector, to carry the whole affair out as quietly and as expeditiously as possible."

"You may rely upon me," the inspector told him.

He waited for no more, but went quickly to the nearest call office and rang up his own department at Scotland Yard. Then he asked for Harbord.

"I have decided that I must stay here," he said, when he got on. "Join me at once and ask for Miles Rashton."

He went back to Stormount's and waited, his sharp eyes scanning the faces of the crowd of guests. Then when he thought Harbord was about due, he went outside and walked up and down on the opposite side of the street, keeping meanwhile a sharp look-out on all who went in and out of the hotel and on one of his own men who was occupied apparently on a little job at the street lamp. He had timed Harbord well. He had not been out five minutes when a taxi drove up with his assistant. Harbord's usually pale face was flushed this morning. His eyes were bright and excited as he sprang out and joined the inspector.

"I met the slavey, sir, and showed her the photograph. She thinks it is that of Mr. Ellerby."

The inspector looked a trifle disappointed. "She is not sure?"

"Well, she did not seem quite certain, sir. She said it was like him, but that when he was with Mrs. Johnson he was growing a beard and his face always looked rough. And he was whiter than the man in that photograph."

"Oh!" The inspector glanced at him. "Did you see it yourself?"

"Yes." Harbord nodded, eyeing his superior keenly.

"Did you recognize it?"

"I think so, though there were a good many – alterations."

"And you were surprised?"

"I was never so amazed in my life."

"And the Burslem Mystery is a mystery no longer to you?" the inspector went on.

"I would not say that, sir," Harbord dissented. "In some ways it seems to me more mysterious than ever. But this main fact is so stupendous, so extraordinary that – that – well, I hardly seem to have grasped that yet. How did you discover it, sir?"

"Really, I hardly know." The inspector looked even a little puzzled himself. "I think the vaguest suspicion of it flashed across my mind in that first minute at Hughlin's Wood. I really think it must have been intuition. Then a succession of the veriest trifles seemed to confirm my theory. Straws which show which way the wind blows, you know."

Harbord coughed. "I wish they had shown me which way it was blowing."

"Well, my lad, you can't be right every time," the inspector observed comfortingly. "Remember that North Withers case. You were perfectly marvellous there. And you have done some real good spade-work in this Burslem affair. I would sooner have you at my side than any man I know."

"You are very good, sir." And Harbord looked intensely gratified at this tribute from his chief. "I suppose the – the arrest is to be made this morning. I heard at the Yard that some of our best men were detailed for special duty to-day."

"The arrest or arrests may be made any minute now," the inspector said, his eyes never relaxing their watch over the entrance to the hotel. "I am merely waiting for her ladyship to return from business. I had to let her go before I was certain of my facts, but I thought she would have been back again before this. I only hope nothing has occurred to warn her. Of course we might have followed her to the City. But, as I could not be in two places at once, I thought it better to wait here and get the whole thing over at one fell swoop. Oh, by Jove, there she is, and the last woman on earth I wanted to see with her!"

To Harbord's amusement he whisked out of sight behind a waiting taxi and watched as a car drove up with Lady Burslem inside, and Mrs. Jimmy sitting next her in luxurious ease.

The car drew up at the lounge entrance and both ladies got out. The commissionaire threw open the glass swing doors and they passed in. The inspector rubbed his handkerchief across his heated brows.

"My hat! Who would have thought of this? There'll be the devil to pay! Just find out what they are doing, Alfred – whether they are staying in the lounge."

Harbord went to investigate and returned with the information that neither of the ladies was to be seen, and that having interviewed the lift man he was able to report that both had gone up to Lady Burslem's rooms.

The inspector drew a deep breath.

"Well, well, it can't be helped. We must put a bold face upon it. Come along, Alfred. You have the darbies, of course?"

By way of answer Harbord put his hand in his over-coat pocket and just let the inspector catch the gleam of bright metal. Then he dropped his hand with a clink of chains.

CHAPTER XXIII

The detectives passed in through the lounge. And it was noticeable as they got in the lift that a couple of men who had been taking a cup of coffee together near the door followed them, while two others went quickly up the stairs at the side.

For a moment the manager appeared under the archway that was the entrance to the larger dining room. His face was white, his eyes were dark with fear as he looked after them. Altogether he might have stood for a tragic figure of despair.

Two men in plain clothes were standing in the passage leading to Lady Burslem's rooms. As the inspector knocked at the door the two who had walked upstairs joined them breathlessly.

The door was opened fairly quickly by the French maid. Her face brightened as she saw the inspector.

"Ah! It ees you," she began, then, as she caught sight of the men behind him, she broke off; her smiles vanished. "But it ees impossible dat you can come in now. Milady, she 'as just come in and she is ver' angry dat I let you look at de electric before. She say she will have no workmen in her rooms at all. And she is going to write to ze manager."

"Quite the best thing she can do," the inspector said equably. "But I am not after repairs this time, mademoiselle. I must see her ladyship at once and also Señor Jaime da Dominiguez."

"You cannot see Milady. I have told you dat she will not 'ave me let you in. Also de Señor. Nevaire, nevaire will he see anyone or go out. You cannot come in, monsieur," giving the door a little angry shake in an endeavour to shut it as the inspector put his foot inside.

"No use, mademoiselle," the inspector said firmly.

He took her hand from the door, and pushed it wide, then beckoned to Harbord and two of the other men to follow. Marie stared at them with wide-open eyes.

In the first room he came to he heard the sound of voices, both of them familiar – Lady Burslem's and Mrs. Jimmy's. He heard the echo of the latter's loud laugh. He hesitated near the door for a moment, then signed to the two men behind to take up their position outside it, while he and Harbord went on to the next. He tried the handle, but the door was locked. Then he knocked loudly on the panel with his bare knuckles. There was silence for a minute, then a man's deep voice with a Spanish accent, the one the inspector had heard earlier in the day, said in clear tones:

"Who's there? No one can come in here."

The inspector's answer was to knock again louder than before.

"Open at once!" he ordered. "Or we break down the door."

Another silence, then footsteps were heard crossing the room, the door was unlocked and a tall, gaunt man stood facing them, his back to the light.

"What is the meaning of this intrusion? Who are you?" he asked; and it was noticeable that there was no trace of any foreign accent; the voice was entirely English now.

"I am Detective Inspector Stoddart of Scotland Yard," the inspector began, then he drew a paper from his pocket.

"I thought as much," the man in the doorway said quietly. "The man to attend to the electric light too, are you not? I have been expecting this visit. Will you come in?" He moved away from the door.

The inspector and Harbord stepped inside.

"You know my errand. I arrest you, John Victor Burslem, alias Jaime da Dominiguez, for the murder of your brother James Burslem on June 3rd last at Hughlin's Wood. And it is my duty to warn you that anything you say in answer to the charge will be taken down and may be used in evidence against you."

He made an almost imperceptible sign to Harbord, and in another moment the younger man with the dexterity of long practice had snapped the handcuffs on the secretary's thin wrists.

"Was this necessary?" the prisoner said reproachfully. "I shall not attempt to escape."

"I think it is necessary," the inspector returned grimly. "As for the rest, there is more than one way of escape, you know, Sir John."

There was a faint smile on Sir John's face.

"I know. But I shall not try them, inspector. I wonder whether you will believe me when I tell you that I am rather glad to see you to-day? Life has been intolerable since – since that 3rd of June. I should have given myself up long ago, but for my dear wife's sake."

As the last word left his lips the door on the opposite side opened and Lady Burslem looked in.

"Are you there, Señor da Dominiguez? There is some copying to be done about that transfer. And I want you to –"

"Not to do any more writing, I hope, my dear," Sir John said with the same sad smile. "Sophie dear, this is the end. You have done everything that a woman could and more than I ought to have let you. Be brave for a few weeks longer, and then your life can be lived in the open again."

Lady Burslem stood like a statue during this speech. Every drop of colour ebbed slowly from cheeks and lips. Then like an avenging fury she sprang between her husband and his captors.

"You shall not! You shall not! I tell you –"

"Sophie!" Sir John made a motion as though he would have caught her in his arms but for his manacled wrists. "We can do nothing but submit to the inevitable." Then he turned to Stoddart again.

"Take me away, please. This is getting more than either of us can stand."

Glancing at Harbord, Stoddart made a sign to the door behind. With one last lingering look at his wife, Sir John Burslem went with his captors.

"The side-door. You will meet no one. I have arranged for that," Stoddart said quietly, as they passed.

Lady Burslem did not speak. She had slipped back against the wall, staring at the detective.

Stoddart looked at her with pity.

"I do not suppose you will believe me, Lady Burslem; but I am more sorry to do what I have to do now than I can say."

Lady Burslem made no reply though her eyes followed the detective's every movement. He came near her and spoke in a slow, gentle voice.

"Sophie Charlotte Ann Burslem, I arrest you as an accessory after the fact to the murder of his brother James Burslem by your husband John Victor Burslem. And it is my duty to tell you that anything you say will be taken down in writing and may be used in evidence against you."

Lady Burslem made no reply. Her eyes looked straight at him with a glassy, unnatural stare.

The inspector waited awhile then he touched the electric bell. When the maid appeared he said:

"Will you put just a few things such as her ladyship will need for one night in a suit-case, please, mademoiselle."

The maid tossed her head, her cheeks were red, and her eyes looked back at him defiantly.

"Ees it zat you tink I take orders from you, monsieur?"

Then at last Lady Burslem spoke:

"Please put the things together. I shall need enough for a week-end visit, Marie. Later I will send for them, and for now I shall take just the things I shall need for the night, as monsieur says."

"*Oui*, milady." Marie looked at her, pointedly turning her back to Stoddart. "And for me, milady, do I come wiz you?"

"Certainly not!" Lady Burslem was pulling herself together now. Her voice was so restrained and cool that the inspector glanced at her with approval. "Bring me my black pull-on hat and my black marocain coat, now. And then – you can go on with the lace you are mending. You will find another piece that wants doing on the shelf in the wardrobe."

Marie disappeared in search of the required garments and very soon reappeared with them. As soon as she had put them on her mistress and handed her her gloves and fur stole, she burst out:

"And me, milady, when you are gone and Señor da Dominiguez, what am I to do?"

"Stay here," Lady Burslem said decidedly. "I will let you know when I make any fresh plans, and where you can join me. Now, inspector, I am ready."

"I have a private car at a side-door, if you will kindly come this way. I thought you would prefer it."

The inspector led the way to the right to the same entrance by which Sir John and Harbord had already left.

As they reached the door of the lift there came a tragic interruption – a loud voice for once rendered unsteady by tears.

"Where are you going, Sophie? Where is this – man – this brute taking you?"

"To prison," Lady Burslem said quietly. "He – he says I helped to murder your husband. Never mind, Kitty. It does not matter. Nothing matters now."

"Indeed, it does matter," Mrs. Jimmy contradicted noisily. "It is a vile thing – a wicked thing. You that are as innocent as a child unborn. And you, sir" – turning with a vicious fury to Stoddart – "what sort of a man do you call yourself? A cheat – a coward – a – a –"

The inspector's eyes fell shamefacedly before hers. But he touched the bell for the lift.

"I am sorry, but I have no time for more this morning."

"You will hear some more, though," Mrs. Jimmy raved as the lift came up.

The inspector moved aside to let Lady Burslem pass in and stepped in after her. Then he barred the entrance with his arm until the door was closed.

"I cannot allow anyone else to come in. Later on, you will be allowed to see Lady Burslem if she wishes it."

"Yes, yes! I will see you later," Lady Burslem said feverishly. "You have been very kind, Kitty. I shall not forget."

CHAPTER XIV

It was the room in which prisoners were allowed to see their friends, a long table ran down the middle and at each end stood a warder. At one side Pamela Burslem was sitting on a visitors' chair, her head bent on her hands, her shoulders shaken by dry, bitter sobs. Her small, piquant face was disfigured by marks of recent weeping, but she was not crying now. Instead, her eyes were hard and bright, though her whole frame was shaken by those hard, tearless sobs. On the other side of the table of division Sir John Burslem was standing, that tall, gaunt figure of a man with the thin, yellowing face that was like and yet so unlike the father Pamela had known and loved all her life.

"Pam, my child, you must be brave," he was saying in the voice that was the one thing that seemed unaltered to Pamela.

Pamela made a desperate attempt to steady herself, but those racking sobs still shook her.

"Can you ever forgive me? Never – never shall I forgive – never can I forget –"

"Forgive you, child?" Sir John put out his hand as though to lay it on her head; then with a glance at the warders drew it back. "It is I who should ask your forgiveness, dear," he said gently. "When I think of all the worry and the suffering I have brought upon you and Sophie, I feel as if I should never forgive myself." Then Pamela raised her head. "Was it fair, dad? You let – her – know, and you let me go on thinking –" Another of those sobs choked her utterance.

"My dear child." Her father's eyes were full of pity; his voice was very gentle. "It was not a question of my letting Sophie know. Fate – Fate brought her into my terrible secret. But you – you were too young. I could not shadow your young life. I thought – I hoped you might never know it. It was too appalling a burden to be shared by a young girl – a child almost."

"Lady Burslem is not very much older," Pamela murmured resentfully.

"My poor Sophie – no!" Sir John said tenderly. "Pam, remember that whatever happens you must be good to Sophie. She has been faithful to me, devoted to me, as I firmly believe no other woman on earth would have been or ever has been to the man she loved. For my sake she has given up the world. I leave her as a sacred charge to you, Pam."

Pamela looked at him for a minute in silence. Then, as some sense of his meaning dawned upon her, every drop of colour drained slowly from her face.

"Dad, oh, dad! You can't – it can't –"

The head warder, who in pity had been looking away from the girl's agonized face, now made a sign to Sir John.

"Time is up, sir."

Sir John looked almost relieved, though the sorrow in his eyes was ever deepening. "Go now, my dear child. You shall see me again before long. And forgive your most unhappy father. Good-bye, my little Pam."

Two warders moved towards him. One stood back and held the door open for Pamela. But the girl waited, looking after Sir John, a world of longing in her eyes.

"Dad!" she whispered brokenly.

Then groping for the wall and the door like a blind woman, she helped herself along to the passage outside where Stanyard and Wilmer were waiting for her. Stanyard took her bodily in his arms and half carried her to the waiting car.

The Burslem Mystery was the talk of London. In the first place, it had excited the popular imagination as no murder case of recent years had done. Ellerby's disappearance had intrigued the public and had intensified the horror of the murder, and recent developments had raised popular excitement to fever height. The daily papers were full of it. Edition after edition was sold out and the wildest rumours were current. When Sir John and Lady Burslem had appeared at the police court, not only was the court thronged, so that even standing-room was impossible, but the enormous crowd that had gathered outside was larger than anything ever seen in that part of London.

Nothing but formal evidence of arrest was taken that first time, and the case was adjourned for a week to give the police time to complete their inquiries and the Burslems time to prepare their defence. In the meantime the public was anticipating the unfolding of a story as dramatic, as absorbing in its human interest as anything that had ever appeared upon the boards.

Inspector Stoddart had been warmly congratulated by his superiors on his successful handling of the case. This evening, however, as he sat in his private office there was no triumph in his face, only a great sadness. Harbord, sitting opposite, had just come in to express his admiration for his superior's acumen and was surprised and puzzled by his reception.

"When I think of that poor, little woman's pluck and her devotion to her husband, how she has planned and schemed to guard and save him, and then remember how I have hunted her, I do not feel proud. I can only think of her despair."

"But, after all, you have to think of the other man," Harbord objected. "From all accounts he was much interested in his life and his exploring work. Why should his brother shoot him? And then there is Mrs. James to consider."

"Pwf!" The inspector snapped his fingers. "That is all that Mrs. James would care. But now Sir John has made a statement in which he says that his brother, who had evidently been waiting for him, stopped his car at Hughlin's Wood and attacked him, reproaching him with having advised the sale of some shares which, low then, went up enormously later. And he had discovered that Sir John had bought the shares himself and thereby made what to James Burslem would have been quite a fortune. He had professed himself dissatisfied with his brother's advice on several occasions before, and this seemed to have put the lid on it. He had always been a man of violent temper, and he rushed at Sir John, stick in hand, and violently assaulted him. Sir John defended himself. Then James Burslem produced a pistol; Sir John tried to snatch it and managed to get hold of it.

"He declares that he had not the slightest intention of using it against his brother, that he did not even know it was loaded, but in the scuffle it went off, and. James Burslem fell back dead. Sir John was horrified, at what he had done and tried this best to restore his brother – in vain. Both he and Lady Burslem got thoroughly panicky. Of course he was a perfect fool. He ought to have gone at once to the police and given himself up that night – probably would have reduced the charge to manslaughter, though the share business was a nasty snag.

"The idea of impersonating his brother came to Lady Burslem first. She got it out of a French novel, she says. The two brothers had always been alike. The change of the contents of the pockets was soon made, and Sir John and Lady Burslem got in their car and drove back to 15 Porthwick Square. There, as we know, Sir John hurriedly made that extraordinary will, giving sole control of his great financial enterprises to his wife. And of course you see the idea – intending for the future to direct them through her."

Harbord looked thoughtful. He had listened with absorbed attention to the story as related by his superior. "Why did he throw his brother's body into the ditch? That looked pretty bad, and would not have worked in well with the plea of manslaughter?"

"It would not," the inspector agreed. "Possibly Sir John sees that, for he swears that he left the body lying by the side of the road, quite near the ditch, but certainly not in it."

"How did it get in, then?" Harbord asked abruptly.

"Ask me another. Lady Burslem told me that the horrible idea had occurred to her several times that possibly James Burslem was not dead when they left him, and receiving consciousness and turning over in his weak condition managed to roll into the ditch and was drowned."

"The medical evidence puts the stopper on that," Harbord said after a pause.

The inspector nodded. "Exactly. James Burslem had been dead some little time before he was put into the water."

"Then this only complicates matters," Harbord remarked.

"I am afraid it will not be regarded as much of a complication at the trial," the inspector said.

Harbord drummed his fingers on the table. "What do you think of Burslem's chances of getting off, sir?"

The inspector shrugged his shoulders. "As far as I can see of the case he does not stand an earthly. But juries are curious things and sometimes take very curious views. If Lady Burslem is put in the dock with Sir John, sentiment may triumph over common sense."

"I cannot even now make out how you got to the bottom of it all," Harbord remarked in a puzzled fashion.

"I think it was something in Ellerby's manner when he made the identification that did not seem to ring true. Then I had the teeth examined, and, though the two brothers had good teeth, all the evidence went to show that Sir John had had a gold-filled tooth on the top jaw which was absent from that of the corpse found in the ditch. Nowhere have I been able to find the dentist who put it in, and of course both Ellerby and Lady Burslem assured me that Sir John had broken it off and neglected to have another put on. However, independent dental testimony did not confirm this. There was no stump left in the mouth that showed any evidence of having been stopped or crowned with gold. Of course that was not conclusive, but it confirmed my previous opinion. Also I felt certain from his manner that Ellerby was deep in the plot."

"By the way, what has become of Ellerby?" Harbord interrupted.

"Sir John merely said he did not know where he was, which I feel certain is a lie. Ellerby is quite safe, though; I always felt certain of that. He managed to do a bunk that night from 15 Porthwick Square. Probably he went to Sir John, who was then lying perdu at Mrs. Johnson's in Lorraine Street, passing as Mrs. Johnson's brother. How the pair of them managed to get out of this country I cannot imagine. Sometimes I think they must have flown over to Spain. For undoubtedly Sir John has been there, and Lady Burslem too. Had this crisis in Sir John's financial affairs not brought them back to England, since Sir John could not bear the thought of the great enterprises he had built up with such indefatigable skill being brought to nothing, there is no doubt that he at any rate would be safe in the Argentine by now; for that was what the sale of Peep o' Day meant. Sir John intended to take as many of his home interests as he could over to South America. Later, of course, Lady Burslem would have joined him and they would have lived in some out-of-the-way spot and hoped never to have been discovered."

"Would they have succeeded – in escaping detection, I mean?" Harbord asked.

The inspector shook his head.

"No. For the simple reason that we were already on the trail. Their discovery could have been only a matter of time."

"There are a lot of minor puzzles though," Harbord said gloomily. "How did Stanyard's cigarette-case get into Sir John's car, and the handkerchief into his?"

"Don't know," the inspector said shortly. "It may be that I have my own ideas, but ideas are not proof."

"And the woman in the case – or I should say the women," Harbord pursued, "the one who watched behind the trees at Hughlin's Wood and the one who drove into the parking ground after Sir John on that fatal night. The one, too, who was seen talking to Stanyard a little way from Epsom."

The inspector stretched out his hand and possessing himself of a box of cigarettes placed it between them.

"Help yourself. Now I am going to ask you a question, Alfred. If you can answer that it may help you with the answers to yours. How did James Burslem get to Hughlin's Wood that night?"

"I don't know," said Harbord, staring at him.

"Have you forgotten the second car?" the inspector said quietly. "The one that was seen before Sir John's with a man and a woman in it?"

"N–o!" Harbord hesitated. "I have always taken it for granted that it was Stanyard's car and that possibly he had brought some one down from town."

"To watch him commit a murder?" the inspector questioned dryly. "No, that idea won't wash, Alfred. As I see it now, Stanyard had nothing to do with the case at all. He does not come into Sir John's story. Nor does he fit into it, anyhow as far as I can see. Somebody else does, though."

Harbord looked at him steadily. "Who is that, sir?"

"Mrs. Jimmy," the inspector said shortly. "She knew her husband was dead right enough. And this sudden friendship between her and Lady Burslem meant only one thing – blackmail. As I reconstruct the events of that night, I imagine that James Burslem, who was furious with his brother over the shares, took his wife into his confidence, and probably she excited him still more. I should say they were near Epsom, and possibly saw Sir John, and finding it out of the question to obtain an interview with him there, discovered the time he would be likely to start back from Epsom somehow. You remember the paper in the bag. They drove down to Hughlin's Wood and, parking the car, came on to the Wood to wait for Sir John. James Burslem on the road, Mrs. Jimmy behind the trees. My own idea is that her husband did not know she was there, but that she waited within ear-shot, meaning, if her husband obtained any large sum of money from his brother, to know how much it was and claim her share. Instead of that she witnessed her husband's death and conceived the idea of making use of her knowledge to obtain a substantial addition to her income."

"Could she have been the woman with Sir Charles Stanyard just outside Epsom?" Harbord debated.

"And the one who followed Sir John into the parking ground in town?"

Stoddart hunched up his shoulders. "Who can tell? That would have given her time to plant the cigarette-case and the handkerchief where they were found. But so far we have no evidence to go upon."

CHAPTER XXV

The Old Bailey was staged for the trial of Sir John and Lady Burslem, the most talked-of murder trial of recent times. It had been decided by the prosecution not to put them in the dock together. Sir John was to be tried first. Then his wife was to be indicted as an accessory after the crime.

That Sir John would be found guilty was certain, in the opinion of the public. But with regard to Lady Burslem people were divided, some holding that she was little less guilty than

Sir John, others opining that she had only done her duty in standing by her husband as a loyal wife should.

An enormous crowd had assembled round the Old Bailey long before the trial was timed to begin. Inside the court itself there was not standing – scarcely even breathing – room. Among the sea of faces turned to the entrance to the dock might be recognized many of Sir John's confreres in the financial world, and actors and actresses in search of thrills, writers of detective novels looking for copy.

Mr. Justice Gower was the judge and there was a great array of counsel for and against the prisoner. Sir William Howse, the Solicitor-General, led for the Crown. With him were Sir Francis Toll Spencer, K.C., and Robert Earle.

Sir Douglas Ames, considered the greatest crossexaminer of his day, was for Sir John Burslem. With him were James Denton and Thomas Mayson, and Sir Frederick Skinner held a watching brief for Sir Charles Stanyard.

The trial was fixed to begin at ten o'clock. Shortly before that time the jury filed into the box, nine men and three women. A minute later an usher drew back a curtain behind the bench, and the Judge entered, a stately figure in scarlet and ermine. After bowing to the Bar he took his seat.

Then every head was craned forward as a door, apparently into some subterranean regions, was thrown open, and Sir John Burslem entered in charge of the warders.

But those who had known Sir John Burslem in the old days rubbed their eyes and looked again. Could this tall, emaciated figure with the thin, white face and the burning eyes really belong to the stout, prosperous-looking Sir John Burslem with whom they were familiar.

The jury was sworn. Called upon to plead, Sir John Burslem said "Not guilty" in a clear, firm voice. Then while the Solicitor-General outlined the case for the Crown the prisoner sat back in a chair that had been placed in the front of the dock. With folded arms and bent head he listened to the indictment put forth by Sir William Howse.

In studiously temperate tones the prisoner was made to feel how terribly it all told against him.

The Solicitor-General, Sir William Howse, began by sketching the business relations between the two brothers. Apparently these had never been satisfactory. James Burslem seemed to have been singularly unfortunate in his speculations, whether advised by his elder brother or not. He seemed to have brooded over his financial troubles, and this last affair of the shares bought by Sir John and their subsequent rise was evidently the culminating point.

Several witnesses would testify to having heard the explorer declare his intention of making his brother disgorge what he regarded as his ill-gotten gain. Then had followed the lying in wait at Hughlin's Wood, and the attack on Sir John. Stress was laid on the fact that though Sir John stated that his brother was the first to produce the pistol, and that it was fired in the struggle, the bullet that killed James Burslem was not fired from his own pistol, the one afterwards found in the ditch at Hughlin's Wood. Of the pistol from which the actual bullet had been fired, the most rigorous search had failed to find a trace. But if the bullet were fired in the course of the struggle, belonging as it might to either brother, how did Sir John Burslem behave? Seeing his brother lying on the ground apparently in the last extremity, would not his first thought have been, had he been an innocent man, to summon assistance, and having ascertained that his brother was dead one would have expected him to report the affair to the police-station and to give himself up for having caused James Burslem's accidental death.

Instead of this straightforward course, James Burslem, having had transferred to his pockets his brother's ring and watch and various small belongings was tumbled face downwards into the ditch, and Sir John and his wife drove back to 15 Porthwick Square, where the new will was executed which would enable Sir John still to manage his many enterprises through the agency of his wife. Then Sir John took his car to the South London parking ground and did everything in his power to make it appear that it was he who had been killed, not his brother. While every newspaper in the land was publishing details of the mysterious murder of Sir John Burslem, the real Sir John remained *perdu* in gloomy lodgings in Lorraine Street, in the house of a Mrs. Johnson who is the sister of his valet Ellerby. From there by means which had not yet been discovered he made his way into Spain. There, later, Lady Burslem joined him.

Then came the great period of stress with regard to some of the biggest enterprises in the Burslem group. From the particulars sent out to Lady Burslem, Sir John no doubt saw that only his hand at the helm could save them. And it was then that the scheme was devised of which the results were seen to-day. Sir John returned to England disguised as his wife's secretary. Detection was only a matter of time. From information received the police were already suspicious of Lady Burslem and were keeping a careful watch upon her movements. Altered as the secretary's appearance was, he was soon recognized as the supposedly defunct Sir John Burslem.

Not a muscle of Sir John's face stirred as he listened; his countenance might have been carved out of ivory so absolutely expressionless and motionless was it.

The witnesses called by the Crown were comparatively few. The medical testimony was taken first; then that of the men who found the body; after them those who had identified it as that of Sir John Burslem, conspicuous among them Inspector Stoddart. Very few questions were asked these witnesses; their identifications had evidently been made in good faith, and it was apparent to the world that they had been mistaken. The attendant at the parking ground identified Sir John as the man who brought his car in and gave various details of the appearance of the woman who had followed him in, but without helping materially to establish her identity.

After him came the gunnery expert, who swore that the bullet which killed James Burslem was not the one fired from the pistol found in the ditch. Other witnesses testified to cleaning Sir John's car and finding Stanyard's cigarette-case in it. Harbord swore to finding the stained overcoat under the thrall in the second wine-cellar in 15 Porthwick Square.

When the case for the prosecution ended it was felt on all sides that it left scarcely a loophole of escape for the prisoner.

Then came the opening of the defence. Sir Douglas Ames looked fully aware of the gravity and the difficulty of the case when he rose. Quite briefly he outlined Sir John's story, dwelling on the fact that it had been put in evidence by the prosecution that James Burslem's feeling against his brother had been very bitter owing to the unsatisfactory state of his finances; that he had sworn to have it out with him in the hearing of several witnesses. It would be proved that earlier in the afternoon of June 2nd James Burslem hired a car at a garage where he was unknown, and that the car was recognized at several different places on the way to Epsom. The only point on which there was any divergence of opinion in testimony was on the question of whether James Burslem was alone or not; some witnesses were prepared to say that there was only one man in the car, others were equally positive that it had two occupants, a man and a woman; other witnesses would prove that the pistol found in the ditch was James Burslem's, and that the bullet that killed him must have been fired from one very similar. The marking on the bullet theory was disputed by some gunnery experts, and altogether the jury was left in a befogged condition on this point.

Sir Douglas made the most of his client's state of panic on discovering that his brother was dead, and of his certainty that he would be accused of having murdered him in order to prevent the truth of the financial transactions between them from coming to light. That the slightest breath of scandal against Sir John Burslem, the faintest suspicion of his probity, would have meant ruin to thousands who had entrusted their money to him was made the most of. Then the tremendous temptation that had assailed him was outlined. Sir John Burslem was a well-known, in some senses a public, man. His brother, great explorer though he might be, was comparatively unknown to the man in the street. Let it be supposed that Sir John Burslem was killed at Hughlin's Wood, James Burslem might never be suspected of the murder, and Sir John might escape while the real assassin was being searched for. Then followed the dramatic account of Sir John's return to 15 Porthwick Square, his signing of the will, deposit of his car in the South London parking ground, and departure into hiding. Told by a counsel with Sir Douglas Ames's forensic skill, the story was one well calculated to arouse sympathy for his client. Several women in court were in tears when he finished, and public opinion, ever fickle, began to veer round in Sir John's favour.

Sir Douglas had announced his intention of putting Sir John in the witness-box, and when the counsel sat down John Victor Burslem was called. Guarded by warders he took his stand and the oath, then, drawing himself to his full height, he faced the jury.

His story as elicited by Sir Douglas Ames differed in no way from that told by his counsel, and very little from that of the prosecution. But when Sir William Howse rose to cross-examine the excitement in court became intense.

"You say that you shot your brother with his own pistol," the Solicitor-General began.

"He was shot by his own pistol by accident in the course of a struggle – a struggle forced upon me by his attack," Sir John replied in a clear, firm voice.

"Are you aware that expert evidence shows that the bullet that killed your brother was not fired from his own pistol?"

Sir John made a gesture of bewilderment.

"I can only say that they are – they must be – mistaken. I had no pistol. There was no pistol there but my brother's. I felt and heard it go off when I was struggling to take it from him."

"Are you also aware that the medical authorities say the pistol was not fired close at hand, as would have been the case if it had gone off during a struggle?"

Sir John shrugged his shoulders. "It went off when I tried to wrest it from him. I can say no more."

"How do you account for there being no blackening of the skin round the hole by which the bullet entered?"

"I do not account for it – I cannot account for it," Sir John replied, with a puzzled air. "I can only reaffirm that the facts are exactly as I have stated."

"Then you say that the medical testimony and the gunnery expert evidence are not true?"

"Are mistaken," Sir John corrected. "That is the only conclusion I can come to."

"Then we will leave it at that. A mistake," the Solicitor-General said severely. "Now, Sir John, matters being as you have stated, your brother having been accidentally shot in a scuffle brought about by himself, why did you not take the straightforward course and at once summon assistance?"

Sir John gulped down something in his throat.

"It would have been no use. I have seen death in too many forms not to know that."

"Then why did you not drive straight to the police-station and say what had happened?"

"Because I was a fool and a coward," Sir John said bitterly. "I felt sure I should be accused of murdering my brother, as is happening now, and I could not face it. It seemed to me that, if the body was supposed to be mine, I should be able to escape altogether, and I yielded to the temptation. My life since has been one long misery and repentance."

"Please confine yourself to answering the questions, Sir John Burslem." Sir William Howse pulled up his gown on his shoulder. "How did your brother's body come to be in the ditch?"

"I do not know; I cannot imagine," Sir John passed his hand wearily over his brow. "When I left it, it was lying by the road-side quite near the ditch, but certainly not in it."

"And the pistol?" the Solicitor-General rapped out. "Did you leave that by the roadside too?"

"No, I threw it away as far as I could and I heard it splash into the ditch."

At this juncture a messenger with a note in his hand was observed making his way through the crowd, after gazing round in a moonstruck fashion. He twisted himself in and out until he reached Inspector Stoddart. The inspector opened the note, read it, and after a word to Harbord, who was seated beside him, followed the boy to the door.

Sir William Howse frowned as he continued his cross-examination.

"You yourself drove your car to the parking ground?"

"I did."

"Who was this woman about whom we have heard so much who followed you in?"

"I have not the slightest idea. I saw no woman. That she was following me was I imagine a flight of fancy on the man's part."

"Did you expect to meet your brother at Hughlin's Wood that night?"

"Certainly not. I had no idea he was in England even."

"Had he any real reason to be dissatisfied with your management of his finances?"

Sir John did not answer for a minute, then he spoke slowly:

"When we embarked on any transaction together we were singularly unfortunate. When I gave him any advice it had an extraordinary knack of turning out badly. I meant, however, to have straightened out his affairs, and returned his shares in the Guayazil Mine if he had given me time, but he would not listen to a word. He seemed mad with rage."

The Solicitor-General looked at him severely.

"You are still prepared to swear that you had nothing to do with placing the body in the ditch?"

Sir John held up his hand. "Absolutely. So help me God!"

"Can you tell us who did?"

Sir John shook his head. "I have no idea. Nothing about the case has puzzled me so much as this question." With another of those penetrating glances of his the Solicitor-General sat down and intimated that his cross-examination of the witness was over.

At this moment Inspector Stoddart re-entered the court, a white paper in his hand. After a momentary hesitation he turned to Sir William and handed it to him. He in his turn waited a minute and conferred with Sir Douglas Ames; then he hurriedly scribbled a line or two and beckoning to an usher passed it up to the Judge.

Mr. Justice Gower read it without one muscle of his stiff, parchment-like face altering. He made an almost imperceptible sign to the Solicitor-General.

Sir William Howse rose.

"May I make an application, my lord? May I move the adjournment of this case until to-morrow?"

The Judge looked at him over the top of his spectacles.

"On what ground do you make this application, Sir William?"

The Solicitor-General looked round from the jury to the prisoners, then he said slowly, every syllable falling with startling distinctness on the listening ears:

"Because I hold in my hand what purports to be the confession of the real criminal, my lord."

CHAPTER XXVI

"The confession of the real criminal." Sir John Burslem looked thunderstruck. At a touch from one of his warders he hastily disappeared down the stairs from the dock. The Judge passed out by the door at the back of the Bench. The Solicitor-General and Sir Douglas Ames went over to a side-door together. With a sign to Harbord, Inspector Stoddart followed them. The general public poured out wonderingly, puzzling, disputing, only to meet a more amazed crowd outside.

Harbord looked at the Inspector. "What does this mean, sir?"

"The woman in the case," Stoddart said briefly. "A few hours ago Mrs. Jimmy was driving herself to the court in her Ford when a runaway butcher's cart got into the way. She lost her nerve, tried to turn, swerved badly, and came into collision with a bus, and got a bad smash. She was pinned down by some of the machinery, and when they got her out it was obvious that she was fatally injured. She was taken at once to St. Jude's Hospital. At first it was thought that an operation might be attempted, but it was soon seen that she was too far gone. For some time she did not realize how serious her condition was. And the hospital authorities, for their part, did not find out her name or her connexion with this case.

"But when she was asked if she had any relatives she wished to see, Mrs. Jimmy realized the situation and desired that a priest, and later a lawyer might be sent for. In his presence and that of the necessary witnesses she made a statement that she, and not her brother-in-law, Sir John Burslem, shot her husband at Hughlin's Wood."

Harbord stared and rubbed his eyes. "But how could such a thing be? Sir John himself says that in the struggle his brother's revolver went off and shot him."

The inspector gave that faint, inscrutable smile of his. "The revolver went off, no doubt, but it did not shoot James Burslem. You remember the medical and expert gunnery testimony, that the bullet that was lodged in the base of the skull was not fired from the revolver found in the ditch, nor at the close quarters indicated by Sir John's account of the struggle."

Harbord nodded. "Both points have always puzzled me. Still, short as has been my career in the C.I.D., I have already discovered that expert evidence is sometimes mistaken."

"This wasn't," Inspector Stoddart said shortly. After a pause he went on, "The bullet that killed James Burslem was fired from the opposite side of the ditch from that spot among the trees where you found the handbag, Alfred. And it was fired from a revolver, the fellow to the one found in the ditch. And it was fired intentionally to kill James Burslem by Mrs. James."

Harbord uttered an incredulous sound. "You are certain that she was not delirious, sir?"

"Absolutely!" the inspector said finally. "Before the case was presented to the Solicitor-General, Inspector Wilkins was sent to Mrs. James's house and found the pistol precisely where her confession indicated."

"That seems to be pretty conclusive," Harbord assented. "But I suppose the markings have not been examined yet?"

"Hasn't been time. But I don't think there is any doubt as to the accuracy of the confession. Mrs. James knew that death was imminent; she was a Roman Catholic and she had to clear her conscience before she died. She began her confession by stating quite frankly that she was thoroughly tired of James Burslem. Most of her time she was a grass widow, and she found him either sickeningly demonstrative when he returned or boringly tiresome with his grievance against his brother. Furthermore, his expeditions absorbed most of his income, and she was always kept short of money, a serious grievance to Mrs. James. He appears to have been especially tiresome in the few days after his return from Tibet on this last occasion, and she found his temper, his fulminations against his brother, and his meanness alike irritating.

"A violent quarrel took place between the pair on the morning of the 2nd of June, and, though a sort of reconciliation was patched up, she admitted that her anger against her husband was still very great. James Burslem remained in his house all the afternoon, apparently brooding over his grievances and keeping her with him, all of which added fuel to her smouldering wrath. Between six and seven o'clock knowing that his brother would be certain to go down and have a look at Peep o' Day, he announced his intention of going down after him and having it out with him. They dined together at a foreign restaurant in Soho, James's already violent temper being aggravated by the wine he drank, and his wrath against his brother increasing. When at last they started for Epsom he produced two pistols and told her that he should challenge his brother to a duel. She managed to abstract one of them when he was not looking, but was unable to get the other.

"A little way outside Epsom he stopped and ordered Mrs. James to go on and ascertain whether Sir John was at Harker's stables as he expected, and if possible to find out, at any rate approximately, what time Sir John would leave.

"She did her best, as is shown by the note you discovered in the handbag. Then the pair drove off to Hughlin's Wood. This was the spot chosen by James Burslem for the encounter, as the sharp bend would oblige the car to slow down. He parked the car by the wayside and Mrs. James with it, and went off to the Wood. But she was not minded to be left behind. She followed him, carefully keeping out of sight, and watched the encounter between the brothers from behind the tree near which you found the handbag. She still held the pistol she had taken from him. Then, when she saw the two men struggling together a sudden temptation assailed her. She was thoroughly sick of Jimmy Burslem, and made up her mind to rid herself of him once and for all. She fired, and at the same moment heard the crack of the other pistol."

"Then, as a matter of fact, she does not know which of them shot her husband," Harbord interjected.

The inspector permitted himself a faint smile. "She had no doubt. Don't you remember she was the crack shot at the Marble Pavilion – couldn't have missed her man at that distance. She says she was puzzled by Sir John and Lady Burslem's conduct afterwards. She could not make out what they were doing, and when they had driven off she came out to investigate. She was amazed to see Sir John's signet ring on her dead husband's little finger. It was she who tumbled the body into the ditch."

"What! His wife! The brute!" Harbord ejaculated.

The inspector moved his hand impatiently. "Not so bad as killing him, was it? She says also she had to get his keys from his pocket, and, turning him over on the right side to do this, he was so close to the ditch that he slipped in. You can believe as much of that as you like."

"That will not be one word!" Harbord assured him.

"Then she drove off in the wake of the others to 15 Porthwick Square, on the way passing Stanyard, with whose appearance and car she was quite familiar, and who was apparently in difficulties. She stopped and offered help, which was refused. Then the brilliant idea of trying to implicate Stanyard occurred to her. She had picked up a handkerchief of Sir John's from the grass. Getting out to see what was the matter with Stanyard's car, while he was occupied with the machinery underneath, she stuffed the handkerchief down between the cushions and seized Stanyard's cigarette-case that lay on the seat. Then she drove quickly to Porthwick Square. Just as she got near, Sir John ran down the steps of No. 15, got into his car and started off. Impelled by curiosity, she followed to the parking ground, parked her car beside his, and after putting Stanyard's cigarette-case where it was found, made off after Sir John, as the man told us. She failed, however, to keep up with him, and at last lost sight of him altogether. Henceforth it was a case of blackmailing poor Lady Burslem. She and her blessed spirits were merely a cloak for extracting money from her. Occasionally, too, when the police watch became very rigorous, by means of her séances she conveyed messages between husband and wife."

"A nice sort of lady, upon my word!" Harbord commented. "It strikes me that hanging is too good for Mrs. James Burslem."

"Well, she will not get it anyway," Stoddart said gravely. "She died just as I entered the hospital this afternoon; without a friend near her, for, though she repeatedly asked for Sophie, of course Lady Burslem was not allowed to go. Well, well, poor thing, after all she was her own worst enemy!"

And that was the best that could be said for Mrs. Jimmy!

CHAPTER 27

The second day of the trial of Sir John Burslem will not soon be forgotten by any of those in court. Enormous as had been the crowds attracted the first day, the rumours that had spread through London like wildfire the night before had almost doubled them on the second. People struggled and fought even for standing room in the street outside the Old Bailey. Inside the court, crammed to suffocation though it was, there was an air of briskness, of expectancy that had altogether been wanting when the case began.

Sir John Burslem stepped into the dock looking as if a burden had slipped off his shoulders, seeming indeed to those who knew him like a shadow of his former self. A dramatic surprise awaited the spectators when the case opened.

"Call Robert Ellerby!" Sir Douglas Ames directed. Robert Ellerby was called loudly by the usher. Those in court who had known Ellerby stared and rubbed their eyes as a quiet looking, elderly man in a well-cut lounge suit rose and made his way to the witness-box. The Robert Ellerby they had known with his clean-shaven face, his somewhat smug expression, had always looked so essentially a gentleman's servant. This man, with the thin, bronzed face and the grey moustache looked more like the colonial rancher, or an explorer. Scarcely a trace of the Robert Ellerby they had known could they discern in him.

Nevertheless, when he had taken the oath in response to Sir Douglas Ames, and began to make his statement, they recognized the quiet, subdued voice, the respectful manner.

It would have been almost possible to hear the proverbial pin drop in the crowded court. For so long had Ellerby been looked upon as dead, and speculation ever been rife as to the disposal of his remains, that to see him there before them, to hear him giving his evidence in this calm, unemotional manner, seemed nothing less than a miracle.

In response to Sir Douglas Ames he stated that when Sir John started for Epsom on the evening of that 2nd of June he told Ellerby that he need not sit up for him. Therefore he was, of course, in bed when the car returned and he was awakened by James, the footman. When he had dressed and had come downstairs and with James had witnessed Sir John's will, he was taken by Sir John and Lady Burslem into their confidence with regard to that evening's happenings. Questioned by Sir Douglas, he said that he had pleaded with Sir John to give up his mad scheme, and to go at once to the police, but without effect. Nothing then remained, witness added simply, but to help Sir John by every means in his power.

"Why did you not go to the police yourself?" Sir Douglas asked.

"Because I could not go against Sir John," the witness answered. "We were boys together. He had been good to me all my life, and I cared for him more than anything on earth."

There was a faint stir in the court, sounding almost like applause. It was instantly suppressed by the ushers, and Sir Douglas proceeded:

"Did Sir John take a revolver with him that night?"

"I am quite sure that he did not," Ellerby said with emphasis. "Sir John had only one revolver in the world. It was kept in a case in his dressing-room, and I saw it there the next day. It was not loaded. I doubt whether it had ever been loaded. I feel certain that Sir John had never fired it. It was a present to him from a Mr. Leadfield. Sir John's initials were on the case and also on the pistol itself, J.V.B. I knew that, when Sir John said his brother's death was an accident, due to his own revolver going off, he was speaking the truth."

"And this made you determined to help him by every means in your power."

"It assured me of his innocence, but, innocent or guilty, I should have done everything in my power to help Sir John," Ellerby said steadily.

Hearing this, the prisoner in the dock shot a quick glance of gratitude to the witness.

Sir Douglas Ames went on:

"And when you disappeared from 15 Porthwick Square, you went to join Sir John?"

The witness bent his head. "Exactly," he said. "In Spain."

"Why did you leave Porthwick Square in such secrecy? There was no warrant out then for your arrest?"

"Because I should have been followed, and so Sir John would have been discovered."

"You and Lady Burslem concealed Sir John's overcoat under the thrall in the second cellar?"

"I concealed it there," the witness said with emphasis. "Her ladyship came down to me because she was unable to believe the hiding-place I had chosen was really safe."

That ended Sir Douglas Ames's examination.

The Solicitor-General stated that he did not intend to cross-examine.

A minute later Mrs. Jimmy's confession was put into court and read aloud in breathless silence. It was then handed to the jury, who perused it with absorbed attention.

After another interval, police evidence was given to show that the pistol was found in the place in Mrs. Jimmy's house in which she had directed them to look. Then followed the gunnery experts who proved by their new system of microscopic lenses that the fine markings on the bullet proved that it had been fired from her pistol.

The medical witness re-entered the box, and repeated that the fatal shot had been fired from a distance, certainly not in the course of a hand-to-hand struggle. One of them had even given twenty yards as his opinion as the nearest distance at which the pistol had been fired, and this practically covered the ground between the tree where the handbag was found and the ditch.

Again the Solicitor-General intimated that he would not cross-examine, and that it was not the intention of the Crown to proceed any further with the case against Sir John Burslem.

Mr. Justice Gower offered no elaborate summing-up. Very briefly he told the jury that if they believed Mrs. James Burslem's confession, corroborated as it was by the medical expert and the expert gunnery evidence, it would be their duty to return a verdict of Not Guilty against Sir John Burslem.

At the conclusion of his speech the jury briefly conferred together in their box, and, as was expected, returned a verdict in accordance with the Judge's direction, and Sir John left the dock a free man. He was immediately surrounded by a crowd of his old friends and new sympathizers.

But the proceedings were not over yet. Indicted as an accessory after the fact, Lady Burslem was placed in the dock. Her father and brothers stood at each side of her and Sir John steadied himself by one hand on the chair that was given her, Mrs. Dolphin and her husband standing behind.

When asked to plead, she said, "Not Guilty" in a clear, low voice.

Sir William Howse said it was not proposed to offer any evidence against her, and the jury returned their formal verdict at once.

With tremendous difficulty the police performed the Herculean task of clearing the way for the Burslems and their party through the court to the corridor, on the other side of which a room had been placed at their disposal. Sir John had his wife on one side, his daughter clinging to his arm. Behind them came Lord Carlford and his son, with Mrs. Dolphin, Sir Charles Stanyard and Ellerby, debonair and happy looking, Aubrey Dolphin bringing up the rear. Even here there penetrated a loud, concentrated cheer from the crowd in the street.

As a racehorse owner, one whose horses invariably ran straight, Sir John had always been popular. Sir John's name, too, had been associated with almost every charitable enterprise in the country, and it had been rumoured that his private charities far exceeded his public ones, and that his purse was always open to any real plea for help. Everything therefore combined to make his acquittal popular with the masses.

But as Sir John entered the room he waved every one back, and handed Pamela gently to Stanyard.

Then when he had closed the door he took his wife in his arms and laid his face on hers.

"How can I thank you, truest of women, most loyal of comrades!"

"Thank me? Thank me?" Sophie echoed, clinging to him. "How silly you are, John! You are my husband! Helping you is just my job!"

THE END